A Prairie-Schooner Princess

CW01082843

Mary K. Maule

Alpha Editions

This edition published in 2024

ISBN 9789361472114

Design and Setting By

Alpha Editions

www.alphaedis.com

Email - info@alphaedis.com

As per information held with us this book is in Public Domain.
This book is a reproduction of an important historical work.
Alpha Editions uses the best technology to reproduce historical work
in the same manner it was first published to preserve its original nature.
Any marks or number seen are left intentionally to preserve.

Contents

CHAPTER I

THE STRANGERS

From under the curving top of a canvas-covered "prairie schooner" a boy of about fifteen leaned out, his eyes straining intently across the brown, level expanse of the prairies.

"Father," he called, with a note of anxiety in his voice, "look back there to the northeast! What is that against the horizon? It looks like a cloud of dust or smoke."

In a second prairie schooner, just ahead of the one the boy was driving, a man with a brown, bearded face looked out hastily, then continued to scan the horizon with anxious gaze.

Beside him in the wagon sat a blue-eyed, comely woman with traces of care in her face. As the boy's voice reached her she started, then leaned out of the wagon, her startled gaze sweeping the lonely untrodden plains over which they were traveling.

Inside the wagon under the canvas cover a boy of nine, two little girls of seven and twelve, a curly-headed little girl of five, and a baby boy of two years, lay on the rolled-up bedding sleeping heavily.

The time was midsummer, 1856, and the family of Joshua Peniman, crossing the plains to the Territory of Nebraska, which had recently been organized, were traveling over the uninhabited prairies of western Iowa.

"Does thee think it could be Indians, Joshua?" asked Hannah Peniman, her face growing white as she viewed the cloud of dust which appeared momentarily to be coming nearer.

"I can't tell——I can't see yet," answered her husband, turning anxious eyes from the musket he was hastily loading toward the cloud of dust. "But whatever it is, it is coming this way. It might be a herd of elk or buffalo, but anyway, we must be prepared. Get inside, Hannah, and thee and the little ones keep well under cover."

In the other wagon two younger boys had joined the lad who was driving. On the seat beside him now sat a merry-faced, brown-eyed lad of fourteen, and leaning on their shoulders peering out between them was a boy of twelve, the twin of the twelve-year-old girl in the other wagon, with red hair, laughing blue eyes, and a round, freckled face.

Sam was the mischief of the family, and was generally larking and laughing, but now his face looked rather pale beneath its coat of tan and freckles, and the eyes which he fastened on the horizon had in them an expression of terror.

"Do you suppose it's Indians, Joe?" he whispered huskily. "Did you hear what that man told Father at Fort Dodge the other day? He said that Indians had set on an emigrant train near Fontanelle and murdered the whole party."

The boy on the driver's seat did not answer. With his wide grey eyes focused intently on the cloud of dust in the distance, his tanned face strained and set, he craned forward, every muscle of his body at rigid attention.

Presently he handed the lines to the brother who sat beside him and reaching up into the curving top of the wagon took down a heavy old muzzle-loading musket.

"Do you think it is Indians?" the boy asked, his hands a bit tremulous on the lines.

"I dunno. Can't tell yet. But we've got to be ready anyhow. Better load up your rifle, Lige."

The brown-eyed boy wound the lines around the whip-stock and took from a rack under the cover a long-barreled rifle.

They had seen many roving bands of Indians on their journey, but had never been molested by them, but at the last settlement they had passed through they had heard horrifying accounts of the scalping and massacre of settlers and emigrants by the red men. On the old Overland Trail between Fort Laramie and the South Fork of the Platte there had occurred an Indian uprising a few days before, the terrifying news of which had reached them at their last stopping place.

As Joe leaned forward with eyes fastened on the horizon he suddenly uttered a cry.

"It's a wagon," he shouted,—"an emigrant wagon—like ours!"

From out of the cloud of dust that drifted across the prairie an object could now be discerned, a large object, with a white canvas cover.

Joshua Peniman, who had never removed his intent gaze from the approaching cloud, echoed the cry.

"It *is* a wagon—an emigrant wagon!" Then as the dust drifted aside and he could see more clearly,—"and they are driving at a fearful pace!"

For many weeks now the family had been traveling over the desolation of the prairies, for days at a time seeing no human creature but one another. For miles all about them lay the prairies, brown, dry, scorched by the hot summer sun, level as a floor, with never a tree, a shrub, a bush, a hill, or a mound to break the dreary monotony of the plains that stretched endlessly away all about them to the very horizon in every direction.

It was therefore with the greater excitement and astonishment that the family saw a wagon drawn by two furiously plunging horses emerge from the cloud of dust that had concealed it, and come swaying and lurching across the plains.

They had stopped their teams now, and the whole family were standing up looking backward.

"Jerusalem! the folks in that wagon must be in a terrible hurry, whoever they are!" ejaculated Elijah, more commonly called "Lige" by his family.

"They'll tip their old schooner over if they don't look out!" cried Sam. "Look at her tilt!"

"Pretty risky driving, I should say," said Mrs. Peniman, shading her eyes with her hand.

"Something must be the matter," cried Ruth, who, wakened by the talking, had come to the rear of the wagon. "I don't believe anybody'd drive like that if they didn't have to! Oh, Mother, do you suppose the Indians are after them?"

"I think not, Ruthie, there does not appear to be any sign of any one after them. What does thee make of it, Joshua?"

"I don't know what to make of it," replied Joshua Peniman, leaping out of the wagon and keeping his gaze fixed on the approaching vehicle. "I never saw such driving. What can they be thinking of to drive their horses like that on such a day! The man must be drunk—or crazy! He'll kill his team!"

The white-topped prairie schooner was now clearly visible, the horses galloping madly, the wagon swaying and lurching from side to side, the white curtain at the back streaming out on the wind.

"Something must be wrong there," cried Joe; "nobody in his senses would drive like that! Do you suppose the team could be running away? No, they're leaving the road! Look, they're turning in here! They must have seen us! I wonder——"

With strained gaze the travelers stood motionless, every faculty absorbed in watching the oncoming vehicle.

Suddenly Mrs. Peniman uttered a startled cry:

"Why, that isn't a man driving—it's a *woman!*"

Joshua Peniman, with hands bowed across his eyes, exclaimed breathlessly, "My God, so it is!"

As the prairie schooner drew nearer the wonder and excitement of the family increased.

On the high driver's seat in the front of the wagon they could now make out a woman; a woman young, beautiful, white and livid as death; a mass of hair that gleamed like molten gold in the sunshine blowing wildly about her shoulders, her eyes distended, her arms bare to the elbows extended far in front of her, one hand clutching the reins, the other lashing the panting, staggering horses, that, lathered with foam and sweat, were heaving and stumbling, ready to drop with exhaustion.

"Help, help, *help!*" her wild, piercing shriek came to them above the clattering of the wagon.

Joshua Peniman, Joe and Lige leaped from their wagons and ran forward to meet her. As they reached her she threw down the reins and reeled and tottered on the seat.

"My husband—my husband!" she gasped, and pointed to the inside of the wagon.

Joshua Peniman took the poor exhausted beasts by their bits and led them up to his own encampment.

"What is it? What has happened?" Hannah Peniman cried, running to the woman and with strong, tender arms lifting her down from the seat.

The woman staggered, and would have fallen if it were not for her strong support.

"My husband—Lee—my husband!" she cried again, and breaking from the supporting arms ran to the rear of the wagon.

Joshua Peniman was there before her.

On the roll of bedding under the canvas cover he saw the figure of a man lying. Springing into the wagon he bent over it, then lifting it in his arms bore it to the opening at the rear, where Joe waited. Between them they carried it to the shade of the wagons, where they laid it on the grass.

As they did so Hannah Peniman stooped over it, then uttered a sharp cry.

"Oh, *look*, look what has happened to him!" she gasped.

Joshua Peniman bent over the prostrate figure. Protruding from the breast, with a great pool of blood staining the shirt about it, was an arrow, buried well up on its feathered shaft.

"*An arrow!*" whispered Hannah Peniman in accents of horror.

"*Indians!*" cried Joe, a creepy chill running down his back.

The strange woman had run to the body and precipitated herself upon it with agonized cries.

"Oh, Lee, Lee!" she shrieked. "Oh, surely he isn't dead! Surely he would not leave us all alone!"

Joshua Peniman motioned to his wife, and with gentle hands she raised the frail, delicate figure of the young wife and bore it away to the other side of the wagon. Mr. Peniman stripped off the coat and laid his hand, then his ear, over the heart of the prostrate figure.

"He is not dead," he whispered, "his heart is beating faintly. Get me a pan of water, Joe, and the spirits of ammonia. Hurry, lad, a life may depend on our efficiency now!"

When he had sponged the blood away he tried to draw the arrow from the wound, but it was too deeply imbedded. His efforts only succeeded in starting a terrific flow of blood, in the midst of which the wounded man moaned and opened his eyes.

"Marian!" his lips shaped rather than spoke the word. Surmising that it must be the name of his wife, Joshua Peniman sent Lige running to call her. Then he bent over the wounded man, saying distinctly, "Thee is with friends, friend. Thy wife is safe, and with my wife back of the wagons."

The wounded man rolled his eyes about, then whispered tensely, "Nina! Nina!"

Not knowing what he meant, the Quaker nodded reassuringly.

"Indians?" he asked, pointing to the arrow.

The man slowly raised his hand and groped toward the wound. To the intense astonishment of both father and sons he shook his head. "Tell—Marian—watch out—watch out for—for——" his head dropped back, the blood gushed from his mouth, and with a gurgling cry he sank back on the grass.

Joshua Peniman knelt beside him.

"Gone!" he said solemnly, reverently removing his hat.

CHAPTER II

THE GRAVE IN THE DESERT

As Joshua Peniman and his two older sons stood looking down upon the dead man, the delicate-featured, high-browed, thoughtful face of a scholar, upon the hands, smooth, white, tapering, with well-kept nails and soft palms, the body worn and thin almost to emaciation, the waxen cheeks hollow and sunken under the blue-rimmed eyes, a strange sense of awe and wonder passed over them.

What was this man—this delicate, scholarly-appearing individual with his soft hands and emaciated body—doing in an emigrant wagon crossing the trackless plains?

Who was the woman who was with him—that young, beautiful, delicately-clad and delicately nurtured woman, whose sobs and moans they could hear from the other side of the wagon?

As these questions forced themselves through the mind of Joshua Peniman the woman came rushing around the end of the wagon and cast herself down beside the body.

"Lee, Lee, Lee!" she shrieked. "Oh, he is not dead, he is not dead! Surely God could not be so cruel as to take him from me! Oh, Lee, my husband, my own, my only love!"

Her voice had risen into a high, wailing cry. Suddenly from the rear end of the wagon from which they had taken the dead man a head appeared.

To the startled eyes of the boys who first saw it it seemed the most beautiful head and face they had ever seen.

It was a small head, fine and delicate, set like a flower on a little swan-like throat, and covered with short curls of sunny gold. Beneath the shining halo of curls a face looked out, pitifully small and frightened, with great terrified violet eyes, a quivering rose-bud mouth, and a skin as fair and delicate as the petals of a flower.

"Father—Mother!" cried a quivering, childish voice, "oh, what is the matter? what has happened? what are you crying so for, Mother?" Then, as the terrified violet eyes caught sight of the body, she leaped to the ground and threw herself upon it with a cry that Joe could never forget.

The children who had gathered about stood transfixed, but Hannah Peniman moved swiftly to the child and took her in her arms.

"Thy father has gone away, dear child," she whispered in her soft, motherly voice. "But thee must be very brave for thy poor young mother's sake. Thou must help her to bear it."

The child uttered a wild sob, then fled to her mother and clasped her arms about her neck.

They clung to each other sobbing bitterly for a time. The boys turned away, and Joe found a lump too big to swallow choking his throat.

After a time Joshua Peniman bent to the woman tenderly.

"Was thy husband ill, my child?" he asked gently.

"Oh yes, yes, very ill," she answered between her sobs. "They told me he had tuberculosis. He was a writer. You must have heard of him. The doctors sent us out West. They told him to get a wagon and spend the whole summer traveling across the plains. We were on our way to Colorado for his health. We have been out three weeks, and he was better, oh, very, very much better. And then yesterday we were driving along near a creek and some Indians set upon us———"

"Indians?" cried Joshua Peniman, remembering that the dying man had answered his question with a shake of the head.

"Yes, Indians—a whole band of them. They began shooting at us. Nina and I happened to be inside the wagon, but Lee—my poor Lee—was on the driver's seat. I don't know when he was hit. I don't know that he knew himself. He shouted out to me to hide, and to hide Nina, and I did, I hid her under the blankets beneath the seat———"

"And you are sure it was Indians that attacked you?" asked Joshua Peniman, while a cold hand of terror clutched his wife's heart.

"Yes, I'm sure. I saw them. I heard them. Oh, they were horrible! Lee never made a sound when he was struck. All at once I saw him reel and totter on the seat, then he came tumbling backward, and I saw the arrow in his breast. I tried to pull it out, but I couldn't, and it bled fearfully, so I stopped. He was conscious then, and said, 'Drive—hurry—wagon ahead!' I got up on the seat and whipped up the horses and drove and drove as fast as I could make them go. The heat was terrible. I thought I should die. But I saw your tracks, and at last I saw the smoke of your fire and knew there was help at hand. I thought I should kill the horses, but I didn't care, all I could think of was help—help for my poor Lee!"

As she said the last words she uttered a long wail, threw her arms above her head and plunged forward over the dead body.

Joshua Peniman lifted her tenderly and bore her in his arms to their own wagon.

All night they worked over her, with every remedy at their command, but before the grey dawn of morning they knew that she would join her husband before many hours.

Heat, exhaustion, terror, the strain of agony and fear, the shock to an already weakened and overstrained heart, were more than nature could bear.

Shortly before daylight she opened her eyes and looked up into the face of Hannah Peniman, who bent above her.

"Who are you?" she asked faintly. "Where do you come from?"

"Our name is Peniman, Hannah and Joshua Peniman. And these are our children. We come from the Muskingum Valley in Ohio."

"You are Quakers?"

"Yes. My husband was a leader in the Society of Friends."

"Then you are good—good and kind, I know," she whispered brokenly. Then clutching Hannah Peniman's hand and fixing her beautiful, burning eyes upon her face she hurried on: "My child—my little Nina— what will become of her? I am going—going to Lee—I could not live without him. Our name is Carroll. My husband was Lee Carroll—a writer—and I am Marian Carroll. The little girl's name is Nina. Will you take her—will you take her with you to the nearest Mission? I know it is asking a good deal with your big family—but you will do it—I know you will do it—for my poor little orphaned child. I will explain to her—give her papers and addresses and all—and they can send her home from there. Our people are all—all——"

She stopped, gasping and struggling for breath. Joshua Peniman lifted her and held a heart stimulant to her lips. After an interval, when they feared all was over, she again opened her eyes. Mother love was stronger than death. "Send—her—to me," she gasped—"I have not long—to— be—with—her."

They laid her back upon the bed, then sent the child to her.

For some moments they heard the low murmur of voices, the sobbing of the child. Then when there had been silence for some time Hannah Peniman quietly parted the curtains of the wagon and looked in.

The young mother lay white and still, her beautiful delicately carved face looking like sculptured marble in the dim grey light of morning, the child with her arms tight clasped about her neck, her cheek on the fast-chilling cheek of her dead mother, sobbing by her side.

Hannah Peniman took her in her arms and carried her out of the wagon. Apart from her own brood of little ones she sat down, the little girl still in her arms, and rocked and crooned to her, talking to her in gentle, soothing tones, telling her of the great happiness her young parents would feel in their reunion, in that place where there is no more parting, no more sickness or suffering or death.

When the sun had risen they buried the man and woman side by side in a grave dug in the virgin soil of the prairie. Over it the sun rose, shining down upon the two pitiful mounds of earth in the loneliness of the desert land, and bringing out upon the two wooden crosses at their head the inscription Joshua Peniman had painted upon them, "Lee and Marian Carroll. Died July 20th, 1856. Buried by Joshua Peniman, emigrant, on way to Nebraska."

Below in smaller letters he had printed the cause of the death. That was all that he knew about them.

He had drawn the arrow from the breast of the dead man before wrapping the still form in the blanket that was its only coffin and shroud, and without asking himself the reason why he preserved the arrow carefully, putting it away in a chest under the seat of his wagon.

The whole family gathered about the graves, while the gentle Quaker said over them the simple, earnest prayer of the Friends, then turned sadly toward the wagons, which were ready to start again on their westward journey.

As they turned away from the lonely graves the child broke from them and with a wild cry ran back and threw herself face downward upon them.

Ruth and Sara broke into loud sobbing, and even the boys were obliged to turn aside.

Hannah Peniman went to the child and raised her.

"Come, little one," she said with tear-wet eyes, "thee must come away. Thy dear parents are not there. That is only the old garments they have laid down to go to the new home that awaits them. They are together now, and will always be happy and well. They are not far away. They will watch over thee. Their spirits will always be near thee. Thou art young, life will bring many joys to thee, of which thy parents will be glad. Come now, little girl, the sun grows high, the day will be hot, and we must be on our way."

As the child, sobbing bitterly and clinging to her, turned toward the wagon that had belonged to her parents, which was hitched on behind the one driven by Joshua Peniman, Mrs. Peniman drew her away.

"Will thee ride in the big wagon with my little girls?" she asked gently; "they would be very glad to have thee."

The child raised her pretty head, looked at the Peniman children with her beautiful, tear-filled eyes, then slowly shook her head.

"I will ride with that boy," she said, pointing to Joe, who, seated on the driver's seat of his own wagon, was valiantly striving to appear manly and keep back his tears. He blushed up to the roots of his fair hair, then leaped down from the seat and very tenderly lifted the little stranger up on the seat of the wagon.

As the cavalcade started forward, now quite a procession with the three teams and wagons, the cow following behind, the collie dog leaping and barking beside the wagons, the faces of all were turned backward and their eyes rested on the lonely mounds on the prairie as long as they were in sight.

The little girl, sitting beside Joe on the high seat with her trimly-dressed little feet swinging far above the wagon-bed, kept her head buried in her arms, and sobbed as if her heart would break. Gentle-hearted Ruth cried with her, Lige beat a hasty retreat to the back of the wagon, while tender-hearted Sam slipped a sympathetic freckled hand into hers and wept openly as he smoothed and patted it.

Joe could do nothing but sit soddenly, with a lump in his throat so big that he could neither speak nor swallow. But his eyes had in them all the sympathy that his lips could not speak, and when the little girl at last looked up it was straight into those bright, wistful, moist grey eyes, after which she snuggled up against him and laid her head against his arm.

CHAPTER III

PRINCESS

As the wagons creaked slowly along over the burning, dusty prairies the little stranger cried more quietly, while the children stared at her with growing interest and wonder.

They had never seen any one quite like her before.

Living as they had in the quiet Friends settlement on their farm in Ohio, they had seen but little of the outside world, and that little had contained nobody in the least like this fairy-like creature, with her dainty clothing, her delicate features and coloring and her sunny golden hair.

"Say," whispered Sam, who was a great devourer of juvenile literature; "she looks just exactly like the fairy princesses you read about in story-books, don't she? Look at her little feet, and her little teeny white hands, and how her hair curls, and how little and white her neck is!"

Lige looked and nodded. "An' look at her clothes, too! City folks' clothes. Wonder why her mother let her wear clothes like that in the wagon? Our mother wouldn't let Sara and Ruth."

"You bet she wouldn't. She makes 'em wear calico aprons."

They glanced again at the little figure on the seat in front of them; at the dainty white dress, the little lace-trimmed petticoat that showed below its edge, the white stockings, the dainty little kid slippers, and then at each other and their own rough clothes and rough red hands.

"Makes you feel kind of like a tramp, don't it?" muttered Lige, and privately resolved to get out his second-best suit and put it on in the morning.

Joe meanwhile was casting sympathetic glances at the little figure beside him, and trying hard to think of something to say or do to comfort her. The sight of a meadow-lark flying up from a little bunch of grass near by gave him an opening.

"Bet there's a nest and some eggs in that bunch of grass," he remarked nonchalantly, and was rewarded by seeing the big violet eyes come up from the little monogramed handkerchief, and the golden head raised to see.

"Where?" she asked, with a child's readily aroused interest.

Joe was enchanted.

"Right over there," he explained, pointing with the whip. "Want to see if there ain't?" He stopped the horses and all the children sprang out and ran to the patch of grass.

Sam reached it first, and made emphatic signs to the others to come quietly. When they had all crept up they found a nest indeed, but better than eggs in it, for there were four big-headed, wide-mouthed speckled little birds, that, when they felt the stir in the grass near them, stretched up their skinny necks and peeped industriously.

The boys laughed, and even Nina managed a little smile. When they went back to the wagon she was not crying, and her three anxious escorts exerted themselves to their utmost to keep her busy and interested for the remainder of the day.

After a time Sara and Paul joined them, and Mr. and Mrs. Peniman, riding in the other wagon with the younger children, were pleased and glad to hear as the day progressed that the voice of the little stranger joined in their talk and laughter.

"What shall we do with her, Hannah?" asked Joshua Peniman anxiously. "Somehow it weighs heavily upon my heart to think of leaving this little orphaned child among strangers at a Mission. I presume they would be kind to her, and perhaps would exert themselves to get her home to her own people, but——"

The sigh with which the sentence ended found an echo in Hannah Peniman's heart. She had been thinking of the matter all day, wondering in what direction lay their duty.

"I agree with thee, Joshua," she answered. "A Mission is no place for a little girl like her. She bears every evidence of delicate and tender rearing, and gives promise of great beauty. She is thirteen years old now, her mother told me, and in a very few years will grow into a beautiful young maiden."

For many miles the couple drove along in silence, the voices from the other wagon coming frequently to their ears. After long and earnest thought Hannah Peniman spoke:

"Joshua," she said, "my heart cannot forget that the hand of the Lord was laid upon us, too, in crossing these prairies. There is always before me the picture of that tiny mound we left behind us in this great trackless desert when our own little girl was taken from us. Perhaps God has intended to comfort us by sending to us this other child, whose sorrow has linked her to us. Somehow I cannot find it in my heart to abandon her to such care as she would find at a Mission."

Joshua Peniman turned to her, love and approval beaming in his eyes.

"Spoken like the true woman thee is, Hannah," he said, clasping her hand. "But I would not that an added burden should be laid upon thee. Thou hast many little ones to attend to, and this stranger child——"

"—Would not make me any more care, dear. She can run wild with Ruth and Sara out there on the plains, and I believe that our boys are kind and chivalrous enough to take care of her."

"But her clothes, Hannah? With eight children of our own to keep covered——"

"One more would not matter. Beside, the child is thirteen years old, and should learn to sew. Soon she will be able to attend to her own clothes. And"—with a little smile that had in it a tinge of pain,—"I imagine few clothes will suffice in the country to which we are going."

"But the cooking——"

"She would be a help to Ruth and Sara in their share of the work. And as for the food she will eat——"

"We must not think of that," cried Joshua Peniman hastily. "The Providence which threw her into our hands will see to it that we are able to feed her. When we reach another town of size I will write to the relatives of which her mother spoke. Until that time——"

"—Until that time," interrupted Mrs. Peniman, with her motherly smile, "she shall be even as our own, and we will care for her as her poor young parents would have wished her to be cared for."

"God bless thee for a good and noble woman, Hannah," said her husband; and so the fate of the little stranger was decided.

Meanwhile as the wagons jogged on through the long, hot, silent afternoon the children grew better acquainted, and presently began to talk of themselves and one another.

"How long have you been on the way, Princess?" asked the irrepressible Sam. "We been out eight weeks now."

The little stranger looked up at him quickly.

"My name isn't 'Princess,' it's Nina," she said.

"But you look just like a princess—like the princess in the fairy stories, don't you know?"

Nina, who had been an indefatigable reader of fairy tales herself, recognized the compliment.

"Aw, no I don't, either!" she ejaculated scornfully. "The princesses in fairy stories are always beautiful."

"So're you," urged the gallant Sam. "You do, too, look like a princess, don't she, Joe?"

Joe glanced up shyly. "I've never seen a princess," he admitted, "but I *think* you do. I think you are beautiful. You are the most beautiful person I have ever seen."

Long years after, when time and fate had wrought many changes in their lives, Joe remembered the speech and thought no differently.

The little girl blushed and hung her head.

"You're a silly boy," she told him. "I don't look a bit like a princess. What makes you boys say such foolish things?"

Joe seldom said anything that he had not thought out pretty thoroughly, and he now puckered his forehead and searched for the reason in his mind that made this little girl seem different from any other he had ever seen.

"I guess," he began thoughtfully, "it's 'cause you're kind of different. You see we've always lived on the farm, and the folks we knew were just plain Friends, who didn't think much about dress or looks, just work and service, you know. But you—well—I dunno, I don't know how to say it— but you look like—like something out of the sky, or the air, or a book or something. Not like us—like you were meant for work and service, but kind o' like the birds and flowers an' the pretty things of life. I guess that's what Sam means when he says you look like a princess."

"W-ell, partly," admitted Sam. "Anyhow I'm going to call you 'Princess.'"

"I don't care what you call me," cried the little girl, with a smile that brought little sparkles into her eyes and made a dimple play hide-and-seek in either rose-hued cheek. Then turning again to Joe, "You're Quakers, aren't you?"

"Yes," he replied, "all our people have been Friends for generations back. Father was the founder of a sect where we lived."

"But you boys don't talk like Quakers!"

"No, we don't use the plain language any more. You see we have been at school with other boys who didn't use it, so we got out of the way.

Father doesn't use it to people of the world, either; we only use it at home. We've always lived in Ohio. Where did you used to live?"

The sadness which the conversation of the last few minutes had driven from the face of the little "Princess" returned.

"We really lived in New York," she said. "But we traveled about so much I don't know just where our home really was. You see Papa was a writer—wrote books, you know, and he had to travel about a lot, and Mama and I always went with him. She could never bear to be away from him, and they always took me. We lived in France and Italy and Germany and Russia, and it was awful cold there in Russia, and Papa took sick. He was awfully sick, we thought he was going to die. The doctors sent us back to America, and we came out West for his health. We got a wagon and team in Chicago and were on our way to Colorado. He was better—lots and lots better, and he might have got well, but then—then——" Her voice broke and the tears welled up into her eyes.

"Oh," broke in Lige, who could not bear to see the clouds obscure the sunshine of the past few minutes, "you ought to see what we've been through! I tell you we've had adventures! We came all the way from Ohio in these wagons, and I tell you what we've had some lively times!"

"What kind of adventures?" queried the Princess, the natural curiosity of a child aroused by these allusions to incidents of a thrilling nature.

"O Jerusalem, all kinds of 'em!" cried the delighted Lige, fairly swelling with importance. "We got into a flood an' nearly lost our wagon, and coyotes got after the horses, and little David got lost an' fell into the river, an'—an'—oh, all kinds of things!"

"Tell me about them," demanded the Princess, who dearly loved a story.

Lige looked at Joe. He was a handsome boy, who was fond of occupying the centre of the stage, but he knew that his brother could do greater justice to the thrilling adventures they had been through than he could.

"You tell her, Joe," he said. And as Joe pulled the horses into a smoother place in the road and threw one leg over the other, the little Princess settled down beside him, her chin in her hand, her great violet eyes fastened upon his face, as he proceeded to tell their story.

THE LITTLE PRINCESS SETTLED DOWN BESIDE HIM, HER CHIN IN HER HAND.—*Page 27*.

The little Princess settled down beside him, her chin in her hand.

That the reader may know as much about the Peniman family and their great adventure of crossing the plains as did the little Princess, we will leave the wagons lumbering slowly along over the baking plains and return to the Muskingum Valley in Ohio from whence they made their start.

CHAPTER IV

LEAVING THE OLD HOME

It was on the morning of May 15, 1856, that Joe Peniman awoke as the first grey streaks of morning were coming in the sky. In the yard beneath his window he could hear the sound of voices, footsteps going to and fro. Inside there was the sound of bumping and thumping of furniture, of much talking, the hurried noises of preparation for some great event.

He started up and glanced at the window. Day was coming! *The Day!* The day he had been dreaming of and hoping for and longing for for months!

He leaped out of bed with a shrill yip of joy and pulled the bedclothes off his slumbering brother.

"Hi, Lige," he shouted, "wake up! It's to-morrow—I mean it's to-day—it's *The Day* at last!"

Lige raised a sleepy face from the pillows, blinked once or twice, rubbed his nose, then sat up with a jerk.

"Jerusalem, is it *morning?*" he ejaculated. "Why, I never slept a wink all night. Couldn't, I was too excited. Oh, golly, this is to-morrow, isn't it? No, it's *to-day* now—and we're going to start right after breakfast! Ki-yi, *ain't I glad!*"

He did an extemporaneous war-dance around the room, then brought up beside the bed where Joe was hastily getting into the new gingham shirt, the dark suit, and strong copper-toed shoes that had been laid out upon it.

Outside in the yard they could hear the sound of talking, of men going to and fro. There was the sound of rumbling wheels, the regular strokes of a hammer, and many directions given in the mild but decisive voice of their father.

It was very early still. In the shadows it was still dark, and over the whole earth there lay that hush, that sense of mystery and silence that comes with the early dawn. The sky above the east pasture showed faint streaks of pink and mauve, and the fragrance of the apple and peach and plum and cherry blossoms in the old orchard came up to them, mingled with the scent of wet grass and clover, the lowing of the cows in the pasture, the crowing of the roosters in the barnyard. It was with something like a pang that Joe recognized the shrill and strident voice of little Dicky, his favorite bantam rooster.

Under the old elm-trees two heavy new wagons were drawn up, and their father, mounted on the dash-board of one of them was fastening in place the white canvas cover, stretching it taut over strong ash bows that were bent from side to side of the wagon.

A thrill passed through the hearts of the boys as they leaned half-dressed out of the window.

The *Prairie Schooners!*

The romantic craft in which they were to embark that day on the most wonderful adventures of their lives!

They had talked of and dreamed about and anticipated the coming of this day for many months. Now it seemed almost too good to be true that it was really here at last.

It seemed to the boys as they hung out of the window that the yard was full of men, and that they all seemed in a great hurry and bustle of preparation, going to and fro between the barn and the house and the wagons carrying boxes and bundles and bedding and furniture and stowing it away in the wagons beneath the canvas covers.

They recognized their Uncle Jonathan among them, and sent forth a loud and triumphant hail to their Cousin Fred, who was standing about wistfully watching the loading of the wagons. Bill Hale, the "hired man," was there, and Uncle Charles, and Friend Robinson, and neighbor Hines, and many more. A queer sort of a sinking sensation seized the pit of Joe's stomach as he saw Friend Robinson carry out his mother's old rocking-chair and the baby's cradle and put them into the wagon.

Through the trees across the creek he could see the red roof of his grandmother's house, the old Quaker homestead where his mother was born and had grown to womanhood, and nearer the woods and stream and lanes where his brothers and sisters and himself had played all their lives.

In the tree outside the window he caught a glimpse of the robin that had nested in that same crotch of a branch for five summers. She was sitting now. The young birds would be out in a few days. Joe turned his eyes hastily away from the bright glance of the little mother as she peered up at him.

"Come, boys—come, Joseph, will thee stand staring out of that window all day?" a voice cried behind him, and he withdrew his head quickly and turned around to see his mother standing in the doorway. She was all dressed and ready for the journey, in a dark grey worsted dress with a white collar, her brown hair neat and shining, her face a little pale, and her sweet blue eyes reddened by recent tears.

"Come, come, boys, thee must hurry," she cried. "Thy father has been afoot for an hour or more, and breakfast is nearly ready. Elijah, did thee put on the new stockings I laid out for thee? Tie thy necktie neatly, Joseph. And hurry, now, the day that thee has been looking forward to so long has come at last, and thee must begin right now to be brave young pioneers."

Her voice quivered a little but she smiled at them bravely, then hurried away.

Out under the elm-trees the boys found preparations for the journey rapidly approaching completion. The great white canvas covers of the wagons were now in place, making a domed shelter for the interior of the wagons, and most of the household goods that the family were going to take with them to their far western home had already been stowed away inside.

As Joe stood watching these preparations something of the finality of the change was borne in upon him. Up to this moment he had thought of nothing but the wonderful journey across the plains, the romance, the adventure, the strange, novel, and interesting things he would see and do along the way. Now it suddenly came over him that he was leaving his childhood home forever.

He thought of the boys, the playmates of his whole life, whom he was leaving behind; of the swimming-hole down under the willows; the nest of young kittens under the barn; the sunfish and croppies in the stream. He thought of his playmates at old-fashioned "round ball," and wondered, with just the suggestion of a pang, who would play in his place this summer.

Just below the house the creek murmured musically over its pebbly bottom, and near it was the old willow-tree in which he could see the platform of their playhouse—all that was left of it—most of it having been torn down and the lumber used for crating furniture and covering boxes.

His thoughts were beginning to grow a bit sombre when a call to breakfast interrupted them. He hurried into the big sunny kitchen, in which he had eaten his breakfast every morning of his life.

It did not look natural this morning. An extemporaneous table had been arranged of planks set on sawhorses, and upon it was spread the breakfast, with odds and ends of dishes and crockery that were to be left behind. About this board the family was gathered, while the kitchen was filled with relatives, neighbors, and friends.

Mrs. Peniman's mother, Mrs. Jennings, sat at the head of the table, with little David in her lap, and her noble placid face looked withered, wan and pale, as if she had not slept for many nights. Mrs. Peniman sat beside her with baby Abigail on her knee, and Joe noticed with a queer constriction in his breast that her face was very pale and her white lips pressed together as if to keep them from trembling. Aunt Sue stood behind her, her handkerchief pressed to her eyes, and Aunt Jenny, his mother's youngest sister, sat on the floor at her feet, her face hidden in baby Abigail's dress, crying as if her heart would break.

Back of them against the wall Uncle Charles and Uncle Henry were biting their lips and surreptitiously blowing their noses, and Uncle Jonathan and Uncle Benjamin, while pretending to be very busy passing around trays of coffee, occasionally found time in a corner to mop their eyes with their handkerchiefs. Old friends and neighbors whom he had known all his life stood about the room looking grave and sober, while there were tears in all the women's eyes.

Joe and Elijah stood in the doorway, loath to go in, but their father beckoned them to him. He was a tall, thin man, with a broad brow upon which waved thick dark hair just tinged with grey. His eyes were dark, with a keen yet very gentle expression, and the almost womanish beauty of his mouth and the square masculinity of his chin were lost in a heavy dark-brown beard which grew high on his cheeks and was trimmed square below the points of his collar.

The boys noticed as they came to him that his eyes were red, and the hand that he laid on Joe's shoulder trembled slightly.

When the breakfast was over and the last preparations being made on the wagons Friend Robinson turned to Mr. Peniman with a heavy sigh. "I tell thee it is a pretty serious business, friend Joshua, to break up a home like this and go away into the wilderness with a family like thine. I don't blame Hannah for feeling sad about it."

"*Blame* her?" cried Joshua Peniman. "Who could blame her? She is the bravest woman in the world. Many women would be prostrated at leaving the home in which they were born and had lived all their lives, their mother, sisters, brothers and all the friends of a lifetime to go away into a wild and unknown country to encounter the dangers and hardships of the life of a pioneer. But she has been our inspiration, she has given courage to us all." After a moment he cleared his throat and went on huskily, "I don't know that any of us particularly enjoy the prospect before us."

"Why does thee persist in going then, Joshua?" broke in his brother Henry. "There is time even yet to reconsider thy decision. It is a great undertaking, a great responsibility thou art laying on thyself. Think of Hannah—think of the children—think of the dangers and the hardships and privations that thee and thine will have to undergo in that desert country——"

"I have thought of nothing else for months, Henry," replied Joshua Peniman solemnly. "I cannot tell thee the struggle I have been through. I fully realize what this breaking up of her lifelong home must mean to Hannah. I know what it will mean to the children—and," with a sudden twitching of his gentle face, "what it will mean to myself. But I feel that it must be done. It is a duty we owe our little family. It is a duty I owe to my religion and my God. Thee knows the condition of the country, Henry. Thee knows that war is inevitable between the North and South. It will be a terrible war, a war of brother against brother, father against son, neighbor against neighbor; one kindred pitted against another. Thee knows our faith, our principles. Could I stay here with my five sons and have them brought up to human slaughter? Could I stay here and have them sent forth to shoot down their fellow-men?"

"But that is all nonsense, Joshua, thy boys are but children yet."

"Joe is almost sixteen. In five years he will be twenty-one. Tell me, brothers, at the rate things are going in this country now how will things stand between the North and South in five years?"

"Well," put in Bill Hale, "there ain't no signs of war *yit*; the trouble between the North and South hain't got no further than shootin' off their mouths, an' so long's they confine themselves to that kind of warfare I reckon you an' th' boys would be middlin' safe here."

"It isn't a question of safety," retorted Joshua Peniman with as near to a flash of anger in his eyes as Joe had ever seen. "It is a question of *principle*. Suppose this country does get into war and there should be a draft. My boys are Quakers. How could they go? And how could they avoid going if they were drafted? Even should there be no real fighting for years to come still those boys would be brought up in an atmosphere of rancor, hostility, and controversy. Hannah and I do not want our children to grow up with hatred in their hearts. We want them to grow up in love and brotherly kindness to all men."

"But thee could keep the children out of it all, Joshua," put in Uncle Charles. "Here on the farm they would not come in touch with the political controversy to any great extent, and both thee and thy boys could keep thyselves entirely aloof from the trouble."

Joshua Peniman shook his head. "No, brother Charles, thee knows that that would not be possible. Thy affectionate heart is speaking now, not thy reason. Thee knows how I stand on this matter of slavery. Thee knows that already I have embroiled myself, have made many and bitter enemies for myself by my connection with the underground railway. I *have* run off runaway slaves, and I will run them off again every chance I get; for I believe it to be a wicked and iniquitous business. No man has a right to own and control another human being. I am a man of peace, who loves my fellow-man, and yet"—he paused and turned his eyes upon Joe, who crimsoned under the scrutiny,—"no longer ago than yesterday I found my oldest son, an offshoot of good old Quaker stock, drilling a company of boys in the manoeuvres of war."

"I didn't mean any harm, Father," burst forth Joe, "thee knows that I would not hurt any one! It is only that it is fun to drill. I love to march and counter-march my men about."

His father nodded. "I know, my son. And therein lies the danger. Thou art breathing in the spirit of warfare with the very air. I do not blame thee, lad; how could it be otherwise? The minds of men are full of it. The papers are full of it, and people talk of little else. I tell thee, friends, war is inevitable, and I will not have my young lads filled with the spirit of it. Hannah thinks as I do, and long before the red carnival of blood-lust is let loose in the land we will be far away, out on the clean, wholesome prairies, where our boys and girls can grow up to noble man and womanhood untouched and untainted by the unholy slaughter."

"But thee should think of the material prosperity of thy children as well as their spiritual good, brother Joshua," argued Charles. "Thee knows that out there in that untrodden wilderness they will have little or no opportunity for education——"

"We are thinking of their material prosperity. What chance in life would our nine children have here? I would be a poor man all my life, and could do nothing to establish a future for them. With a big family like ours we need room, more opportunity for development, and that we will find in the new country. If we go west now, while the children and the country are both young they will have great opportunities. I will take up a homestead and make them a good home, and as the boys grow old enough they can take up timber-claims and homesteads so that by the time they reach manhood they will each have a valuable property, a good start in life, and a chance to make of themselves whatever they see fit."

"Yes, but their education——" urged Charles, whose heart was sore at the thought of seeing his brother and his young family set forth for that strange, far land, and hoped even now at the last moment to turn him from the purpose.

"That does not trouble us, Charles. Thee knows that I was once a teacher in a college, and that Hannah has also had a good education. There is nothing to prevent us from conducting a little school of our own for our children until such time as there will be good schools in that growing country for them to attend."

"But what good'll schoolin' do 'em if they was all to get skulped by them bloody Injuns out there?" put in Bill Hale. "My wife's sister-in-law's cousin went out west onct, an' he never come back. The Injuns got him. Like's not they made soup of him. But I'm bound to say that if he was anything like the rest of that family he'd 'a' made dern poor soup, even fer a cannibal."

Joshua Peniman did not join in the general laugh that followed Bill's remark. He glanced uneasily at his watch, then at the house.

"Call thy mother, Joe," he said; "it is growing late, the sun is up, and we should be on our way. Ah, here they come now!"

As he spoke Mrs. Peniman came down the steps, the baby in her arms, leading little David by the hand. Her sister Jenny followed with Mary, and Ruth and Sara walked on either side of their grandmother, their hands in hers, while Sam and Paul, with red noses and watery eyes, followed.

The powerful bay team, Jim and Charley, hitched to the big wagon, were prancing and fidgeting, and the sorrel team, Kit and Billy, hitched to the lighter wagon, which it had been decided that Joe should drive, were harnessed and ready, when Bill Hale came racing from the house waving a bundle in his hand.

"What's the matter?" cried Joe, checking them up. "We must have left something behind!"

"Couldn't have forgotten the baby, could we?" queried Sam.

By this time Bill Hale had reached them, carrying a large bundle tied up in a napkin in one hand, and in the other swinging a pair of squawking chickens by the legs.

"Ye 'most missed it, I tell ye," he grinned. "Ol' Mis' Perkins brought ye over some things t' take on your journey, an' she never got here until jist now. I've et Ma Perkins' pies an' things an' I couldn't abear fer ye to miss 'em."

He handed the package tied up in the napkin to Mr. Peniman.

"Mis' Perkins 'lowed she wanted to send some chicken along fer yer lunch," he went on, looking down at the squawking fowls in his hand, "but hearin' that the Friends had cooked up s' much fer ye she figgered she hadn't better cook hern, but send 'em along on th' hoof like, so's ye could have 'em any time ye liked."

The children all laughed, and even Mr. Peniman smiled.

"That was very kind of Friend Perkins," he said. "Thank her for us, won't you, Bill? But I declare I don't see how we are going to take those live chickens! We've got about all the live stock we can handle now."

"Oh, we must take them, Joshua," said Mrs. Peniman. "It would never do to send them back when she was so kind. We can manage to take care of them somehow."

"I've got a box in my wagon that hasn't much in it, Father," said Joe; "we could turn the things out and put them in that."

"You can kill and eat them any time they get to be a bother, you know," said Uncle Charles, who stood by.

Ruth, who loved every living creature, and who would have fed and mothered any number of pets, protested loudly.

"Oh, we will *not* kill them, Uncle Charles!" she cried. "Look at them, Father, aren't they perfect darlings? Let's take them along for pets, Father, I'll take care of them!"

By this time Joe and Lige had cleared the box of its contents, and with Bill Hale's help soon had the struggling fowls shut up in it, with slats nailed up in front to keep them in.

"Oh, aren't they *lovely* chickies?" cooed Ruth, who had jumped out of the wagon to watch the operation. "We'll call this one Dicky, and this one Mother Feathertop, to always remind us of our old Mother Feathertop at home."

"All right; ready there?" called Mr. Peniman.

Cherry, the red cow, that was tied behind the big wagon, looked back and gave a mournful bellow, as if she knew that she was leaving her old home forever; Spotty, the collie dog, leaped forward with a bark, and the children scrambled to their places in the wagons.

Joe never liked to remember the few moments that followed, as relatives, friends, neighbors, chums, and playmates of a lifetime crowded close about the wagons to bid them good-bye. There were sobs and tears, close embraces, choked words of love and farewell; hands were shaken, tears shed, husky good-byes spoken. But it was soon over.

The boys sprang to their places, the reins were gathered up, the word of command spoken, and the prairie schooners drove slowly out of the farmyard, en route for the Golden West.

CHAPTER V

WESTWARD HO!

The road over which the Peniman family set forth led through southern and eastern Ohio, where the roads were good, shade and water abundant, and where pretty towns and villages lined the way, so that their larder was always plentifully supplied with fresh meat, fruits, and vegetables.

The wagons in which they were to make their long overland journey to the new territory of Nebraska had been carefully prepared for the comfort of the travelers, and the first part of the trip was like nothing so much as a prolonged family picnic. Their night camp was made in beautiful woods beside murmuring streams, and if bad weather came a town or village was always within easy reach, where the wagons could be put in a stable and the family repair to a hotel until the storm was over.

On their seventh day out they reached Columbus, and during the week that followed traveled across the western part of Ohio and crossed into Indiana, where they made a stop of a few days with old Quaker friends.

Their progress was necessarily slow, averaging not more than fifteen to twenty miles a day. On June seventh they arrived in Indianapolis, then but a small and inconsequential town, where they made a stop of a few hours to lay in a fresh suppy of meat, fresh fruits, bread, butter, and vegetables, then struck into the main road leading north and west to Crawfordsville, where they stopped long enough to buy a doll for little Mary, a tin trumpet for David, and ice-cream for the rest of the family.

This part of the journey, while pleasant and interesting, was uneventful, and though the boys enjoyed it, much as they would have enjoyed a prolonged picnic, they were looking eagerly forward to the adventures which lay in the wild and untrodden land beyond the Missouri River.

On June fourteenth they arrived at the beautiful Wabash River, and made their camp upon its banks for the night, where the whole family had a refreshing bath in its sparkling waters.

Up to this time the weather had been fine, the roads excellent, and the traveling pleasant. But the day they began their journey across the State of Illinois the weather changed and a heavy rain set in which materially interfered with both their comfort and their progress.

At first the children found it rather fun sitting snug and dry under their canvas roof while the rain pattered down upon it. But when day followed day and the rain continued to fall, when they had to make camp at night in wet groves with a fire that would not burn and clothes and shoes that were never dry, it was not quite so pleasant.

Betrayed into neglecting his canvas covers by the long dry spell Mr. Peniman now found that they had shrunken from the sun and were beginning to leak, and the family woke morning after morning to find the rain spraying down into their faces, and to crawl out of damp beds to find the ground a mush of wet grass and mud, and no dry wood obtainable with which to start their fire.

There was no running before or behind the wagons these days, no playing in the fields, picking wild-flowers or frolicking on the road as the white-topped wagons crawled along; all day long while the horses plodded monotonously along through puddles of water or mud that went over their fetlocks and ruts that let the wagons down almost to the hubs of the wheels, they sat tired, bored, and hoping for fair weather and sunshine.

On the fourth day of the rain, when the wagons had become so damp that they were decidedly uncomfortable, they came to a house toward evening, and Mr. Peniman alighted to ask if the people who lived in it would give them shelter for the night. They found both husband and wife down with the ague, and little cheer or comfort in the neglected house, but were glad to accept the shelter of its roof and the chance to dry their clothes by the fire. When they were starting on in the morning Mr. Peniman tried to buy some hay and grain from the owner of the place, whose name was Grigsby, but he refused to sell.

"Nope," he said, drooping listlessly against the door-post with a shawl over his shoulders, "I cain't sell you no grain nor hay. Had th' shakes so bad this spring I hain't got to do much farmin', and I hain't got hardly enough to feed my stock." Then, as a shrill squeal pierced the air his eyes brightened and an idea seemed to strike him. "But I tell you what I will do," he drawled, "I'll sell you two of the nicest little suckin' pigs you ever see. Their mother up an' died of the cholery a few nights ago, and they ain't old enough to eat yit. Me an' the old woman, havin' th' shakes so, cain't bother to feed 'em, so I'll let you have the pair of 'em for two dollars. Goin' off in th' wilderness like you be they might come in handy."

He shuffled off to the barn, and soon returned carrying a basket in which were two tiny pigs only a few days old. With a grin he drew from his pocket a nursing-bottle filled with warm milk and held it to the little white pig's mouth. It took hold like an old hand at the business, and the children shouted with glee while the little spotted brother squealed shrilly with envy.

When the nursing-bottle had been refilled Ruth demanded the privilege of feeding the protesting young porker, and sitting down in the straw took the little pig in her lap and fed it so dexterously that her brothers yelled with delight.

Of course that settled it.

With one accord the children demanded the possession of the two little pigs, and with a long-headed thought for the possible needs of the future Mr. Peniman agreed, and the listless Grigsby filled a box with straw and packed the little fellows cosily into it.

"What shall we name them, Father?" cried Ruth, hanging lovingly over them. "They are such darlings they ought to have real lovely names."

"Call them Romeo and Juliet," said Mr. Peniman, with a twinkle in his eyes.

In talking with the Grigsbys Mr. Peniman had learned that they had chosen a bad road, and were traveling through a poor and swampy part of Illinois, where the roads were all bad and chills and fever prevalent, and by their advice had left the road over which they came and striking north and west came out upon a much better road, that in the course of a few days' traveling brought them to the Sangamon River, and a few days later to Decatur. Here they remained a few days to dry out their clothes and wagons and renew their supply of provisions, being regaled at supper that night with sweet corn and watermelons.

It was now July first, and very hot weather. The travelers were burned and tanned as brown as Indians, and were beginning to feel like real pioneers. They drove into Springfield, the capital of the State, on the evening of the third of July, and Joshua Peniman suggested to his wife that the wagons be put up in a livery stable and the whole family go to a hotel, where they could all have a good tub bath, a night's rest in a real bed, and a few meals at a real table.

"We are going far away into the wilderness," he said, "and it may be years before our children will have a chance to see a Fourth of July celebration again. I believe that all young Americans should love and honor that day. I think we had better stay over to-morrow in Springfield, let the little ones have a good time, and take the boys to see the celebration we see advertised, while thee has a good rest at a hotel."

When told of this plan the young Penimans were delighted. The novelty of traveling in the wagons had begun to pall a trifle, and the thought of a day in a city, a night at a hotel, and the exciting events promised by the great posters that lined the roads, gave them great pleasure.

It turned out to be a great day for them. They started out immediately after breakfast, and firecrackers, torpedoes, flags, and rockets were purchased at the first store they came to, and in the intervals of other excitement the boys revelled in pops and bangs and explosions, while the girls exploded their torpedoes on the sidewalks, and they all marched gaily to the music of many bands.

There was a great parade in the forenoon, in which the Whigs and Democrats vied with each other in the exhibition of floats, bands, and flower-decked carriages. Long columns of men of both parties marched and shouted, bearing transparencies extolling the virtues of their particular candidates. The Buchanan men wore white coats and caps, and carried huge portraits of their candidate.

There was to be a great political rally at the park in the afternoon, and after dinner the boys and their father followed the crowd to the pretty shaded inclosure, where a great pavilion had been erected, gorgeously decorated with flags and bunting.

The place was already crowded when they arrived, but they pushed their way through the throng and succeeded in getting seats on a long bench before the speakers' stand.

It seemed a little thing that they should be so placed that Joe should be able to look directly into the speaker's face and hear his every word, but upon such trifling things the whole course of a life sometimes depends.

Bands played, a great chorus upon the platform stood up and sang "America," and then a stir and flutter passed through the crowd as a party of gentlemen in frock coats with tall "chimney-pot" hats, made their way to the platform, where they were greeted with great bursts of applause.

The Peniman boys had never heard a public speech in their lives. Partly owing to the fact that their father was a Quaker and avoided discussion of the question that was beginning to seethe and burn through the length and breadth of the land, partly because of the remote and quiet farm from which they had come, they had heard little of the agitation of the times.

Politics were at a white heat throughout the country. The pro-slavery and anti-slavery parties were each using every artifice in their power to elect their candidates. Arguments, discussions, public speeches and inflammatory meetings were taking place in every part of the United States, and the fire that later burst into so fierce a conflagration was beginning to smoulder hotly beneath the surface.

There was something in the very air of that meeting that breathed tension, excitement. And Joshua Peniman felt a cold chill smite his heart, as sitting with his young sons he listened to the conversation that went on about him. Joe, too, felt the electric atmosphere. His eyes brightened and his color rose. When a dapper little gentleman with a massive head and a keen, ruddy face mounted the platform and began to speak he leaned forward eagerly.

He liked the speech. The cultured voice, the smooth periods, the forceful gestures of the man fascinated him. Yet he found his mind continually protesting against the statements he made. The boy knew nothing of the Kansas-Nebraska Bill, the Wilmot Proviso, or the Missouri Compromise, but as the speaker proceeded he found himself arguing passionately against him in his own mind. When the speaker sat down, amid terrific applause, Joe turned to his father.

"Who is he, Father?" he asked in a whisper.

"His name is Douglas—Stephen A. Douglas. He is a United States Senator from Illinois," replied Mr. Peniman.

"He's a great speaker," whispered Joe thoughtfully; then half-hesitatingly, as if trying to put into words a thing that was not clear in his own mind, "but somehow—I suppose it's pretty presumptuous of me to say so—but somehow I don't agree with what he says."

Joshua Peniman turned a quick, pleased look upon his son's face.

"Nor do I, Joe. His reasoning is false, spurious. Such a policy as he is advocating could only plunge our country into endless trouble. He is a Democrat, and though he claims that he does not care whether 'the cause of slavery be voted up or voted down' he is doing more, perhaps, than any other one man in the Senate to uphold it and increase its power and territory."

"But, Father——" began Joe, but his whispering voice was lost in a terrific storm of cheers and hoots and yells as a tall, gaunt man in a long-tailed coat of shabby black, mounted the platform.

As he began to speak, in a deep, earnest voice, that had in it now and then a whimsical quality of humor, now and then a deep note of pathos, there was a general craning forward in the crowd, a stillness, a breathless attention, that had not been accorded the previous speaker.

From his first words Joe sat entranced. In every statement that he made the boy found an echo in his own heart. His blood tingled, his color rose, he clenched and unclenched his hands, a great surge of exultation, excitement, a stir that he had never before known passed through all his being.

The crowd about him seemed equally roused and swayed by the words of the speaker. At times as the impassioned sentences rose and swelled through the air they were stopped by the wild cheers that burst from the throats of the thousands of listeners. And when he leaned forward, pointing his long, gaunt finger at them, his deep, sad eyes fixed as if in prophetic vision, a stillness so great passed over the audience that the breathing of the man next him was perfectly audible.

"And I contend," thundered the orator, "that no man is good enough to own and govern another man without that other's consent. Slavery is founded on the selfishness of man's nature; opposition to it is founded on the love of justice. These principles are in eternal antagonism, and when brought into collision so fiercely as slavery extension brings them, shocks and throes and convulsions must ceaselessly follow. These two principles cannot stand together. They are as opposite as God and Mammon; and whoever holds to one must despise the other. 'A house divided against itself cannot stand.' I believe that this government cannot endure permanently half slave and half free. I do not expect the Union to be dissolved—I do not expect the house to fall—but I do expect that it will cease to be divided."

The last words rang out in such an earnest, impressive, almost prophetic tone as to make a cold shiver run through the audience. For a moment the speaker stood silent, his black hair fallen forward over his forehead, his sad grey eyes, deep-set and hollow, gazing out over the assembled people. Then as a great storm of applause broke out and the people made a rush for the platform he bowed and retired.

Joe woke as from a trance when the audience began to file out.

"Who was he, Father?" he asked breathlessly. "Who was that man?"

As he looked up into his father's face he saw that his cheeks were flushed and his usually gentle, kindly eyes were blazing.

"His name is Lincoln, I believe," he answered, rousing himself with an effort from the thoughts the address had set running in his mind. "He is a lawyer, a member of the legislature from Sangamon County, some one told me."

For a long time Joe was silent. Lige spoke to him about something else, but he did not hear him. When he spoke again they were out on the street and on their way back to the hotel.

"Do you believe I could ever be a lawyer, Father?" he asked.

His father smiled, then answered gravely, "I have no doubt you could, Joe, if you set your mind on it."

"And a member of the legislature—like that man?"

Joshua Peniman laughed outright. "Well, I don't know about that, my son. That man appears to me to be a rather unusual sort of a person. But you might become a member of the legislature, perhaps."

"Then that's what I'm going to do when I'm a man," said Joe decisively.

After a long pause he lifted his eyes to his father's face.

"Do you believe in the abolition of slavery, Father?"

"I do indeed, my son," replied Mr. Peniman earnestly. "As Mr. Lincoln said 'No man has a right to own and govern another without that other's consent.'"

"Do you believe in the abolition of slavery enough to fight for it, Father,—if our country should have to go to war?"

"Quakers cannot fight, Joe. We are bound to peace."

"But if war should come," urged the boy, "if we should have to fight—if the South should secede——"

"*God forbid!*" cried Joshua Peniman, in a voice whose deep, quavering earnestness was a slight indication of the storm that was raging in his heart. "May God forbid such a catastrophe! Let us not talk of it. Let us not *think* of it. Let us pray the Almighty Ruler of the Universe to avert so frightful a calamity to our nation!"

Joe glanced up quickly and opened his lips to speak, but the expression that he surprised upon his father's face caused him to close them promptly, avert his eyes, and walk silently beside him.

In the evening there was a great torchlight procession, followed by more speaking at the Opera House. But this function the Peniman family did not attend. Mr. Peniman, stirred, anxious, feeling a prescience of the storm that was brewing in the country, was eager to get away; to get his young lads out of the spirit of rancor and bitterness that was abroad in the land, and out onto the clean, quiet prairies where the inhumanity of man to man would not throw its baleful shadow over them.

In the morning long before the celebrators of the night before had opened their eyes the two prairie schooners were on their way, and the young pioneers, with faces turned westward, were starting upon the most exciting part of their journey.

CHAPTER VI

IN WHICH THE PIONEERS HEAR ALARMING NEWS

Their Fourth of July spent in Springfield was a day long to be remembered by the Peniman family. The children talked of it many days as the canvas-covered wagons rumbled slowly along the dusty, rutted Illinois roads, and years later, when the events then being so darkly foreshadowed on the horizon had come to be matters of fact, it helped to shape the destiny of Joshua Peniman's sons.

Joe had something new to think about now as he sat in the wagon holding the reins in his hands while the horses plodded on through the long, hot, silent days, and his mind was often busy with the future that lay before him, while plans, dreams, ambitions began to unfold themselves in his mind.

They passed through Beardstown and camped on the Illinois River, then struck off again to the west, and twelve days later sighted the Mississippi River.

It was Lige who first caught sight of the great brown swiftly-flowing waters.

"Look," he cried, breaking into Joe's day-dream by poking him in the ribs, "look what a big river we're coming to! Wonder what river it is?"

"Mighty big one—and a mighty dirty one, too," commented Sam, hanging away out of the wagon to get a better look at it. "Look at the whopping big bridge across it!" he whooped, pointing at the great bridge that spanned the muddy waters. "Hey, Father, what river is that? It's a mighty big one!"

Mr. Peniman turned and looked back with a smile.

"What river is that? That's a great question for a boy your age to ask! Don't you know where we are? What have you studied geography for if you don't know what river that is?"

"Oh, I know!" shouted Ruth, "I know, Father! It's the Mississippi! This is Illinois, that State over there is Iowa, and that is the Mississippi that flows between!"

"Ah, good girl!" applauded her father. "Of course! The Mississippi— the great Father of Waters. And the boundary line "—he continued thoughtfully, speaking more to himself than the children,—"between the old East and the new West."

"The Mississippi at last—hurray!" shouted Joe.

"Huh, I knew it all the time," grunted Sam. "Ruth needn't think she's so smart. Golly, when I got kept in last winter 'cause I couldn't tell what States were bounded by the Mississippi I didn't think I'd be crossing it so soon!"

They spent the night at Rock Island, then the terminus of the Chicago and Rock Island Railroad, and the next day crossed the Mississippi at Davenport, on the first bridge built across the river, which had been completed but a few weeks before. They stayed there that night, then started on, and two days later drove into Iowa City, then the capital of the State.

As the two wagons progressed slowly through the bare, wide clayey streets, which were flanked on either side by one-story unpainted buildings, as if dumped unceremoniously into their present location with no view to permanency, they observed groups of men gathered together talking excitedly. Presently a troop of cavalry dashed through the streets, followed by a company of infantry.

"*Soldiers!*" ejaculated Lige. "Wonder what soldiers are doing out here?"

As they drew up before the bare, unpainted general store Mr. Peniman turned to the boys and told them to stay in the wagons.

This was most unusual, as the boys were always glad to get out at these stops, stretch their legs, buy candy and gum, and exchange greetings with the boys and dogs they generally found congregated about the door.

"Aw, why not, Father?" protested Sam. But his protestations were cut short by his father's uplifted hand and the expression on his face.

"Because I wish you to," he said with unusual curtness, and disappeared within the store.

"Don't see why he wouldn't let us get out," grumbled Sam, "I wanted to buy some candy."

It seemed a long time before their father returned to the wagons, and when he did Joe noticed that he looked pale and grim and that his lips were compressed into a close, white line.

He went from store to store swiftly, with absorbed attention, and greatly astonished the occupants of the wagons by coming back with a new

Enfield rifle in his hand, followed by a man carrying a keg of powder and a big box of cartridges.

"Who's the new gun for, Father—me?" cried Joe with delight.

"Yes, you can shoot well enough now to be trusted with a gun. Lige can use the old rifle. I bought one of those new Colt's revolvers for you, Mother."

"For *me*, Joshua?" Hannah Peniman opened her blue eyes very wide. "Why, dear man, thee knows that I could never use a gun. I am deathly afraid of them."

"We are going away into the wilderness, Hannah," he said very gravely, "thee must learn." And the words were spoken in a tone and with an expression that made her start and look at him closely.

When they were once more upon their way she turned to him and asked in a low voice, "What is it, Joshua?"

They had never had any reservations from one another, and though he wished now with all his heart that he might spare her he knew that he stood in need of her courage, her help, her calm, cool judgment.

"There has been a massacre of whites by the Indians not far from here," he told her. "The white settlers along the Little Sioux have been obliged to flee, and many of them have been murdered. I cannot tell thee the horrible details. They are sending out State troops. It was all brought about by the treachery of a white man, they tell me, but——" He broke off abruptly and sat gazing into her horrified face.

"They say," he continued, "that most of the Indians around here are friendly, but a white trader deceived and murdered the brother of Chief Inkpaducah, and he has roused his whole tribe to vengeance."

"And they have killed the settlers—and women—and children?" she gasped, every vestige of color leaving her face.

"They killed the children. They have carried the women away into captivity."

"Oh, God, have mercy on us!"

"In God's care and mercy alone can we trust, Hannah," he answered. "We will never give these red brothers cause for anger against us, and perhaps we may escape harm at their hands. But I must confess it has given me a great shock. I wish——"

"The children—the children——" she whispered in anguish. "Oh, Joshua, I wish we had never come to this terrible country. I wish we had stayed at home——"

"I have been wishing the same thing. But it is too late now. We have come too far on our way. Thee—thee would not advise that we turn back now, would thee, Hannah? When we are so near the goal?"

For a moment she sat silent, her sweet blue eyes, wide and filled with horror, fixed upon the western horizon, her arms clasped tightly about the baby, which she pressed almost fiercely to her breast. After a time she turned to her husband and laid her hand on his arm, saying bravely:

"No, Joshua. My heart is filled with fears, but thee has sacrificed too much to turn back now. We can only go on, and pray that Almighty God will protect us."

"My brave, noble wife," he whispered, and kissed her.

That night when they made their camp the two wagons were drawn close together and the cow and horses instead of being picketed out were placed beside them. No camp-fire was built that night, and the supper was prepared over as small a fire as possible, a piece of sacking placed over the top of the stove-pipe to absorb and keep down the smoke. Before they retired their father gave each of the three older boys a gun and ammunition.

"We have reached the real West now, lads," he told them, "and must be prepared for some of the adventures you have been looking forward to for so long. I have no idea that you will have occasion to use those guns to-night, but like good pioneers you must keep them ready and in order for whatever might happen."

A thrill passed through the hearts of Joe and Lige as they listened to his words. Not even then did they appreciate the menace they portended.

That night Joshua Peniman did not sleep in the wagon as he had been accustomed to do, but with Spotty beside him and a loaded musket at hand lay down beside the wagons wrapped in his blanket.

There was little sleep for the elders of the party. The children, who had been allowed to hear nothing of the horrors of the massacre, slept tranquilly, but Joshua Peniman patrolled his camp all night, while his wife lay among her little ones in the wagon with her heart like an ice-cold stone within her breast.

They were now traveling through an almost uninhabited part of western Iowa, where settlers were far apart and shade and water grew scarcer and farther apart every day.

The weather had grown intensely hot, and the poor animals, forced to travel all day through the heat of the sun without sufficient water, suffered greatly.

The cow especially seemed to feel the strain, and after one intensely hot day, during which the pioneers had all suffered, she gave but a small portion of milk, and lay down when they made camp refusing to graze.

That night the baby was taken ill. Both father and mother did all that they knew for her, but she grew steadily worse, and two days later, while they were traveling over a barren, desolate expanse of country with no living creature in sight but themselves, she passed away.

They stopped and made a little grave in the desolate prairies, over which they placed a tiny cross marked with her name and age. Then the bereaved parents went on their way, with what agony of spirit only those who have lost a precious little one may know.

CHAPTER VII

A NIGHT OF HORROR

"And so," Joe concluded his long story, during which the afternoon had waned and the long shadows over the prairies told of the coming night, "we left little Abby behind us and started on again. Father and Mother were terribly sad. Sometimes I was afraid that Mother could not live through it. They seemed awfully nervous and afraid all the time, too. Father never went to bed at night, but sat or lay beside the wagons with Spotty beside him and his gun in his hand, and Mother would not let any of us get away from the wagons.

"It was fearful hot all that time—hotter even than it is to-day—and we had to travel slow on account of the cow. We just plugged along, and then toward night we hauled up beside the road and camped. Nobody had any heart to eat, so it didn't matter. Once in a while we came to a little town, or some houses, but we seldom stopped. Father seemed in a hurry to get where we were going, and Mother didn't seem to care about anything. Two or three times we had a scare about Indians, but they never came very near to us. Then one day when it had been so hot and dusty that we were all almost suffocated we saw a kind of a draw ahead and made for it, thinking we would camp there that night. It wasn't much of a place to camp, but we didn't see any sign of water anywhere, and Mother was just about beat out.

"Golly, I bet I'll never forget that evening! We were all feeling mighty miserable. I happened to look off toward the wagon road, and I saw a big cloud of dust. First I thought it was just a whirlwind, and then we were afraid it was Indians. But after a while we made out that it was an emigrant wagon, being driven by a woman. That surprised us a lot. She was driving like the old Harry, and Father ran out toward the road to meet her when we heard her yelling for help. When the wagon came nearer we saw——"

"Stop, stop, oh *don't!*" cried the little Princess, covering her eyes with her hands while shudders shook her frame. "Don't," she cried again, "I can't bear it—I can't *bear* it! I know—I know the rest!"

"Yes," Joe took her hand very gently, "you know the rest. It was your wagon—and—and—it brought us—*you.*"

For a little while all the children were silent. Ruth crept up and put her arm about the little stranger's waist.

"I guess God sent you to us to be a little sister to us in baby's place," she said chokily.

Nina turned and put her arm about her neck.

"Perhaps He did. I never had any sisters or brothers. I'd like to be your sister. I like you."

"I'm glad," said honest Ruth, and kissed her.

"So'm I," cried Lige; but Joe said nothing.

That night when camp was struck the three wagons were drawn into a circle with the horses and cow inside.

Joshua Peniman did not remove his clothing, but having seen his family comfortably disposed, with the strange child in the wagon with his wife and the younger children, he stretched himself out beside the wagons, with Spotty near him and his musket by his side. Joe refused to go to his place in his own wagon, but lay down beside his father.

The prairies looked vast and still under the glimmering starlight with no sound but the sough of the wind through the grass and the occasional howling of a coyote. For a long time he lay awake, some vague, haunting uneasiness upon him. Twice he sprang up, his musket leveled, every nerve and muscle strained to attention.

They had agreed that Mr. Peniman was to take the first watch of the night and Joe the second. At two o'clock Joe woke, and seeing his father patrolling up and down beside the wagons insisted that he should go to bed. This the weary man refused to do, but wrapping himself in his blankets lay down upon the ground.

Joe sat beside him, his gun leaning against his knees, and looked up at the silent stars, feeling them companions in his loneliness.

It was between two and three o'clock, and he was beginning to doze, when a low, ominous growl from Spotty caused him to start wide awake, his gun clenched in his hand.

Spotty was standing, stiff-legged, the hair on his neck raised, his lips drawn back showing his teeth, growling deeply and staring into the shadows back of the wagons.

Joe did not move, but remained motionless listening.

Presently he heard a soft rustling in the grass.

A moment later by the light of the stars he made out a dim silhouette creeping toward the wagons.

"Stop," he cried, "or I'll shoot!"

Instantly Joshua Peniman was on his feet.

"What is it?" he whispered huskily.

"Man—Indian—over there by the wagons!"

The whispered words had scarcely left his lips when an arrow whizzed by his ear.

Instantly Joshua Peniman's gun, leveled at the point from which the arrow came, barked through the darkness. The shot was answered by a wild, shrill whoop, and suddenly the night seemed to be filled with flitting figures.

Joe's gun was at his shoulder, and as one huge naked savage leaped at his father he fired. The Indian fell with a groan, but almost before he had touched the ground another had taken his place, rushing toward the white man with uplifted tomahawk and blood-curdling yell. He was almost upon him when a sharp "crack" spoke from the back of one of the wagons, and the Indian dropped and lay motionless, while Lige, half-dressed, leaped out and ran to his father's side.

Sam on the seat of Joe's wagon held the rifle firmly at his shoulder. His freckled face was very pale, but the blue eyes were shining in a way that boded ill to the Indian who should come within range of the old rifle.

In the opening of the big wagon, between its curtains stood Hannah Peniman, her revolver in her hand. Her face was white and set, but the hand that held the weapon did not tremble.

The night was now hideous with yells. With the blood-curdling war-whoop that had carried terror to the hearts of so many early settlers on the plains the Indians were now circling about the camp, watching their opportunity to break through.

Suddenly from somewhere in the distance rose another cry. The heart of Joshua Peniman almost died in his breast.

"Another band!" he muttered, as he crowded down the charge in the old musket. Their case had seemed hopeless before, but they had firearms while the savages seemed to be armed only with bows and arrows, and might have had a chance. But if another band of savages joined those already upon them——

"Ki-ki-ee-ee-ee!" rang the cry through the night.

The Indians who were creeping up toward the wagons suddenly paused and stood still. Some sudden instinct made Joe raise his musket and fire into the air. Then at the top of his lungs shout, "Ki-ki-ee-ee-ee!"

He had no idea from whom the cry had come, whether from white man or Indian, friend or foe; but some sure instinct told him that whoever they might be their presence was unwelcome to the marauders.

While the sound of his shot and cry were still reverberating in the air there came a swift rush from the darkness outside the circle of wagons, and in the starlight they could make out the naked outlines of a band of Indians who made a rush for the wagons.

In the terror and excitement of the moment they did not notice that one of the band separated himself from the rest, and slipping into the shadows made his way noiselessly as a serpent to the rear of the Carroll wagon, where he climbed under the curtain and was lost to view.

Joshua Peniman uttering a warning shout sprang to the front of the wagon in which were his wife and younger children, with the child of the deceased Carrolls. Hannah Peniman was guarding the rear of the wagon, her revolver cocked and ready in her hand, while Joe and Lige at the front and back of the other wagon were making good use of their firearms, and Sam, standing up in the front was banging away with the rifle as fast as he could load and fire.

As the Indians rushed toward them it looked for a moment to the travelers as if all hope was lost. At the moment when the savages burst through their guard the shrill "Ki-ki-ee-ee-ee!" again smote upon their ears, and an instant later the sound of wild yelps and thundering hoofs was all about them, and another band of Indians, mounted and in full war panoply, burst into the encampment.

The travelers thought their last hour had come.

"To the wagons, to the wagons!" shouted Joshua Peniman. "Inside, Sam! Lige, help thy mother guard the rear! To me, to me, Joe! We must try to keep them away from this wagon at least! Now, is thee ready? *Fire!*"

As his words rang out above the tumult a tawny chief with eagle feathers in his hair, who was riding by, checked his horse so abruptly that he threw it back upon its haunches. He cast a swift, searching look at the man and boys who stood so resolutely before their wagons, and suddenly threw up his hand. Riding toward them he waved a piece of white cloth above his head, then halted his horse before them.

"Is thee a Quaker?" he surprised them by asking in fairly good English.

"Yes, I am," replied Joshua Peniman, looking not at all like a Quaker with his wild, disordered hair, his set white face and his gun at his shoulder. In the excitement of the moment he had no time to think of the strangeness, the incongruity of the question. All he could think of was that for some unknown reason the other Indians seemed to have drawn off, and for a moment at least there appeared to be a pause in the savage onslaught.

The Indian who had spoken to him whirled his pony about and shouted a few words in a language they could not understand. Instantly there came a wild yelp in answer, and a moment later there was the clamor of a battle cry, the wild thundering of hoofs, the crash of blows, the uproar of battle. Before the horrified pioneers knew what was happening the sound of battle began to recede from them, had grown faint and fainter, had died away across the plain, and the night was still about them.

Even then they could not realize that they had been saved; that death—horrible death—and worse than death—had in some miraculous way been averted from them.

They expected momentarily that the savages would return. Joshua Peniman and the boys reloaded their muskets. Mr. Peniman snatching the axe from the wagon laid it beside him. Joe slipped a long sharp knife inside his belt.

Strangely enough none of them spoke. The moment was too tense, the struggle for life too imminent for words.

Moments passed. The shrill yelps and cries grew fainter and fainter and finally died away.

An intense, silent half hour went by. Then Joshua Peniman lowered his gun to the ground and looked about him.

"I believe they have gone!" he whispered.

"I believe so too!" replied Joe in the same tone.

"Keep on guard. I'll look around."

Cautiously and with musket ready he made a tour around the wagons.

Two Indians, both dead, lay in the grass not far away, but there was no sign of any living creature about the place but themselves.

He returned to the wagons relieved but perplexed.

What did it mean? He could not account for it.

"They appear to be gone," he said. "For the life of me I cannot understand what happened, but somehow, by God's merciful providence, we have been spared."

"But how—why—why did they go away like that?" Joe demanded. "Does thee think they will return, Father?"

"It is a most mysterious proceeding. I do not know what to think of it. But I scarcely think they will return—at least not immediately."

The children, who had been hidden under the wagon seats covered with blankets, now crept out, still too terrified to speak.

"I don't believe they'll come back," said Joe, who had been thinking hard. "Do you know, Father, I believe that there must have been two tribes. I believe they are at war with one another, and that the last ones that came—those that came on horseback—drove the others away. They didn't come together. There weren't many of those Indians that attacked us first, and they came on foot. We would have heard horses, but they crept up on us like shadows. If Spotty hadn't warned us we might all have been murdered in our sleep. I didn't hear a sound until he began to growl."

"Nor I either," answered his father. "Thee may be right." Then suddenly for the first time the peculiarity of the question that the big chief had asked him flashed into his mind. "Why, I guess thee is right, Joe," he cried. "That big fellow with the eagle feathers in his hair held up a flag of truce. He asked me if I was a Quaker! I never thought about it until this moment. How strange—how passing strange! How did he guess—how could he know—it must have been he who saved us!" Then suddenly catching sight of his wife's deathly face he turned to her. "Go lie down, Hannah, thee is all used up. The danger is past for the time. What ever miraculous interposition of God's mercy saved us it seems clear that we are saved. Our enemies have gone and we can sleep in peace. Go to thy rest, too, Joe. Thee has done well. I feel that I have a real man to depend on in these trying times."

The look in his eyes, the pressure of the hand on his shoulder, sent Joe away to bed with a warm glow in his heart.

Presently the camp was still again, and Joshua Peniman patrolled up and down and all about it, with his musket over his shoulder and Spotty at his heels until the rosy glow of morning was tinting the eastern sky.

Just before sunrise he received a severe shock, when looking across the pathless prairies toward the north he saw an Indian riding toward him.

For many moments he watched the advancing figure. When it came within musket range he raised his gun to his shoulder and shouted:

"Stop, or I'll fire!"

The Indian did not check his pony, but held up a bit of white rag. As he came nearer, riding his pony as erect and motionless as a bronze statue, the pioneer saw with a start that it was the Indian who had spoken to him the night before.

"How!" he said, bringing his pony to a halt before the white man and sliding down from its back.

"How!" answered Joshua Peniman, answering the western salutation.

The Indian came closer.

"You Quaker, eh?"

Wondering, the white man answered as he had answered the night before, "Yes, I am."

"Me Quaker too."

"*You? You a Quaker?*"

A grave smile broke over the impassive, copper-colored face.

"Me Neowage, Chief Winnebagoes. Live Omaha Reservation. Friends' Mission."

"Oh-h!" A great light began to dawn on Joshua Peniman. "Oh, you are one of the tribe who were put in charge of the Friends' Mission?[#] Then it was *you* who saved us last night?"

[#] During the year 1856-1857 the Winnebago tribe, being much depleted by continual wars with the Sioux and Arapahoes, sought protection at the Reservation in Omaha. There the remnants of the tribe were put under the protection of the Friends' Mission, and many of them became converts to the faith.—SHELDON'S *History of Nebraska.*

The big chief nodded.

"Me hear you say 'thee' to you boy. Me know you Friend."

"And because I was a Friend you saved me—me and my family! Oh, Friend, I thank thee!"

He stepped forward and grasped the Indian's hand.

With a dignity equal to his own the chief shook it warmly.

"Friends good people. Good heart. Good friend to Winnebagoes."

"Then you are a Winnebago? Who were the others—those Indians that attacked us?"

"Dirty Sioux." He turned and spurned the dead body in the grass with his foot.

"Ah, they were Sioux, eh? Are the Sioux hostile to white men?"

"Sioux bad Indian. Heap bad heart. Winnebago good Indian. Heap white man's friend."

"I am glad, glad indeed to hear it. You don't know how you relieve my anxious heart. But how did it happen that you came to our aid so opportunely last night?"

The Indian folded his arms across his brawny chest.

"My tribe war with Sioux," he said. "Heap much trouble now. Inkpaducah on war-path. Kill heap white men. Me hear gun, know trouble. My young men on war-path. Fight Sioux all time. Me come, drive Sioux away."

"God be thanked you did come. You saved our lives. How can I thank you?"

The Indian waved his hand with a royal gesture. As his keen eyes roved about the encampment they fell upon a scrap of paper which lay under the Carroll wagon. He strode over to it and picked it up, then remained gazing at the ground for some minutes.

The wagons stood backed up to the edge of the ravine, and back of them the ground was soft, in some places muddy.

Neowage pointed silently. Joshua Peniman hurried to his side.

"White man print," he grunted, indicating a well-defined footmark in the muddy earth at the back of the Carroll wagon.

Joshua Peniman stooped and examined it carefully.

The sharp edges of a hard leather sole and the imprint of a boot heel were plainly discernible.

A white man!

With perplexed face he stood staring at the imprint.

That Indians might attack them was perfectly understandable, but that a white man should be among them—that *a white man* was one of those howling demons who had set upon his camp the night before—was a thing that he could not understand.

Neowage glanced sharply at his feet.

"Not you mark?"

"No, I was not near the back of that wagon. It was unoccupied. And you see that is a much larger foot than mine."

"You boy?"

"No, my boys are all going barefooted."

"Who?"

"I wish I knew."

The Indian was turning the scrap of paper he had picked up under the wagon over and over in his hands.

"Tore," he said, pointing to the ragged edges.

Mr. Peniman took the paper and scrutinized it carefully. It was but a small scrap, and its edges showed that it had been torn recently and hastily. As he turned it over the words: "and the said Lee C. Carroll———" caught his eye.

With a strange leap of his pulses he turned and ran to the Carroll wagon.

As he threw aside the rear curtain and looked in he uttered a loud exclamation.

The inside of the neatly-arranged wagon was in chaos, trunks torn open, boxes and bundles rifled of their contents, clothes, books, papers scattered about; and the dispatch-box, placed in the hands of Nina Carroll by her dying mother, which contained all her money, deeds, papers, and all the information that had been left her regarding herself and her parents and the relatives to whom she was to be sent—*was gone!*

CHAPTER VIII

JOE MEETS A FRIEND AND MAKES AN ENEMY

The sound of the voices outside had wakened the boys, who, worn out from the excitement of the night, had fallen into a fitful slumber.

As the fact of the looting of the Carroll wagon, with its disastrous consequences to the young survivor of the tragedy, forced itself upon him Joshua Peniman uttered a loud exclamation.

Instantly Joe and Lige leaped from the wagon, their guns in their hands, and Mrs. Peniman, still grasping her revolver, parted the rear curtains of the wagon and looked out.

When their eyes fell upon the Indian both boys started violently, and Joe raised his gun.

"No, no, son, put down thy gun," cried his father. "This is a friend. It was he who so mysteriously saved us last night. He is a Friend, and has learned to speak a little English at a Friends' Mission."

"Oh," cried Hannah Peniman, and in the little exclamation was wonder, relief and surprise.

"But see, Hannah," went on Mr. Peniman, "see what those miscreants have done! They have rifled the Carroll wagon and carried off everything of value in it, including the dispatch-box."

"The *dispatch-box*?" Hannah Peniman's face whitened and her eyes grew dark with horror. "They have taken the dispatch-box? Oh, Joshua, that box had in it everything relating to the property and identity of that little girl!"

Her husband nodded.

"I know," he said. "It is a terrible catastrophe. I should have put that box in my own wagon."

"But who would have thought—who would have supposed that Indians——"

Neowage who had been looking and listening impassively, interrupted her.

"Indian no want papers."

Mr. and Mrs. Peniman started and looked at one another.

"True," said Joshua Peniman, pulling at his beard, "that is true, Neowage."

Presently he looked up at his wife with a troubled face. "There is more in this than we see now," he said in a low tone, and told her of the scrap of paper, the print of a white man's boot at the rear of the wagon, of the broken locks and opened trunks and scattered books and papers in the wagon.

"There is something very strange about it," he concluded. "Our own wagons were not disturbed, our horses were not taken; it almost looks to me as if the assault was made upon us to cover the rifling of the Carroll wagon."

He stopped abruptly and stood for some moments with head bent thinking intently. Then going to his own wagon he returned with the arrow he had taken from the body of Lee Carroll.

Silently he handed it to Neowage. Silently the Indian inspected it.

"Santee Sioux," he said after a moment, handing it back.

"Are you sure?"

"Sure. See plenty. My young men fight Santee Sioux. Kill my people, two, t'ree, five hunnerd. Drive my people way from hunting grounds. My people starve. Go Omaha Reservation. They put us in Friends' care."

"And this is a Sioux arrow?"

The Indian nodded.

"I took that arrow out of the dead body of a white man. When he was dying he told me that it was not an Indian that had killed him."

Then by a sudden impulse he told the chief the whole story.

When it was finished the Indian remained standing with his arms folded across his bare brown chest, his head bent, his face impassive. After an interval he spoke.

"You got papoose now?"

"Yes."

"She sleep in wagon?"

"No, she has never slept there since her father and mother died. She sleeps with my little girls in that wagon," pointing to the canvas-covered prairie schooner where his own children lay asleep.

"Indian no want papoose. Indian no want paper. White man want papoose and paper."

Joshua Peniman nodded. "Yes, I see your point. But I don't know. It's beyond me. I don't know what to think."

The children, awakened by the talking, had now crowded to the back of the wagon, and Ruth, Nina, Sam, and Paul were staring out with bulging eyes.

For the first time they were gazing upon a real Red Man of the Plains, and strange to say their father was not shooting at him nor scalping him, nor even being scalped by him, but was standing quietly talking to him, evidently asking his advice.

The younger children were also awake now, and Mrs. Peniman got down from the wagon and began preparing the breakfast.

"Thee must stay and break bread with us, friend Neowage," said Joshua Peniman; and presently the whole family were gathered about the oilcloth on the grass, with Neowage cross-legged and silent among them.

It seemed very strange to be thus eating breakfast with one of the savages of whom they had stood in such deadly terror the night before; the little girls shrank closer to their mother and peered at him with fearful eyes, but the boys watched his every movement with fascinated gaze, and Lige began mentally composing a letter to Simeon Fisher, in which he meant to tell him all about his friend Neowage, the great and mighty chief of the Winnebago tribe.

The chief, however, after one keen glance from his black eyes seemed to pay little attention to them. His eyes were fastened upon Nina, and whether it was her tragic story or her winning beauty that held his attention they could not tell.

When he had finished eating he rose abruptly and said, "Me go now." Then turning to Mr. Peniman he extended his hand.

"No be 'fraid," he said in his deep guttural voice. "Neowage you friend. He watch over you. No let Quaker family get harm." Then as he turned to where his pony was standing, its bridle trailing on the ground, he included them all in one quick glance and muttered a guttural "goo-bye."

Mrs. Peniman rose and gave him her hand, thanking him for his protection. The boys also hastened to shake hands with him. But Nina sprang up from her place and ran to him, taking from her neck a pretty little blue chain, and laid it in his hand.

"Keep it," she said, smiling up at him; "you were good and saved us. Keep that to remember us by."

"KEEP IT; YOU WERE GOOD AND SAVED US."—*Page 83.*

"KEEP IT; YOU WERE GOOD AND SAVED US."

The Indian looked down from his great height upon the golden-haired little girl, then to the chain in his hand.

"Umph!" he grunted, but they knew from the smile on his face that he was pleased.

"What you name?" he asked.

"Nina—Nina Carroll." Then with a shy little smile, "The boys call me 'Princess.'"

"Umph!" again grunted the Indian, and mounting his pony rode swiftly away.

As the pioneers traveled on through the heat and dust of that day the hearts of Joshua Peniman and his wife were deeply troubled. It was not alone that their worst fears of the perils of the plains had been realized in the attack of the night before, but the menace and mystery of the theft of the dispatch-box left a deep sense of fear and depression upon them.

"I cannot but fear for the child," Joshua Peniman said, after long study. "We know nothing about her, who she is, what her life may represent, or what enemies her family may have had. The thought is forcing itself upon me that we should not keep her with us, that we must leave her at the first Mission we come to, as her mother requested. They may be able to get her back to her own people."

"But who are her people? How can we ever tell that now? Every bit of information, every letter, address, paper, everything relating to her or her relatives, was in that box."

"But surely the girl herself knows——"

"Very little. I have talked with her. It appears that she and her parents have been traveling abroad a great deal of the time since she was born. She knows that they lived in New York, also for a time in St. Louis, but she does not remember the address in either place. Her mother's parents are dead, I believe, and I judge from things she has told me that there must have been some trouble with her father's family, and that the young couple lived rather an independent existence." Then after a long pause, "Somehow I cannot bear to leave the child at a Mission. Think of leaving our Ruth——"

"I know, Hannah, but her safety——"

"Yes, I realize that. We have the right, perhaps, to jeopardize the lives of our own family in this trip across the plains, but have we the right to expose the life and safety of this child, that has been left in our care?"

They sat in deep thought for some minutes. From the other wagon they could hear the chatter of the children's voices, as Ruth, Lige, Sam, Joe, and Nina excitedly discussed the events of the night before. She still grieved for her parents, but little by little the society of the wholesome, healthy-minded young Penimans was winning the little Princess back to cheerfulness.

"She seems very happy with us," sighed Mrs. Peniman.

"Yes, I believe she is. I wish we might keep her with us," answered her husband gravely.

The next day they reached the Des Moines River, and after making their night camp by the beautiful stream made their way the next morning to Fort Dodge, which had been built on the east side of the Des Moines two years before. Here they found other travelers and heard the horrible details of the Spring Lake massacre, and also of the depredations of the Sioux on the South Fork of the Platte. Sam and Lige, who were standing near, overheard a mover relating to their father the circumstances of a hideous murder of a party of emigrants which had occurred near Fontanelle but a few days before. These accounts, while they thrilled the boys with a sense of adventure, made their parents more anxious than ever, and many times the temptation assailed them to give up the hazardous journey and return to safety and civilization.

But there was something in the make-up of the early pioneers that forbade them to turn back, and after a few hours of rest they replenished their supplies and went on their way.

While at Fort Dodge Joshua Peniman made inquiries in regard to Missions, and learned that a Presbyterian Mission had been founded at Bellevue, the first permanent white settlement in Nebraska, on the west side of the Missouri River. To this he determined to make his way, and leave in safety the child of the strangers who had been entrusted to his care.

The travelers had now left civilization far behind them. The boys, who had so eagerly anticipated the adventures of the journey, now had more than sufficient of it to satisfy them. What white settlers there were in the country at that time were settled along the streams and rivers, leaving the space between unorganized and wild. As they traveled on trees and water grew farther and farther apart. There were some trees, mostly willows and cottonwoods, along the borders of the streams, all the rest was grass and sky.

They often saw large bands of Indians sweeping across the plains, hunting the wild game that was everywhere in great abundance. They saw great herds of elk and antelope, and wild turkeys were plentiful, with great flocks of prairie-chickens and quail.

They had no difficulty in providing their table with fresh meat now, for the boys and their father had but to go out with their guns for an hour or two in the evening and come back with their game-bags full.

But while they had meat in plenty they could no longer get fruit or vegetables. They could not supply their daily needs at towns or villages, for there were no towns, and the settlements were so far apart that many times they traveled for days without ever seeing a house or human. When they did find a "settler" or squatter, his home was on the bank of some river or stream, and his food consisted mostly of "sow-belly" and coffee, with little enough of either for himself, and none whatever for guest or traveler.

The lack of green food troubled Mrs. Peniman greatly, for with the voracious appetites of her young brood she realized that they should have vegetables to offset their constant consumption of the heavier diet.

One morning while they were traveling through western Iowa she suddenly leaned out of the wagon peering down into the grass.

"Stop a minute, Joshua," she cried, "I see something over there I want to investigate. It looks to me as if the Lord might be sending us the vegetables we have been wanting."

Mr. Peniman stopped the team and she scrambled nimbly down. Seeing her leave the wagon, Ruth, Nina, Sam and Paul eagerly followed her.

"What is it, Mother? What do you see?" cried Ruth.

Just then Sam stooped down and held up a small green object between his fingers. "Look, Mother," he cried, "look at the funny little green balls!"

"Ah," cried Mrs. Peniman, seizing it eagerly, "that's what I thought! That's what I was looking for! Look here, see?"

She stooped down, pointing to a delicate green vine with small leaves and delicate tendrils that grew in the grass at her feet.

"Pea-vines!" exclaimed Ruth.

"Yes, pea-vines! and these are some kind of a wild pea. I am almost sure they would be good to eat."

By this time Mr. Peniman, Lige and Joe had joined them.

"Oh," said Mr. Peniman, "*buffalo peas*! I have often read of them growing on the plains."

"Are they good to eat, Father?" asked Sam, who was in a chronic state of being hungry.

"I think so; we might try them. Run about and gather all you can, children; we'll cook them when we camp to-night."

With pails and baskets the young people ran about gathering the peas from the low trailing vines.

"They're the queerest peas I ever saw," said Joe; "they haven't any pods, and they're so *big*, look!" and he held up a round green ball about as large as a marble, pale green on one side and on the other a dull, purplish red.

When camp was struck that evening there was great interest shown in the preparation of the buffalo peas. After soaking them in water Mrs. Peniman put them on to boil with a pinch of soda, then drained off that water, put fresh water upon them, let them boil again, and when they were tender served them with a dressing of milk.

The family ate them, but it was the general opinion that the peas had grown too old to be prepared in that way, and on the next evening Mrs. Peniman made them into a pea soup, which was pronounced delicious by the entire family, and became a distinct addition to their diet as long as the buffalo-pea season lasted.

The boys had often remarked as they traveled farther and farther westward into the uninhabited wilderness that the road over which their prairie schooners rumbled was a broad, hard highway, with scarcely a blade of grass upon its surface. Joe wondered at this, and asked his father why it should be so.

"We are traveling over the old Oregon Trail, my boy," Mr. Peniman told him. "It is an old, old trail, the first highway made into the wilderness of the west by the feet of white men."

"Who made it?" demanded Lige, who resented any one having been ahead of them in pioneer life.

"The trail was first made in 1813 by what was known as the Astorian Expedition, which set out from St. Louis with about a hundred men, intending to cross the mountains and build a fort for the American Fur Trading Company in Oregon. You boys should read the history of that expedition; you would find it most interesting."

"Did they get there?" asked Sam, who was always interested in the result of any adventure.

His father smiled. "Yes, Sam, they got there. When I knew that a part of our journey would lead us along the old Oregon Trail I read up its history. They had a terrible journey, but after great losses and hardships seven men reached the Columbia River, where they built a fort which they called Astoria, after John Jacob Astor of New York, the president of the fur company. The Indians set upon them and stole their goods and their stock, and they returned to St. Louis with only one old horse, which they had succeeded in trading for with a friendly Indian."

"But that was so long ago, Father," put in Joe, "I should think the trail would have been lost since."

"It probably would have been," answered his father, "but that it was kept open by the Oregon emigration of 1832. But it was beaten into its present good condition and has been kept so by the gold-seekers and emigrant trains that began the rush to California in 1849. This is also sometimes called the 'Mormon Trail,' because it was over this very road that we are traveling now that the Mormons passed on their pilgrimage to Salt Lake in 1847. They, too, had great hardships and losses, and had to winter at Florence, a little trading-station on the Missouri River, which we should reach very soon now."

"Jiminy, that's interesting," cried Joe, who had been listening intently; "it makes it so much more interesting when you think of who's been over this old road before. How much easier and pleasanter it is to learn history and geography when you're right on the spot than when you are sitting on a hard bench at school!"

Toward evening the country became more rolling, and shortly before sunset they saw in the distance a blue haze and high steep bluffs.

Joe, whose eyes were always on the alert, cried, "River ahead!"

Mr. Peniman, who was studying a map spread out on his knees, looked up.

"Yes," he said, "that is the Missouri River."

"*The Missouri*—at last!" whooped Lige, "hurray, now the fun will begin!"

Mr. and Mrs. Peniman looked at one another. To them the experiences that lay beyond the Missouri did not appeal in the light of *fun*.

The day had been hot and clear, and as the sun sank in the west it left a sky of intense brilliancy, shot with crimson and gold, fading away toward the horizon in tender pink and mauve and lavender. They drove into the straggling little trading-post of Florence, where the unhappy Mormons had passed such a tragic winter many years before, and as they left it and drove over a small hill their eyes fell upon a sight grander and more beautiful than Moses saw from the top of Nebo's Mountain. The valley of the Missouri lay before them, and with the great river sweeping by long lines of bluffs covered with waving trees it presented to them a panorama both magnificent and inspiring.

"See that great bluff over there, Joe?" called his father. "That's where the Lewis and Clark Expedition held their first great council with the Indians. It was called *Council Bluffs* in memory of that event, which was the beginning of the opening up of this great western country. I am told it has come to be a great Indian trading-station."

Twilight was beginning to fall as they drove into the trading-post, which is now the city of Council Bluffs.

It was a great sight to the young easterners. On every hand were Indians, Indians and more Indians. Some wearing the cotton shirt and trousers of civilization, others blankets, others rejoicing in the garb of nature, augmented by a breech-clout and a few feathers in their hair. The squaws with their papooses strapped on their backs stood stolidly about, some in blankets, some in ugly calico "Mother Hubbard" wrappers. These Indians were mostly Omahas, with some Pawnees, Arapahoes and Potawatamis, all friendly to the white man. The Omaha Reservation was but a short distance away, and the Indians were bringing in skins, furs, and buffalo hides and exchanging them for blankets, flour, coffee, and the white man's "fire-water."

There were many emigrant wagons gathered in the wide straggling street, between two rows of one-story shanties, and white men were trading with red men, home-seekers anxiously seeking information, dogs were barking, children crying, men arguing and swearing, while the patient oxen hitched to the wagons breathed gusty sighs of rest, and the few women who were on their way to a home in the new country west of the Missouri looked on with troubled eyes or hurried in and out of the few straggling shops making their purchases.

The Peniman family had all alighted from their wagons before the general store, and while Mr. and Mrs. Peniman went in to make some purchases, followed by David and the little girls, Joe and Lige stood outside, looking with interested attention at the strange, novel spectacle of an Indian trading-station.

They were watching some white men who were talking with a group of Indians. Suddenly Joe pricked up his ears and walked nearer.

A tall, slenderly-built man, with a red, dissipated face, watery red-lidded eyes, and longish red hair was holding out a string of beads and jabbering in his own language to a tall, handsome young Indian who had an otter pelt over his arm.

"Aw, don't you *do* it," Joe burst out suddenly. "He's stringin' you! That string of beads ain't worth twenty-five cents."

The young Indian turned and looked at him, and the man, turning several shades redder than before, wheeled upon him with an oath.

"Mind your own business, you little pup," he roared, "who's askin' your advice!"

Whether he understood what had been said or not, Joe did not know, but the Indian turned and walked away, carrying the pelt with him. The man strode up to Joe with a menacing attitude.

"I'll teach you to interfere in my business again, you meddlesome young fool," he shouted, and raised his clenched fist. At this moment Mr. and Mrs. Peniman came out of the store, followed by Ruth, Sara, and Nina Carroll. Joshua Peniman, seeing his son threatened, hurried to his side, and the man, with another great oath, turned and faced him.

As he did so the oath died on his lips, his eyes flew wide and his mouth fell open, and the fiery color receded from his face, leaving it grey and ashen.

Joe, staring at him, saw that his eyes were fixed upon Nina, with the look of a man who sees an apparition from another world.

"What's the matter here?" cried Joshua Peniman. "Joe, what has this man been doing to you?"

"Nothing," answered Joe with a laugh, "he's just mad because I busted up his trade with an Indian. Say, what do you think, the old cheat was tryin' to trade that young buck out of a splendid otter skin for a string of nasty little cheap yellow beads!"

Joshua Peniman turned to the man, but he was paying no attention to them. With eyes fixed on the face of the little Princess he stood motionless, his thin, dissipated face almost white through its coat of tan.

Mrs. Peniman, who saw the look, seized Nina by the hand and hurried her away.

The man whirled upon Joshua Peniman.

"Who is that?" he demanded. "What's her name?"

"Who?" asked Mr. Peniman coolly. He too had seen the expression, and was on his guard immediately.

"That—that girl! Where did she come from? What's her name?"

Ruth and Nina had come out of the store together. Joshua Peniman, whose conscience would not let him lie, purposely misunderstood which little girl he meant.

"That little girl is my daughter. Her name is Ruth Peniman. She comes from the Muskingum Valley in Ohio," he answered.

The man stared at him with fiery eyes.

"Are you lying to me? If you are you'd better make your will right now."

"I am not lying to you. I never lie. My name is Joshua Peniman. I and my family are crossing the plains to Nebraska. The little girl you just saw come out of that store with my wife is my daughter Ruth. This is my son Joe."

The stranger turned and cast a snarling glance at the boy.

"He'd better not interfere in my business again, or his name'll be on a coffin-plate," he growled, and moved away.

Joshua Peniman motioned to the wagons. "In with you, boys," he said in a low voice, "we'll have to get away from here."

When they were in the wagons again and on the road he turned to his wife.

"What does it mean?" he said in a voice so low that the little girls who were in the back of the wagon dressing the china dolls they had bought at the trading-station could not hear him. "What is this mystery that is following us? It is evident that Nina is in danger from some one—for some reason that we know nothing about. I shall be thankful when we can put her into the hands of those who are in a better position to protect her than we are."

"That man back there," breathed Mrs. Peniman, scarcely above a whisper, "that horrible creature—thought—acted—*as if he knew her*!"

"He did know her—or he thought he did! He had some sort of a shock when his eyes fell upon her. He was not sure, and I think I threw him off the trail."

"It is strange—strange—in this vast new country—what can it mean?" cried Mrs. Peniman, and gazed out over the prairies with brooding eyes.

CHAPTER IX

RED SNAKE

It had been Joshua Peniman's intention to pass the night at Council Bluffs and cross the Missouri in the morning. But the events that had transpired at the general store so alarmed him that he decided to leave the trading-station at once, anxious to get the child who appeared to be so surrounded by mystery away from the proximity of the stranger with the degenerate, fox-like face.

They drove until dark along the banks of the river, then made their camp in the woods in a place that looked sheltered and secure. They had finished their supper and were preparing for bed when the young Indian, whom Joe had advised not to trade his otter skin for the stranger's worthless string of beads, came striding into their camp.

He walked straight up to Joe and held out his hand.

"Good boy," he said, greatly to the lad's astonishment. Then without another word laid the otter skin in his hands.

"Hello," cried Joe, "where'd you come from?"

"Me Pashepaho. Son Pawnee chief. Spik li'le." Then looking down at the otter skin—"Heap bad man."

"Who? Oh, the feller that was tryin' to do you out of this skin for a string of beads? I should sa-ay so. He's a crook, he is. But say, P—p——"

"Pashepaho. Son chief."

"Uh-huh," nodded Joe, to whom the son of a chief was no different from any other Indian, "but look here, Pashepaho, you fellers ought to learn the value of your goods and not let those thieving white men skin you like that. I happen to know that this is a good otter skin, because my uncle used to deal in furs and I've seen lots of 'em. Those beads he was tryin' to trade you weren't worth a quarter."

"No?" the young Indian looked at him and a slow fire smouldered in his eyes.

"White brother liar. Take 'way red man's land, take 'way red man's furs, take 'way red man's wife, give red man fire-water."

Mr. Peniman had come up to hear what the Indian was saying. "That's true," he said gravely, "the white men are setting a bad example to their red brothers, I fear." Then after a moment's pause, "Do you know who that man was, Pashepaho?"

"Red Snake. Heap bad man. Got bad heart. Trade with Indian. Live Santee Sioux."

Joshua Peniman started. "He lives with the *Santee Sioux*?"

The Indian nodded.

"But he is not an Indian, he's a white man, isn't he?"

"Squaw-man."

For a moment Joshua Peniman stood staring at him, his brain whirling.

A white man—lived with the Santee Sioux! Had evidently recognized—or partly recognized—Nina Carroll! Who could he be? What the relation between him and the departed Carrolls? What could be the meaning of this tangle in which he had involved himself by taking into his custody the friendless child of the white man who had been slain by a Sioux arrow!

The young Indian pointed to the pelt, which still hung carelessly over Joe's arm.

"Me give," he said. "Pawnee heap white man's friend."

"You mean you want to give me this skin?" cried Joe.

The young Indian grinned and nodded.

"Oh, no, Pashepaho! That pelt's worth good money. I have no use for it, and you ought to get a good price for it. I'm awfully much obliged all the same; it was fine of you to want to make me a present. I like you. You're square. Shake. You and I will be friends, shan't we?"

Pashepaho shook the hand that Joe extended to him. Joe dashed into the wagon and scrambled out again a moment later carrying a bright red necktie in his hand.

"Here, you take this. I'd like to make you a present. I know you like red. It'll look good on you."

Pashepaho took it eagerly, scrutinizing the brilliant bit of silk with the pleased smile of a child. Then he proceeded to wind it about his head, tying it in a knot in the back and letting the ends hang down over his shoulders.

"There! That looks fine! I knew it would be becoming to you," cried Joe, without an intimation that that was not the accustomed manner of wearing neckties.

The Indian looked from the boy to his father with a pleased grin. "You sleep?" he asked.

"Yes, we're going to camp here to-night," answered Joe.

"Me sleep, too."

Joe brought him out a substantial supper, which he ate squatted on the grass beside the wagons, and when the family settled down to their night's rest he lay down beside them with his blanket over his head.

It was long past midnight when Joe was awakened by a slight movement at his feet. He had heard no sound. Spotty was standing, his ears cocked forward, and the young Indian, motionless as a statue, stood with bow bent, an arrow in rest.

"What's the matter? What do you see?" cried Joe, springing up.

"Sh-sh!" whispered the Indian.

For a moment longer he stood, then discharged the arrow and at the same moment let loose a blood-curdling yell that roused the family and set the children to screaming.

Mr. Peniman leaped wildly to his feet.

"What is it? Where are they?" he shouted, but the young Indian laughed and snapped his fingers.

"Gone!" he said with a gesture of wide flight, "Red Snake coward. Think Big Chief come."

"*Red Snake!* Was Red Snake here? How do you know? What was he doing? Were there other Indians with him?"

Pashepaho shrugged his shoulders.

"Me know he come. Me come. He scare. He run 'way. He no come more. Think heap much Pawnee here."

He chuckled to himself, but Joshua Peniman did not join in his merriment. He knew now that a deadly enemy was following them, and that while Nina Carroll was in their hands there could be neither rest nor security for the family.

They rose early, and taking a grateful farewell of Pashepaho started on their way.

In the fresh light of early morning, they caught their first glimpse of Nebraska.

The land all about them lay smiling, with tall prairie grass waving to and fro and flickering with constantly changing shades and colors, the river glinted like a sheet of silver, and over all arched the sky, blue as an amethyst, with the delicate shades of early sunrise coloring the east.

They crossed the Missouri on the ferry-boat *General Marion*, which had been running only since the spring of the year before, and found themselves in Omaha, taking their first view of the bare, straggling settlement which is now the chief city of the great agricultural State of Nebraska.

At that time Omaha was the centre of the reservation of the Maha, or Omaha, tribe, and a trading post for the trappers and traders who had come to profit by the credulity and ignorance of the Indians. Missionaries were here who had come to carry Christianity into the wilderness, and a few white settlers who at that date had found their way across the river into the newly organized territory. The great motionless prairies lay spread out in striking contrast to the uplands and valleys along the river, with the sombre brown of the vegetation lighted up by the sunrise through a soft haze that cast a glamour over the picture.

The Omahas were camped in their teepees on the lowlands, bucks, squaws, papooses, dogs, wigwams and ponies huddled together, just as they had come from their great annual hunt in the Elkhorn valley, where elk, bison, antelope and other game abounded. There were a few shanties and log huts scattered about, but at this date, August of 1856, there were not more than fifty white families in the whole of Douglas County.

Joshua Peniman inquired the way to Bellevue, and after a brief stop in Omaha set forth for the Mission at that point.

Before leaving Omaha, Hannah Peniman had sent the children into the other wagon, and drew the little Princess to her, reminding her of her dead mother's wishes, and telling her that they were now near Bellevue, where they would leave her at the Mission, from which she hoped that she might be sent home to her own people.

Somewhat to her surprise, the little girl received the announcement with grief and terror.

"Oh, no, no, no," she cried, "I don't want to be left there! I'd *die* of homesickness there! Oh, Mother Peniman, don't leave me, don't leave me, please don't go away and leave me!"

"But you would only be there a short time, Nina," said Mrs. Peniman gently; "they would soon send you home."

"I *have* no home," she cried, bursting into a wild storm of weeping; "I don't know any of my people. My papa and mama are dead, and there is no one who wants me or cares for me! Oh, don't leave me, Mother Peniman, please, please take me with you!"

"Can you tell me the names of any of your relatives, Nina? Don't you remember your grandfather or grandmother? Haven't you any aunts or uncles or cousins? Who is there back there where you used to live that you could go to?"

"I don't know, I don't know!" sobbed the child. "I never knew any of them. My grandma and grandpa on Mama's side are both dead, and I think Papa must have quarreled with his parents, for he never talked about them. We lived abroad 'most all the time, and when we were in this country we lived all by ourselves in New York."

"But can't you tell us the names of any people who would know who your relatives are? Your mother said——"

"No, no, I can't, I can't!" sobbed the child. "Everything was in the box Mama gave me. She told me that full particulars were in there. I don't know who they can send me to—I have no friends—no one who loves me——"

Hannah Peniman looked at her husband over the head that was buried on her breast. The past few months had drawn lines in the comely face, had silvered the shining brown hair with threads of grey, and left deep shadows in the sweet blue eyes.

"She doesn't know—she doesn't understand, the poor lamb," she said tremulously.

"Oh, yes, I do know, yes I do understand," sobbed the child. "I know that my papa and mama are dead and that I am left all alone in the world— I have no one who loves or cares for me—and now you are going to send me away—leave me all alone at a Mission—and I'll die—I'll just *die*——"

Her voice had risen into a loud sobbing wail, and the children in the other wagon heard it. In a twinkling Joe, Lige and Ruth were running back to them.

"Mother—what's the matter with Princess—I heard her crying," panted Ruth, scrambling into the wagon.

"They're going to leave me—leave me—at the M-M-Mission," sobbed Princess. "They're tired of me—they don't love me—and they're going to send me back h-h-home!"

Joe sprang into the wagon, his face looking strangely pale and set.

"Leave her at a Mission? Father—what does she mean?"

His father explained, as gently as he could, omitting, for the sake of the little girl, the danger that threatened them on her account, and which seemed to be so relentlessly following her.

The child had thrown herself into Joe's arms, and he listened with his arms clasped about her.

"It was the dying wish of her mother, Joe," Mr. Peniman concluded.

"But she is dead—and Nina is alive. If she doesn't know her own people—if she doesn't want to go to them—isn't it better that she should be allowed to do what she wants to with her own life?"

"But the danger, Joe——"

Joe clasped his arms more tightly about her. "I'll take care of her, Father," he said, with an expression that made the words like a vow.

A few hours later they reached Bellevue, the oldest town in Nebraska, and once designed to be its capital, and Mr. Peniman drove directly to the Mission.

They left Nina in the wagon with the other children while they went inside. What was said or done, what discoveries they made, or what caused them to so quickly reach a decision the children never knew; but only a few minutes had passed before they saw them returning, and Hannah Peniman's head was held high and an angry spot was burning on either cheek as she climbed into the wagon.

Nina, with tear-stained face and eyes swollen and red with weeping, was clasped in Ruth's arms, and both of them were crying together. When they heard the approach of Mr. and Mrs. Peniman Nina raised her head with a gasping sob, but Mrs. Peniman bent over her, took her in her arms and pressed her to her breast.

"Don't cry, poor lamb," she comforted, "thee shall not be taken from us. I believe your chances are better with us than they would ever have been there. God took our baby daughter from us, and I believe that He has given us thee to comfort us. Cry no more, dear child, thee shall stay with us, and our fortunes shall be thy fortunes, to the end of the chapter."

There was great joy in the wagons when the news went forth that Princess was not to be taken from them. The children had all become devotedly attached to their little comrade, and her happiness was no greater than theirs when they learned that they were not to be parted. Mr. and Mrs. Peniman, too, felt a great weight lifted from their hearts.

"He who never faileth us will guard her, Joshua," said Hannah Peniman, a mist in her brave blue eyes. "I could never have found it in my conscience to abandon the poor lamb. She will be to us as one of our own children, and I know that her mother will rest more tranquilly there in her grave on the lonely prairies knowing that her little one is with us. Her spirit will watch over her, her love will guide her safely through all dangers and alarms."

"God grant that it may be so," answered Joshua Peniman solemnly.

CHAPTER X

NEBRASKA

The Peniman family found the little town of Bellevue the most pleasant and attractive place they had struck in many days' travel, and it comforted the hearts of the elders of the party to find that after all Nebraska was not the treeless and verdureless wilderness they had been led to expect.

Located on the banks of the great Missouri, overlooking the green wood-crowned bluffs, with the soft verdant valley winding its way below, they were not surprised as they gazed upon it that the old fur-trader, Manuel Lisa, had named it "belle vue," or "beautiful view," so many years before.

This was the stopping-place of all the adventurers to the far western land. Trappers, traders, travelers and prospective settlers all stopped here for rest and refreshment before making the plunge into the wilderness that lay beyond on the trackless plains. Missionaries here made their first attempt to civilize and Christianize the Territory, and Mr. and Mrs. Peniman found great comfort and solace in sitting again in a church, even though not of their own particular faith, and listening to the word of God.

They made their preparations to leave this last anchor to civilization with much reluctance and regret. They wished many times that they might consider their journey ended here. But the object of that journey had been to so locate that each of their growing lads might be enabled to homestead his 160 acres as soon as he was old enough, and the bottom lands of the Missouri were already pretty well squatted by trappers and settlers. So after a pleasant and restful day at Bellevue they purchased the last essentials for their home in the wilderness, loaded them into the Carroll wagon, and started westward on the most trying and perilous part of their journey.

They crossed the Platte River, a winding, shallow stream twisting along over its flat sandy bottom, which gave the Territory the Indian name of "Ne-bras-kah," or "Flat Water," and started across the prairies.

After leaving the Oregon Trail there was not even a track to be seen on the prairies. There was no road, nor any sign of a road. All to the westward seemed an unbroken wilderness. Meadow-larks sang in the grass, deer or antelope now and then flitted across their vision far away in the knee-high sage-brush, and their eyes strained westward over an ocean of immensity that looked as if it stretched away unbroken to the very edge of the world.

They watched the sun go down that night as the voyager sees it go down at sea, sinking inch by inch with no obstructing obstacle between, until its red rim sank below the horizon, leaving them alone on the vast solitude of the prairies.

It was well for the family that they had carried wood and water from their last camp at Bellevue, for there was neither wood nor water in sight.

The wagons were drawn up in a semicircle, the cow and horses placed inside, and the family gathered close together about their supper table, as if feeling the need of human contact in the vast loneliness that brooded about them.

They woke the next morning with the blaze of sunshine in their faces. It was a marvelous thing, this awakening on the silent unbroken surface of the plains, with the sun coming up like a great crimson hogshead over the flat rim of the earth, changing it from black to grey, from grey to pink, from pink to rose and blue and green and purple; and in all that great expanse, over which the eye could travel in every direction to the very limits of the horizon, to see no living creature but each other.

The day was hot and cloudless, and as the wagons bumped and crawled along through the grass something of the dread silence and loneliness of the prairies crept into their hearts, and a sort of awe came over them. The children found themselves dropping their voices and speaking low, as if they were in church; and Mr. and Mrs. Peniman avoided each other's eyes and spoke but seldom, as their gaze stared out over the interminable plains.

There were no trees in this land through which they were now traveling, and the only bird that gladdened their ears or eyes for many a long day to come were the little meadow-larks, which perched upon a swaying stalk or weed uttered its clear, gurgling melody.

One morning as they were jogging along, Lige, who sat beside Joe in the wagon, suddenly jogged his arm.

"Look, Joe," he cried, "what are all those little humps in the ground? See, there are thousands of them! Aren't they queer? Let's ask Father what they are."

His father heard and smiled. "Just watch," he said. "And Ruthie, thee and Sam and Paul should watch, too. Those are little houses, and some queer little fellows live in them."

"What lives in them?" asked Joe. At the same moment Sam, who was lying on the beds in the back of the wagon, stuck his head out of the rear curtains and gave a squeal of delight.

"Oh, I see!" he shouted. "Look at that queer little feller sittin' right up on the roof of his house! Come on out, Ruth, greatest sight you ever saw! Queerest little things, bigger'n gophers and not striped, just kind o' plain brown, with their arms folded across their chests. What in the world are they, Father?"

"They are prairie dogs," answered Mr. Peniman. "We are passing through what is called a 'prairie dog town.' I have read of them many times, but have never seen them before."

They had stopped the teams, and the family all scrambled out of the wagons to see this strange and novel sight of a "town" in which nothing lived but prairie dogs.

"Why, just see," cried Joe, "there are *millions* of them! Just look at that fellow over there, Ruth, sitting up on the roof of his house scolding at us!"

And truly there did appear to be millions of them. The whole surface of the ground as far as they could see was dotted over with the queer little dome-like houses, made of the clayey soil of the prairies thrown up into small heaps or mounds; and on each sat a small reddish-grey animal, a little larger than a squirrel, with tail cocked up saucily over their backs, and paws folded demurely across their fat little stomachs, gazing with bright, bead-like eyes at the intruders, of whom they did not seem to be in the least afraid. On each side of the face were pouches, in which they carry out the dirt when burrowing the holes in which they live, and in which they pouch nuts, roots, and other dainties. They seemed filled with curiosity, and as they came swarming up out of their holes to sit on the tops of their houses, they made a peculiar barking noise, something like the bark of a young puppy.

This amused the children immensely. "How deep are their holes, Father?" asked Sam.

"I have read that they are tunneled back long distances, and that many of the underground passages connect the mounds with one another. I have also read," he continued with a twinkle in his eyes, "that a prairie dog, an owl, and a rattlesnake lives in every hole."

"A *rattlesnake?*" cried Ruth. "Wouldn't it bite the prairie dogs?"

Joshua Peniman laughed. "Well, I don't know, Ruth, that is what I read; but my own opinion is that as the main business of little Mrs. Prairie Dog is to keep snakes and other varmints from eating her little ones I hardly think she would tolerate a rattler in her house. But come now, jump in, we must not spend any more time here. No doubt there are many just as interesting and curious things to see farther on."

They stopped early that night on account of the heat, wanting to save the horses all they could. A strong wind came up about sundown, which soon grew to be a gale, and which almost blew them off their feet as they scampered about on the prairie trying to find something of which to make their fire.

It was their first taste of the "Nebraska zephyrs," of which they were to see so much later on, and it kept the whole family busy chasing about after hats and bonnets, brooms, dish-pans, and all sorts of things that blew out of the wagons.

"I can't find anything to build a fire of, Mother," cried Joe after a vain search, "there's nothing out here, only wind and grass. Don't you think we'd better use some of our stored-up wood?"

Lige, who was just returning from a prolonged chase after Ruth's sunbonnet, suddenly stopped short and pointed away across the prairies. Joe turned and looked, then remained staring.

"What in the name of goodness——" he ejaculated.

"Look, Mother, what are those things over there?" called Lige. "Do you think they are some kind of animals?"

"Sheep!" ventured Sam, staring away intently toward where a number of dark objects were moving rapidly toward them from the south.

"No, they're too small for sheep," said Mrs. Peniman, puckering her forehead and narrowing her eyes; "what in the world *are* they?"

"They've got a queer gait," cried Joe, "and they're coming a-whizzing. Could they be wild turkeys?"

"Oh, no, they're not fowl of any kind."

"Will they bite, Mother?" queried little Mary.

"Maybe they're coyotes," suggested Paul.

Just then Mr. Peniman, who had been out looking after the horses, appeared.

"Look, Father, what are those things over yonder?" cried Lige.

Mr. Peniman shaded his eyes with his hand and gazed intently out over the prairies. Then he began to laugh.

"Hurry up, boys," he cried, "here's the stuff for your fire coming to you! Catch as much of it as you can as it goes by, for I warn you that with this wind it won't wait long on anybody."

"But what is it, Father?" asked Joe curiously.

"It is called 'tumble-weed.' It is a sort of bush, with a small, slender stalk. During the summer this bush grows almost round, and when the fibre of the plant dries the stalk becomes brittle and the first hard wind breaks it off; then the bush rolls over and over across the plains, sometimes traveling for miles before a high wind."

"Oh-h," cried Lige, with a falling inflection of disappointment in his voice, "I thought it might be something interesting."

"So it is something interesting," said Mrs. Peniman. "Did you ever see a more interesting sight than that? It looks like a Lilliputian army marching toward us! Hurry up everybody, get in line, let's stop all we can. I know they will make a splendid fire."

Always ready for anything new the children hastened to form in a line, even down to small David, who was continually being blown off his short legs. As the tumble-weeds came toward them, rolling over and over before the strong south wind, they had a great game, stopping them, chasing after them and running them down, while Mr. Peniman piled them up and threw a horse-blanket over them to keep them from blowing away.

It was a great romp, and the children shrieked with laughter as they all chased after the strange, grotesque bundles, with the wind beating in their faces and almost carrying them away.

"Whew! that's more fun than pom-pom-pull-away!" puffed Lige, throwing himself flat on a great tumble-weed which was trying hard to elude him. And Mrs. Peniman, with her hair blown down and her cheeks as red as Ruth's, declared it was the liveliest game she had taken part in for many a long day.

When broken up and crowded under the pot and into the little sheet-iron camp-stove they found it excellent fuel. It burned out quickly, but made a hot fire, little smoke, and saved the precious store of firewood so laboriously gathered up and so carefully hoarded for emergencies.

That night the moon was full, and the boys begged to sleep in their blankets outside. As the night was very hot and it was close and stifling under the canvas their mother gave her consent. The dry prairie grass made a good mattress, and rolled up in their blankets like old campaigners they lay looking up into the wonderful night sky for a long time before they could fall asleep.

At last the fatigues of the day and the deep quiet of the prairies lulled them to rest. Sam and Lige were fast asleep and Joe was beginning to doze, when there came to his ears a sound so weird, so blood-curdling that he sprang up, his heart beating heavily.

His first instinct was to grab for his musket. Spotty was standing up, with hair bristling and lips drawn back, growling fiercely.

The wagons were, as was their custom these days, drawn up into a semicircle, and the boys were lying within it close to the big wagon. Just back of the wagon the three teams of horses were picketed, and just beyond them the cow.

As Joe stood listening intently, his musket in his hand, he heard the horses begin to plunge and snort.

He glanced at his father, but the sight of the thin, tired face of the sleeping man stopped him.

For a moment all was silent as the grave. Then again came the long, hoarse, raucous cry.

He stooped and shook Lige.

"Wake up," he whispered in his ear, "there's something after the horses!"

Lige woke with a start, and grabbed his rifle as he sprang to his feet.

"Where?" he whispered. At the same moment the howling was repeated, and the horses back of the wagons began to rear and snort with fear. Suddenly the cow sent forth a terrified bellow.

With musket over his shoulder Joe dashed between the wagons, followed by Lige.

The moon was at its full, and the flat surface of the prairies was dimly visible all about them. Outlined against the horizon they saw a number of gaunt, shadowy forms flitting silently. At no great distance from them a creature, larger than a big dog, sat up on its haunches and with head raised to the moon uttered a long, wailing howl.

From far away across the prairie it was answered, and while they stood listening the night grew hideous by the calling and answering of the deep-chested howl of grey wolves.

"Wolves—grey wolves!" whispered Joe, "they are after the horses!"

Presently as they stood with suspended breath dim grey shapes came gliding across the prairies toward them.

Almost as he spoke they heard the cow give a terrified bellow, and heard her tugging wildly at her rope.

"The cow, the cow!" shouted Lige, and together the boys leaped forward.

They saw the poor animal crouched and cringing with terror, and as they sprang forward, gun at shoulder, they saw a huge, gaunt grey figure leap at her throat.

Scarcely waiting to aim, Joe shot. The reverberation had scarcely ceased when his father was at his side.

"What is it?" he cried.

"Wolves—wolves! They are after the horses—they almost got the cow!" shouted Lige, and fired again into the shadows, where he could make out the slinking grey figures.

Joe too was loading and firing. The horses, half mad with terror, were rearing and snorting, and the cow plunged in wide circles, blowing and bellowing with fear.

Mr. Peniman, musket in hand, ran to them, but the wolves had been frightened away. He found two great, gaunt, grey marauders dead, but the others, frightened by the shots, had disappeared as swiftly and silently as shadows.

The boys were greatly disappointed to find that they had not killed more of the midnight thieves. "There were such a lot of them," cried Joe; "what became of the rest? I thought I would kill half a dozen at least."

"Wolves are great cowards. When they heard the shots they probably made off with all speed. I think you did exceedingly well to get two in this uncertain light. Too bad we can't skin these fellows and keep the pelts as souvenirs of your first wolves. But you will no doubt have the chance to get plenty more, so we will let these fellows go. We'll have to watch for them after this. It would have been a bad lookout for us if they had got the horses or the cow."

This incident served to show the pioneers that other dangers than those of Indian raids menaced their night camp on the plains, and served to make them more watchful than ever.

CHAPTER XI

THE PRAIRIE FIRE

A few days later the travelers drove into a dreary, straggling little settlement of a few log and sod shanties on a little stream called Salt Creek. Here they spent the night, glad of the company of other white settlers. There was a general store in the little settlement, at which Joshua Peniman bought a barrel of salt pork, a barrel of flour, sugar, coffee, rice, tea, beans, dried peas, and a bucket of lard and a firkin of butter.

"I am doubtful," he said as he loaded them into his wagon, "whether we will come to another place where we could get supplies."

Early the next morning they loaded up their wagons, bade farewell to the other movers, and struck off across the trackless prairies.

It was still early, and the drum of the prairie-chickens came to their ears across the silence of the plains. Joe and Lige took their guns and went in search of them, and soon returned with a couple of fine young hens, which Mrs. Peniman cooked for their dinner.

A strong, hot south wind was blowing, which toward evening increased to a gale. Even the shadows of night did not bring relief from the heat, which seemed to increase rather than diminish. Mrs. Peniman could not sleep. With a feeling of suffocation and uneasiness upon her she tossed from side to side. The air was hot and close, and in her nostrils there was a pungent smell. With the instinct of danger strong upon her she sprang up, and jumping out of the wagon looked about her.

Off to the south the sky was red, and straining her eyes through the darkness she saw, low against the horizon, a leaping tongue of flame.

She ran to where her husband lay sleeping. "Joshua," she whispered, laying her hand on his arm, "Joshua, wake up! I smell smoke, and away over yonder I think I see a fire——"

"*Fire!*" the sleeping man was wide awake and on his feet in a moment. "Fire? Where?"

Mrs. Peniman pointed.

For an instant he stood staring at the little tongues of flame that licked up over the horizon, then sprang to the pickets and began untying the horses.

"Prairie fire!" he cried. "And there's no telling where it will stop in this wind! Call the boys!"

When the boys were roused he gave them no time to ask questions. In quick, nervous tones he issued his orders.

"Hitch up as quick as you can, Joe," he shouted, "there's a prairie fire over yonder! Lige, get up the black team. Sam, run and bring in the cow. Pack those things in the wagons, Hannah, never mind order now. Ruth, get a couple of pails of water out of the kegs. Paul, pull up those stake-pins, wind up the ropes and throw them in the wagons! Hurry, hurry, all of you, we haven't a moment to lose!"

Working with feverish haste he turned often and glanced at the line of red on the horizon.

"It's miles away yet," he said in a low voice to his wife; "we may be able to get out of its path, but with this wind——"

He stopped abruptly, then leaping into the wagon shouted, "Come on, in with you, never mind those things, Hannah, never mind anything now! The wind has changed, and that fire will be down upon us in less than half an hour. Whip up your horses, boys, don't spare them now! With that fire behind us——"

He leaned forward as he spoke and lashed his team; the horses plunged forward with a leap that made the wagon careen.

Over the coarse prairie grass they fled, the horses straining and plunging, while they looked continually behind them to where the red line had left the horizon now and was creeping toward them, the red tongues of flame leaping higher and higher as they caught the dry grass and rosin weeds.

The air grew suffocatingly hot, and before long particles of burned grass and weeds, carried by the gale, began to fall about them.

"Watch that nothing catches fire in the wagon, Hannah," shouted Joshua Peniman, bending forward and laying the whip across the backs of the petted team that had scarcely ever felt a blow in their lives before. "Watch the children's clothing. Have wet cloths handy!"

The wind, a gale before, now seemed to have increased in fury, and before it the fire leaped and roared like a furnace.

"Faster, Joe, faster!" yelled his father; "it's gaining on us, we've got to reach a stream or draw of some kind——"

Leaning far forward on his seat with the whip in his hand and the reins clutched hard, Joe did not wait for the finish of the sentence. With voice and whip and lines he urged the horses forward, shouting at them, shaking the lines over their straining backs, whirling the whip about their heads, as in a blinding reek of smoke and dust they thundered on, while closer and closer behind them came the roaring flames.

The horses were soon panting and lathered with sweat, staggering and stumbling under the strain of the heavy wagons, and poor Cherry, fastened on behind, was almost pulled off her feet, and slid and stumbled bawling wildly.

The whole sky was illuminated now, and the air so filled with smoke that they could hardly breathe. Behind them the ominous crackling and snapping of dry grass grew louder and louder, as the fire, fanned by the high wind, rushed through the tall, dry prairie grass with the velocity of a cyclone.

All at once without decreasing the pace of his horses, Mr. Peniman stood up in the wagon and looked back.

They heard him utter a sharp, inarticulate sound, and the horses were stopped with a jerk that almost threw them upon their haunches.

"No use," he shouted, leaping out, "we can never make it! Got to fight it out here! *Out everybody*, and fight for your lives!"

Joe and Lige stopped their teams, and drawing the wagons up together they leaped out and tied their teams to the rings in the side of the other wagon.

"The kegs!" shouted Joshua Peniman, "roll out the kegs, and those gunny-sacks! We've got to back-fire, it's our only chance now!"

With frantic haste the boys rolled out the precious kegs of water, while Mrs. Peniman, with an instinctive knowledge of what to do, threw out a couple of brooms, some old coats, and a bundle of gunny-sacks.

The children, aroused at the first call of danger, had all gotten into their clothes by this time. With their heads enveloped in wet towels, wet brooms and gunny-sacks in their hands, they stood ready to do as their father commanded.

Having secured the horses firmly to the wagons Joshua Peniman rushed back over the way they had come for some two hundred feet, and called the family to him.

"We've got to set a back-fire here," he shouted; "watch it closely, don't let it get away from you, and beat out every tongue of fire that tries to get beyond you. Have your brooms and sacks ready. *Now!*"

The whole family, with the exception of Mary and David, who had been left asleep in the wagons with Spotty to guard them, were now lined up at a distance of some two hundred yards nearer to the oncoming fire than the wagons. It required courage for young people who had never, until they had begun this journey, encountered real danger, to face the roaring wall of flame that rushed toward them, but they were well disciplined and obeyed their father's orders implicitly.

Seeing that they were all in readiness Joshua Peniman stooped and put a match to the grass at his feet. Instantly it leaped into a flame. He let it burn a little way, then whipped out the edges, making a straight track of fire of about a hundred and fifty feet wide. This Joe instantly recognized as a "fire-guard." Then backing up a few steps at a time, and keeping the flames under control, they let this second or "back-fire" burn toward the wagon, leaving between them and the oncoming wall of flame a large area of burned-over ground. This they continued to do until they had described a complete circle about the wagons.

"Watch out there, Joe, keep your eye to the right there," yelled Mr. Peniman, black and smoke-begrimed and beating with all his might at a vicious tongue of flame that threatened to get beyond him. "Look out there, Lige! Nina, be careful to keep your skirts out of the fire! Watch behind you, Sam; better wet your broom again! Beat out that fire on your left there, Hannah!"

With her skirts pinned up about her, her hair blown down, and her sleeves rolled to her elbows, Mrs. Peniman wielded broom and sack, beating and firing as she went backwards, step at a time.

"Oh, Mother, will it get us?" cried Ruth, as a great gust of wind enveloped them in smoke and increased the roar and crackle of the flames that rushed toward them.

"Don't be frightened, Ruthie," she shouted above the wind. "Keep your broom going! Don't stop to look. God will take care of us. Watch your side there, Nina; beat it out—*beat it out*! Here, Sam, come here and work by Nina; she needs help!"

As Sam left his station she ran to where he had been and with furious strokes of broom and sack beat out the fire that was creeping away from them.

Back-firing and beating out the flames as they went, they gradually worked back toward the wagons, leaving behind them a smoking black ring nearly two hundred feet in circumference.

Their faces and hands were black and blistered, their feet scorched, their eyes burning and smarting, and their lungs wheezed with the effort to breathe through the suffocating smoke and ashes that filled the air.

The horses, half-wild with terror, were rearing and plunging, and poor Cherry running madly in circles as far as her rope permitted.

"Run to the horses, Joe," shouted his father, after a swift backward glance at the wagons. "Put wet sacks over their heads and throw wet blankets over them! Lige, here, you take Joe's place! Watch out there, Mother, beat out that fire on thy right!"

Joe threw down his sack and ran with all speed to the horses. With soothing words and pats he did his best to quiet them, throwing their blankets over their backs to protect them from flying sparks, and enveloping their heads in wet sacks, wrung from the precious and fast-disappearing kegs of water.

He had difficulty in getting near enough to the distracted Cherry to do anything for her, but after a wild struggle, during which he was dragged in a wide circle by her rope, he succeeded in getting a wet sack over her head and a blanket on her back. The chickens were squawking and the little pigs squealing in their boxes, and he stopped long enough to throw a bucketful of water over them, and pitch a tarpaulin over their boxes. Then he rushed back to the wildly beating family.

As they backed and fired they began to see outside the ring of fire grey spectral shapes dashing by in the shadows, running madly, frantically, with the terror of the crackling flames behind.

All at once the ground under their feet seemed to tremble, and the horses, crouching and shivering with terror, began again to rear and plunge.

Dropping his sack Joe ran to the heads of one, Lige to the other, while Mr. Peniman dashed to the heads of the third team.

"To the wagons, to the wagons!" he shouted, and saw his wife and the other children drop their sacks and dash for the wagons as the quaking of the ground and a great roar like that of an approaching cyclone rose above the crackling of the flames.

"What is it? What is it?" shouted Joe, terror-stricken.

"*Buffaloes!*" yelled his father. "Stampeded by the fire! Get your guns—fire into them as they come—please God our back-fire may keep us from being trampled by them!"

There was a moment of awful suspense, while the ground beneath their feet seemed to rock and tremble with the impact of the wildly charging herd. Through the smoke and dust they could make out a great mass of enormous reddish-brown bodies being hurled madly forward before the pursuing flames. Then the terrified creatures made a wide circle to avoid the black ring of burned ground, which they seemed to fear, and the herd of buffaloes, grim, monstrous shapes in the dusk of early morning, thundered by and passed out of sight.

When the circle of back-fire was completed the nearly exhausted family leaned for a moment on their wet brooms to breathe. The last of the water in the kegs went to wet blankets and tarpaulins to spread over the canvas covers of the wagons, and as the flames swept toward them they took their stand about the wagons, still armed with their wet brooms and sacks, to make a last struggle against the fire that came crackling and rushing toward them.

CHAPTER XII

A NEBRASKA DUGOUT

With the roar of a tornado the prairie fire swept down upon them.

The high grass, dry as tinder after the long hot spell, burned as if covered with turpentine.

The tall rosin-weeds and sunflowers, blazing like torches, sent up showers of sparks that the wind carried through the air, setting fresh fires and raining down upon the travelers, burning their clothes and singeing their faces and hair.

Once Mrs. Peniman's calico apron caught fire, but she tore it off and trampled it under her feet.

At times it looked as if the wall of flame must leap the narrow boundary of burned-over ground and sweep down upon them, destroying them all in the roaring furnace that raced toward them.

The heat grew fiercer; the horses screamed and tugged at their halters, the cow bellowed pitifully, and the little pigs at the back of the wagon squealed as if the knife of the executioner were at their throats.

For a moment the flames seemed to fairly tower over them, hissing and crackling in its wrath.

Would it leap the back-fire?

The hearts of the pioneers almost stopped breathing. An agonized prayer went up from the hearts of the parents that they and their little ones might be spared.

Then the wall of flame flickered, fell—and swept on around them.

Their back-fire had saved them.

With cracked and parching lips they uttered prayers of thanksgiving, and worn out with the struggle let sacks and brooms drop from their nerveless hands and stood still.

They realized now for the first time the extent of their exhaustion. They felt the pain of their burned hands, their scorched faces, their parched and burning throats.

Daylight came before they were able to realize the fact that they were saved.

The broadening light revealed a sad and dismal prospect. If the prairie had seemed monotonous to them before in its sombre dress of grey, and brown, and green, it seemed desolate beyond all description now, covered as far as the eye could see with a pall of funereal blackness.

Suffering as they were with burns and thirst it was noon before the ground was cool enough so that they could drive over the still smoking prairies.

All the afternoon they drove, straining their eyes in every direction for the sight of a town, a house, a sign of shade and water.

As fast as possible they veered away from the burned district, and about sundown got out of the track of the fire and onto the brown dry prairies.

Back of them and far away to the south and east they could still see the devastating trail of the fire, but away to the north and west the wind had turned the direction of the flames and the prairie remained untouched by its fury.

It was a tremendous relief to escape from the scorched and blackened ground, the stifling smell of burned grass, the acrid smoke that made their eyes smart and water and their throats sting, and to drive out on the unscorched prairies, which, hot as they were, seemed cool in comparison.

It was nearing nightfall when they saw, not far away, a small column of smoke rising in the air. Joshua Peniman scanned it with eager eyes.

"It might be an Indian camp," said his wife anxiously.

"White men or red we must have water to-night," he said, and drove on.

As they drew nearer they saw a low, squat outline against a small rise in the ground, and from it rose a stove-pipe, from which the smoke they had seen was coming.

"What is it?" called Joe. "Is it an Indian's hut?"

"No, thank God," cried Joshua Peniman fervently; "no Indians live there. It must be a dugout, and if it is white people are living in it."

He clucked to the horses and drove eagerly forward.

As they approached the low, dark object they saw that it had a roof, and that the sides were dug back in the rise of ground behind it. They could also see that it had two windows in front, and a door, which was thrown open as they drew nearer, and a tall, raw-boned red-haired woman with a good-natured freckled face stood framed in the opening.

"Wal of all things!" she ejaculated, "if it ain't a bunch o' emigrants! Hello, mister, where'd you come from?"

"From Ohio," called out Joshua Peniman, and made all possible haste toward the dugout.

As the wagon drew up before the door she looked at its occupants, then laughed aloud.

"Fer th' land sakes," she cried; "what be ye? Air ye niggers or Mexicans or Portuguese, or what?"

"We're Americans—and white," said Mr. Peniman laughing, as he leaped from the wagon. "At least we were white once, and we hope to be again. We've just escaped with our lives from a terrible prairie fire, and are covered with its smoke and grime."

"Lord save us!" ejaculated the woman. "Was you in the track o' that fire? We been watchin' it all day. We was skeered it might ketch us, but the wind wa'n't in th' right direction. Them prairie fires is terrible things. We mighty nigh got burned out last fall."

"We used all the water we had fighting fire," Mr. Peniman continued, "and are all suffering from thirst. I wonder if you could let us have a little drinking water?"

"*Kin* I? Wal I should say I could! Me an' Jim never turned a thirsty man or woman or horse or dog away from our place yit! Git out, git out, all of ye! We've got a good well and you can have all the water ye want to drink and wash up, too, and I will say you sure do need it."

The travelers came scrambling out of the wagon, and there were tears of relief and gratitude in Hannah Peniman's eyes.

"Jim," a husky-looking pioneer over six feet tall, with a good-humored sunburned face and a shock of tow-colored hair sticking up through a hole in his hat, came hurrying up at this moment, drawn from his work in his cornfield near by by the unwonted sight of a caravan of moving wagons before his door. As he came he cast a sharp, inquiring look at the company of sooty, grimy individuals gathered before his dugout.

"We aren't quite such desperate characters as we appear," saluted Joshua Peniman with his pleasant smile. "We have barely escaped with our lives from a prairie fire, had to use all the water we had, and have had no chance to wash. My name is Peniman—Joshua Peniman, a Quaker, from the Muskingum Valley in Ohio, and these are my wife and children."

"Glad t' meet ye, Mr. Peniman," said the pioneer, extending a hairy, work-worn hand. "So you was in the track o' that fire, was ye? Sa-ay, I wonder ye ever got out alive. It was sure a fire, all right. Me an' the old woman been watchin' it. Thought fer a spell it might come this way, but th' wind favored us. Glad ye got through all right. Ye sure have got a likely-lookin' family. My name's Ward—Jim Ward. B'en out here goin' on three years. Homesteaded a piece o' land back here that ye can't beat in the hull nation. Travelin' across country? Be'n pretty hot, ain't it? But that's what makes good corn. We're going to have a hummer of a crop this season. But come in, come in! Ye shore do look all tuckered out. Wife'll git ye chairs, an' I'll go out an' draw up some fresh water. I reckon ye must be dry."

When the thirst of the family had been satisfied they felt greatly refreshed, and for the first time began to look about them. Mrs. Ward saw the curious glances the young people were casting about the queer-looking underground house and burst into a good-natured laugh.

"I'll bet you folks ain't never seen a dugout before," she exclaimed jovially. "Well it's sure a queer way to live, but me an' Jim think it's a good way—to begin with. We ain't always goin' to live this way, but a dugout's safe from cyclones and blizzards and Indians, an' it's warm in winter an' cool in summer—an' what more does a pioneer want?"

"I see that it has great advantages," said Joshua Peniman gazing with interest about the dwelling. "Do you see how it is done, Hannah? You see they have chosen a place where there is a rise in the ground, and have dug back into the earth so that the house is protected on every side but the front. You have had to build up side walls, of course, where the earth slopes away, and a front wall, but that was all. I see how safe and sheltered it must be, both from weather and possible enemies."

"Yes, an' a feller has to think a heap about both o' them out here," said Jim Ward, standing with his hands in his pockets and his legs wide apart as the travelers admired his dwelling.

The excavation, which was about twenty by thirty feet square, was dug back into the bank of a piece of rolling ground on the prairie, and made into a chamber about nine feet high. The entire rear part of the dwelling was protected by the embankment, and a part of the sides, while a stout, thick wall of sods was built up on the sides and in front, in which was let a door and two windows. An ivy-vine was trained up over the window casements, clean white curtains shaded the spotless panes, which had broad sills, upon which were placed pots of geraniums in full bloom.

The floor was made of matched flooring, and was as white as hands could make it, with braided rag rugs spread before the shining stove and the red-covered table, upon which were a Bible, a vase of wild-flowers, and a shining lamp. In a corner of the room was a large double bed, made up with a spotless blue-and-white patchwork counterpane, and "shams," elaborately worked in red cotton, with "Good Night" on one pillow and "Good Morning" on the other. At the other end of the room was a shining cook-stove, with a tea-kettle steaming cozily upon it, and a row of packing cases, which had been placed one on top of another and cleverly converted into a kitchen cupboard.

"It's wonderfully clean and cozy and comfortable-looking," exclaimed Mrs. Peniman. "I wonder how you keep it so. I would not dream that a house just dug into the ground could be so attractive."

"Lots of 'em ain't," vouchsafed Jim Ward. "Some of the folks that come out here is content to live like pigs. But me an' Mary ain't. She always was a good housekeeper, an' she keeps this place so nice I sometimes almost forget we live in a dugout."

"Now you quit talkin', Jim," put in "Mary," "and go an' draw up a tubful o' fresh water. I reckon these folks don't want nothin' so much in this world as a bath. I'll set a wash-tub out in th' back yard, an' when it comes dark ye can all take a bath. I sh'd think ye could begin now with th' little fellers."

One after another the Peniman family slipped out and took their turn in the tub in the back yard, and it was indeed a cleansed and changed family that gathered at last on the "front stoop," as Jim Ward facetiously called the hard, beaten place before the door.

When supper was over they sat on the "stoop" until the moon rose, listening eagerly to the many curious and interesting tales the pioneer homesteader and his wife had to tell.

"Has thee ever been troubled with Indians, friend Ward?" asked Joshua Peniman, a bit anxiously.

"No," answered the pioneer, "we ain't never had any trouble with 'em. A lot of the settlers has, but I've always figgered it was their own fault. We've been livin' out here three years now, an' we've never had a thing stolen or molested or a bit o' trouble ourselves."

"But why haven't you?" demanded Joe, "when the others have?"

"Because I've always figgered on treatin' the Indians like they was *human*. Some folks treats 'em worse'n dogs. Good land, this is their country, ain't it? They was here first! Us folks that comes in now is just takin' what they've owned for God knows how many years. Ain't it so?"

"Yes," said Joshua Peniman, "it is. I have always felt so. But we have so often been warned of danger——"

"An' there *is* danger; don't ye ever forgit that. Some o' these here Indians is bad medicine. They're mad about havin' white settlers come in, an' they'll plug ye the fust chance they get. But I figger that Indians is jest like other folks. Some is bad an' some good—they're all just human. Me an' Mary has always thought if we treated them all right they'd treat us right. So fur it's worked all right."

During the long talk that Mr. Peniman had with Jim Ward after the women and children had retired to get ready for bed, he discussed land and locations, and when the family set forth the next morning it was with the firm intention of going to the northwestern part of Nebraska, where the land along the Niobrara was particularly recommended, and where there were still thousands of acres of government land to be homesteaded upon for the choice.

They bade their kind host and hostess a reluctant good-bye, and having promised that they would write them when they had arrived at their destination they started on, turning to wave their hands again and again to the last white people they were to see for many a long day.

CHAPTER XIII

THE MINNE-TO-WAUK-PALA

It was with the greatest reluctance that the travelers parted with Jim Ward and his good-natured wife. For many days they had seen no other human beings, and the relief of being with and talking with them was so great that it took a determined effort to leave the cheerful dugout and its occupants and turn their faces once more toward the uninhabited plains.

They had traveled but a few miles in the calm clear light of morning when they saw not a quarter of a mile ahead of them thirty or forty beautiful antelope. They were cantering across the prairie, their little white cotton tails shining in the sunshine, the light gleaming on their pretty dappled sides. They were playing and leaping, and their curious antics made the boys shout with laughter.

"Wonderful chance to get an antelope," said Lige with shining eyes; but Joe shook his head. "Could you shoot one of those beautiful creatures?" he asked. "I swear I couldn't."

The antelope seemed to have but little fear of them, and cantered along for some distance, stopping now and then to crop the grass. After a time they raced away toward the south, and were lost to view.

It was now well on in August. Even at the early hour at which they had started there was a scorching wind blowing, and as the day advanced the sun beat down on the prairies from a cloudless sky with an intensity that promised a day of intolerable heat.

The family dispensed with every garment possible, and sat under the canvas covers fairly parching with heat, while the hot wind seemed fairly to scorch the prairies, and to burn and shrivel their skins.

Many times during the day they had to stop the horses, and at last Joe conceived the idea of making pads for their heads from the prairie grass, which he kept wet with water, brought from the well of the hospitable Wards.

It was toward three o'clock in the afternoon, at the very hottest part of the day, that Mrs. Peniman looking out of the front of the wagon suddenly exclaimed aloud.

"Why," she cried, "look, look, Joshua, there is a lake before us!"

Mr. Peniman, who was half-dozing on his seat, started wide awake.

"A *lake?*" he cried. "A lake in this country? Where?"

"Why, see, over there," pointing ahead of them, "a beautiful blue lake! See how the water ripples in the sunshine?"

The children, roused from the dull stupor into which they had fallen, were all crowding to the front of the wagon to look out. Joe and Lige on the high seats of the two other wagons craned their necks to see. They all set up a great hurrahing, but Mr. Peniman, after one long look, said nothing.

Suddenly his wife, who had been gazing with steadfast gaze at the entrancing sight, caught his arm.

"Joshua"—she cried,—"that lake—it looks very strange to me! Could it be that—I have read—oh, could it be that there is no lake—that it is— that it is——"

He laid his hand over hers with a tender, sympathetic pressure.

"Yes, dear heart, I hate to dispel thy illusion, but there is no lake there. It is a mirage."

"A *mirage?* What's a mirage, Father?" asked Sam, his face reflecting his bitter disappointment.

"It is just an air-picture, my son, an optical illusion."

"You mean"—cried Joe, incredulously—"you mean that there is no lake there? Why, how can that be, Father? We can *see* it; it is right there before our eyes——"

Mr. Peniman shook his head wearily.

"It is a trick of the plains," he said. "It almost seems that its only purpose is to torture and mislead thirsty travelers like ourselves."

"But if it isn't a lake," propounded Lige, "what is it? We see it, it is there before us——"

"But don't you notice, my boy, that the trees that appear to surround it are upside down?"

The whole family gazed fixedly at the supposed "lake."

Blue as the heavens, ruffled by the breath of early morning, surrounded by waving trees, it lay tantalizingly before their eyes.

"I have never seen a mirage before," said Mr. Peniman, "but I know that they are a common occurrence on the plains, and in all arid and desert country. They are due to a condition existing in the atmosphere, caused by the reflection of light. What we see over there is probably the reflection of the sky, and as the reflection surface is irregular and constantly varies its position the reflected image will be constantly varying, and is what gives it the appearance of a body of water ruffled by the wind."

For a time the mirage endured, tantalizing them with its beauty, then suddenly faded, the alluring vision disappeared, and its place was filled by the parched grass of the prairies.

It was a bitter disappointment, the more bitter because of the hope it had aroused in their breasts.

Toward evening they saw, outlined against the western sky, two emigrant wagons crawling along over the plains. But so great was the distance, so wide and expressionless the plains that they scarcely seemed to move forward, but to remain stationary against the brazen sky.

There was no sign of shade or water on all the great expanse as the sun went down, and having traveled until twilight had fallen they made their night camp on the dry, barren prairie, with stars and sky and grass their only company.

They had now been two months on the road, and both horses and individuals were feeling the strain.

The horses were stiff, thin and lame, the cow a mere bag of bones, and the children cross and fretful.

Mrs. Peniman had lost her round curves and pretty complexion, and her husband's beard had grown long, and he was so brown and sinewy that his friends in Ohio would scarcely have known him.

They were all heartily tired of the weary crawling and jolting of the wagons across the barren prairies, and rose with aching heads and dragging limbs and moved wearily about the business of getting under way again without enthusiasm.

The day came up, as do so many days upon the western prairies, with a cloudless sky, blue as amethyst, and a sun that rode triumphant in a blazing chariot from rim to rim of a blistering world.

At noon the teams were so exhausted that the travelers were obliged to stop and unhitch them, leading them into the shade of the wagons to relieve them for a while from the rays of the broiling sun.

As the hot afternoon sun climbed into the heavens the very prairies seemed to drowse and sleep. Over their heads a few buzzards flapped lazily, and before them the gauzy heat-waves rose from the ground shimmering and dancing while the slow, monotonous klop, klop, klop of the horses' feet was the only sound to be heard.

Inside the wagons David and Mary had fallen asleep, Ruth and Nina, with their heads upon their sun-browned arms, had passed away into dreamland, Sam read, Lige dozed, Joe was nodding over his book, and even Mr. Peniman was drowsing.

Only Mrs. Peniman, sitting upon the front seat of the wagon, with her chin in her hands, and her eyes fixed on the distant horizon, was awake.

Thoughts were too busy in the aching head under the faded sunbonnet to let her sleep.

No one—not the husband so close at her side, not the children about whom the chords of her heart were knit—knew what this journey into the wilderness was costing her.

The lonely little mound back there on the prairies was seldom out of her mind, and the homesick longing for her home and her mothers and sisters so far away in the East, was sometimes almost more than she could bear.

As the thoughts of her lost baby, and all that she had left behind back there in that sweet and verdant country crossed her mind, hot tears rushed into her eyes. She blinked them resolutely away. She thought at first as she looked up that it was the tears that blinded her. Then as she wiped them away she drew a little gasping breath and looked—and looked again. At first her heart gave a great leap, then sank down drearily as she thought of the experience of the previous afternoon.

With a determined effort she turned her head away. Then when the torture of suspense would be no longer borne, she looked back.

Away on the distant western horizon there was a bluish haze.

She laid her hand very gently on her husband's arm.

"Joshua," she whispered, "I hate to rouse thee, but—look off there to the west; what is it we see? Is it—is it another mirage? It looks as if there were trees there. I have been looking and looking, but I was afraid to speak. I hated to awaken your hopes—it is so hard——"

The weary man roused himself. With hands clasped above his eyes he gazed off over the prairies.

After a long interval he said, "'I think—I believe—it *does* look like timber! Of course it is a long way off yet—but——"

His voice ceased, as he fixed his whole attention on the horizon.

Presently he spoke again, this time more decidedly.

"I believe there is a patch of timber over there. There must be a stream of some sort near. Don't wake the children, let them sleep; we will make for it as fast as we can."

Pushing the limping horses forward as fast as they were able to travel, the prairie schooners rolled on across the prairie, and the man and woman upon the wagon seat leaned forward and watched the horizon with straining eyes.

It was near evening when a breeze, bearing something fresh and fragrant on its breath, blew into the wagons and roused their drowsy occupants.

Joe woke with a start. His team was plodding along steadily, but his father's wagon was some distance in advance of it, while the Carroll wagon, with Lige nodding upon the driver's seat, was far in the rear.

He rubbed his eyes, caught up the lines and puckered his lips for a whistle. But the whistle was never uttered.

Instead there came from his chapped lips a startled exclamation.

Rubbing his eyes he looked and looked, and looked again. Then reaching behind him he grabbed Sam by one of his bare brown feet and shook it vigorously.

"Say, Sam, wake up here!" he shouted. "I want you to tell me if I'm crazy or if my eyes have gone bad or if I'm seeing another mirage! If I'm not plumb crazy there's a river over there, and trees——"

"Who said 'river'—who said 'trees'?" cried Sam, starting up; then he stopped short, staring ahead with an incredulous expression.

"Is it—it ain't—it can't be another mirage, can it?"

Joe gave a loud, joyous laugh and cracked his whip over the backs of the horses. He had had time to look again and he was satisfied.

"Mirage nothin'!" he exulted, "nary a mirage this time! Can't you smell it? Can't you taste it? Can't you feel the moisture in the air? You bet your life this isn't a mirage, it's the real thing, shade, water, grass, trees! And it ain't far off either!"

By this time the blur of bluish haze had developed into a tone of decided green, and there was no more doubt that trees and water were in sight. Mr. Peniman was stooping forward gazing intently.

"I was told that there was a river not far from here," he said to his wife, "and I think it should be in just about this location. It is called by the Indian name 'Minne-to-wauk-pala,' or Blue Waters."

"I don't care what it is called," said Mrs. Peniman, laughing joyously, "if it is only *there*. I don't think I could stand another shock like that mirage."

"You won't have to, my dear," said Mr. Peniman, his face lighting, "for, look, we can begin to see the trees and water now."

CHAPTER XIV

THE NEW HOME

No promised land of Paradise ever looked fairer to longing eyes than looked the scene that lay before the parched and weary travelers as they approached the Minne-to-wauk-pala or Blue Waters.

Crossing a broad plateau they drove up a gentle incline, and just as the blazing sun was sinking below the horizon there opened before their view a beautiful valley with waving green grass, welcoming trees and flower-strewn glades, and a blue, sparkling river with rock-strewn shady banks flowing swiftly over a rocky bottom, and long lines of timber stretching away to the north and south.

For a moment the travelers stood transfixed, as if the very gates of heaven had opened before them. Then Ruth, with a little gasping breath, cried out:

"Oh, Mother, Mother, isn't it *beautiful!* It looks so green, so fresh, so *lovely*—as if God had just finished it!"

And indeed the fair green land, with no mar of civilization upon it, with its fresh virginal beauty untouched and unspoiled by the hand of man, did look as if newly created.

The tired beasts had sniffed the fragrance of the water and with pricked ears were pushing eagerly forward.

"*What a camping-place!*" shouted Joe, springing eagerly down as the wagons were drawn up in the shade of the trees. "Come, Mother, jump down and come take a look at this river! Cricky, we haven't seen anything like this since we left Ohio. This water isn't red or brown or dirty, it's just what its name calls it—*blue!*"

It didn't take many moments for the tired, thirsty party to scramble out of the wagons and race down to the river, where their thirst was soon quenched by water that was cold, sweet, and free from the alkali which had made the water they had been drinking ever since they entered the Territory almost unbearable to them.

How welcome after the parching heat of the prairies was this cool, green, quiet place! How restful was the ripple of the water, the rustle of the willow and cottonwood trees, the caress of the long, soft grass!

While Mr. Peniman, Joe and Lige were getting the exhausted horses out of their harness and leading them down to drink, Ruth and Sam untied the cow, that manifested almost as much joy in the prospect of grass and shade and water as did the rest of the family.

They all threw themselves down under the trees too worn out and exhausted from the heat, too grateful for the blessed relief, to even explore this Paradise in the desert.

Slowly the fiery globe of the sun sank below the horizon, slowly a pink and purple splendor spread over the evening sky. A hawk flew by, wheeling majestically through the intensely blue dome. Joshua Peniman knelt upon the grass. "Let us thank God," he said in a low, reverent voice, "who has led us through the perils of the day and brought us to this His holy temple to-night."

That night while the others slept Hannah Peniman sat long on the banks of the Minne-to-wauk-pala, her eyes fastened upon its blue waters, her thoughts busy with many things.

When they arose the next morning she laid her hand upon her husband's arm.

"Come down to the river with me, Joshua," she said. "I want to talk to you."

She led him to the wide flat rock upon which she had sat and thought the night before, and sitting down beside him took his hand.

"Isn't it a heavenly place?" she sighed.

"It is indeed. We could have found no lovelier to make our camp."

"Our *home*, Joshua."

"Our *home?*" He turned quickly and looked at her.

"Yes, dear, our home. I came here last night after you had all gone to bed and communed long with God. I feel that it is His hand that led us here. Why go farther into the wilderness, dear heart? Why brave farther the perils of heat and drought and physical suffering? Here we have timber, water, grass for our cow and horses, shade and protection for ourselves, good land, apparently everything that we need to make our new home. Why go any farther? Why not call our journey ended and locate right here?"

Joshua Peniman stared at her in amazement.

"Thee has taken me completely by surprise, Hannah!" he said after a blank silence. "I had never thought of such a thing. Thee knows that from the first our plan was to go to the Niobrara——"

"But why go to the Niobrara? Why not locate right here on the Blue?" she answered with a little laugh. "Isn't it just as good? There appears to be land enough around here, heaven knows!"

He sat silent for some moments turning the matter over in his mind. The thought of stopping where they were had never occurred to him. Weary though they were, and suffering from heat and long journeying, he had never once wavered in his purpose of crossing the Territory to its northwestern side, to the lands which had been recommended to him between the Elkhorn and the Niobrara Rivers.

With thoughtful face he cast a slow appraising glance all about him.

"Ye-es," he said musingly, "that is all true. There is plenty of land about here—I do not believe there is a human creature within twenty or thirty miles of this place. The country lies well, and by the looks of the soil the land should be good. There is shade, and wood, and water—three absolute essentials to the comfort and safety of the settler, and an inestimable blessing in this barren country. There is timber along the creeks—a settler must have timber—and along the bottom land over there we would have good forage for the horses. The land that I was making for on the Niobrara——"

"—Is probably not a bit better than this," urged Mrs. Peniman. "And, Joshua, look at the horses, look at that poor cow! Think of the many, many weary miles we should have to travel over those desolate burning plains before we got there! It is now the middle of August—the hottest part of the summer—does it not seem like tempting Providence to strike out across the prairies again with our teams in the condition they are?"

Joshua Peniman was silent, thinking intently. Presently he rose and walked up and down the banks of the river, then out toward the plateau, where he stood for a long time, his eyes turning in a keen, critical survey in every direction.

Presently he returned to the rock upon which his wife was sitting.

"Thee has a long head, Hannah," he said, falling into the old Quaker form of speech which he often used when they were alone or when he was deeply stirred; "and I will not say that thee is not in the right of it. But this is a serious matter. We have gone far and sacrificed much to make our home in this new country, and we must not make a mistake now. Let us stop here to-day and think it over. I will go out and look the land about here over carefully, and I feel that we should consult with the children. For you and me the time in this new land will not be so long, but for them it is their whole lives and the happiness and prosperity of their future. I feel that they should have their say about our location. Does thee not agree with me?"

"I do indeed. That is best. Let us stay here to-day, rest, think, pray to God for wisdom, and look the ground over carefully with a view to our permanent location. And let us have a family consultation after prayers."

When the boys tumbled out of bed for an early swim before hitching up their teams for the start, they were astonished to find their father walking thoughtfully up and down on the bank of the river and none of the usual active preparations for the day's travel under way.

"We have decided to take a day off to rest, lads," he told them gravely. "This is going to be a very hot day, and both we and the horses need it. Will thee enjoy having a day here by the river?"

"Will we?" shouted Joe, who was beginning to be sadly weary of the hot, dusty days on the monotonous prairies. "I should say we would! This is such a lovely place I hate to leave it."

As they all darted off for their swim, followed nimbly by Ruth and Nina in calico wrappers, Joshua Peniman looked about him. Down in the bottoms the horses, turned out to enjoy their well-earned rest, were cropping the sweet short grass along the stream, the cow lying down in a bed of wild clover chewing her cud and exhaling long sighs of contentment, and under the shade of the trees Sara and David and Mary were playing, with the collie lolling with tongue out beside them, while the two little pigs that had traveled all the long journey in their box at the back of the wagon had been turned loose in a pen made of loose boards, and were tranquilly grunting their appreciation.

The table was spread on the long, soft grass, and about it moved Mrs. Peniman, humming softly to herself as she prepared the breakfast. The scene was a peaceful and pleasant one, and Joshua Peniman looked long and earnestly upon it, weighing and judging and trying to make up his mind.

When the morning chapter had been read and the silent prayer over, he turned to his family.

"Children," he said, "thy mother and I have been having a grave discussion this morning. We have called thee into our council because we believe that each of thee should have a voice in a decision that will so materially affect all thy after lives."

The young people looked at him with startled faces. What could this decision be that so materially affected them? That made father look so grave, and mother so eager?

"Thy mother thinks," their father continued, "that perhaps it would be well to change our plans, give up the idea of going any farther west, and stay here."

"*Stay here?*" The words were shouted in a chorus.

"What, *locate* here? Take up land—make this our home?" cried Joe.

"Exactly. We have been going over its possibilities as a future home this morning, and I must admit that I am much impressed with them. We have water here, shade, timber, grass for pasture, the land appears rich and the soil deep, and of course there is no scarcity of land about here for homesteading. Now, as you will have to live your lives and make your future in this new country, we want to know what you all think about it."

The discussion that followed was eager, enthusiastic and noisy, but the general consensus of opinion was one of hearty approval of the plan. The children were all tired of the journey, and the prospect of having that journey definitely ended, of remaining here in the green and pleasant place was one that appealed to them all.

The day was spent in going over the land, laying out in fancy where the house should stand, where corn and wheat and oats and potatoes should be put in, where the barn should be built, and the fruit trees set out, and the vegetable garden planted.

About half a mile above the point at which their camp had been made they came upon a piece of ground that sloped gently down to the river, with a broad, level expanse to the south of it that appealed to Mr. Peniman's practical mind as fine farming land. Nearer the river was a grove of cottonwood trees, and in a fern-lined hollow beneath the bank an ice-cold spring of sweet water.

"Here shall be the place for the house!" cried Mrs. Peniman, her eyes sparkling. "What could be lovelier? Where could we find anything finer if we searched the whole Territory of Nebraska? Here we would have shade, water, shelter from the wind, a spring, and a world of good farming land all about us!"

"That field over there has a southern exposure and would be fine for corn," mused Mr. Peniman. "We could sow oats and wheat over there on the plateau, that point running down to the river would make good pasture-land——"

"And we could build a little spring-house over the creek down there in that little bend," cried Mrs. Peniman, still absorbed in her household plans.

"Yes," said Joshua Peniman, thoughtfully knitting his heavy brows, "I believe that it would do—I believe that it would do well. But to make sure that we are all accord in this important matter we will take a vote. Think now, my children, for upon your decision this morning may rest the beginnings of a colony—a town—a city—perhaps, the beginning of civilization in this part of the Territory. The place where you will probably all carve out your futures, and where, I hope, you will leave your mark upon the civilization of the West."

For a moment there was a solemn pause. Youthful as they were the young Penimans were impressed with the thought that upon the decision of that moment the environment of their whole after lives might depend.

"Are you ready?" asked Joshua Peniman. Then, "As many as favor remaining here and locating our new home upon the Blue River hold up your right hand."

"Am I to vote, too?" queried Nina timidly.

"To be sure, my child. You are one of us. We look upon you now as one of our own children," answered Mr. Peniman kindly.

When the vote was put every hand went up.

"It seems to be a unanimous decision," he smiled. "Then this spot shall be our future home. Here let us kneel and ask God's blessing upon it."

On the green grass by the river the little colony knelt down, and the father's voice went up in earnest supplication for heavenly protection for the new home. Overhead the trees whispered softly, and the river mingled with the earnest voices when they uttered a fervent "Amen."

CHAPTER XV

BUILDING THE SOD HOUSE

The Peniman family spent that evening sitting on the banks of the Minne-to-wauk-pala, feeling no longer like homeless wanderers, but as those who after long tribulation have come into their own.

The whole family were in high spirits, and their camp that night was made with more comfort and permanence than any camp they had yet had.

Four young saplings were dragged out of the dead timber along the stream, and cut into lengths of the proper height for a table, and these were driven firmly into the ground. Upon them Joe nailed a few saplings crosswise, and over these was fastened a strong piece of canvas. Upon this canvas the children piled wet sand from the river bottom, patting it down and making a firm, level surface. When it was dry the oil-cloth was tacked over it, making an excellent substitute for a "boughten" table. Stakes were driven into the ground on either side of the table and more fallen saplings nailed upon them, and when the family sat down to their evening meal it was once more at a table with comfortable seats and a place to enjoy their meal without the discomfort of cramped legs or the disturbing inroads of bugs and ants.

In the shade near by they drove stakes in the ground (always taking care to select only dead and broken timber, for a tree had become too rare and precious a thing for them to sacrifice willingly), and over it they stretched a tarpaulin, making a shelter to serve as a kitchen. Joe and Lige constructed a fireplace and oven near by of small round stones from the bed of the stream, and fixed a firm and level place on a rock to set up the stove. Around it they nailed small boxes and receptacles for the cooking utensils, and set two packing-cases on end with a calico curtain before them to serve as a china-closet, and Mrs. Peniman speedily emptied a packing-case and set it up in the improvised kitchen to use as a kitchen table.

"It will take some time to build our house," she said brightly as she hurried about getting her new cooking-place in order, "and we might as well be as comfortable as we can until it is done."

The family, tired enough of living in the cramped space of the wagons, readily agreed to this, and the next day was spent unloading the wagons, unpacking boxes, and making their temporary home as comfortable and convenient as possible.

When the comfort of the family had been looked after Mr. Peniman turned his attention to the animals.

The little pigs had grown and thriven so, even under the hard conditions that had beset the rest of the travelers, that they were now entirely too big for their box, and squealed their protest continually.

They had long ago outgrown the necessity of bottle-feeding and took their sustenance out of a pan like regular porkers.

Joe and Lige found their father, late in the afternoon, standing beside the box looking down at the little squealers with a speculative expression.

"I was thinking," he said as they approached him, "that we must provide better quarters for Romeo and Juliet. They've outgrown their box, and I don't see that we can spare them another. They ought to have more room."

"Couldn't we build them a pen out of logs?" asked Joe.

"Can't spare any of our precious timber for pigs," said Mr. Peniman. Then with a sudden smile breaking over his face, "Now I have it! Come along, boys, get your spades, and I'll soon show you how we can make Romeo and Juliet a fine home."

The boys had learned long since that the humorous little twinkle in the corner of their father's eye always meant fun ahead, so grabbing up their spades they followed him to a spot some distance back of the spot they had marked out for their future home on the river bank.

With a few quick strokes of his boot-heel Mr. Peniman described a circle on the ground. Then, throwing off his coat, he fell to digging.

Somewhat puzzled as to how a pig-pen was to be constructed with shovels, the boys followed his example.

"But I can't see," puffed Lige, "how this is going to make a place for *live* pigs. If they were dead ones, and we were going to bury them——"

Suddenly Joe burst out laughing.

"Oh, I know," he cried. "Why, of course! It's a bully idea! Don't you see that we can *dig* a pen for them? A mighty good kind of a pen, too, that they can't break down or squeeze through or get out of."

Mr. Peniman stopped digging long enough to mop his face.

"Surely! We'll make a pit about three feet deep, and big enough around so that the little fellows will have a chance to chase around and grow. This pair," he smiled, casting a smiling glance at the little porkers, "may be the beginning of our stock-farm." After a moment he continued, digging busily, "People who come out to the plains in wagons can't carry much with them, so they have to use everything they have at hand. There's not much of anything to work with on the prairies but dirt and grass, and we not only have to make them furnish our stock a home but ourselves as well."

Lige stopped and leaned on his spade.

"We aren't going to dig a hole like this for us to live in, are we?" he demanded in a tone of horror.

The shout of laughter with which his father and brother received this remark caused him to resume digging hastily. Mr. Peniman hastened to reassure him.

"Don't fear, Lige, we won't do that, but I'll show you a better way, and yet the prairies will have to furnish the material."

Lige was still unconvinced that the plan for the pig-pen was a good one, until when it was finished, a fine round pit of about twelve feet in circumference and three feet deep, the whole family came in a body to see Romeo and Juliet established in their new home.

This was accomplished after a good deal of squealing and struggling on the part of the tenants, but when they were finally established, with a roof across one end covered with a thatch of prairie grass to keep off the sun, they ran about and about in an ecstasy of glee, nosing the walls, rooting in the dirt, and expressing their pleasure with skips and grunts of delight.

"Well," admitted Lige a bit reluctantly, "I'll agree that that's an all-right pig-pen, but I don't see yet how you're ever going to make a house for us to live in out of dirt!"

"Wait for a few days and I'll show you," said his father cheerfully.

It was not even that long before his curiosity was gratified. The very next morning they were roused by their father's voice calling them.

"Come along, my lads," he cried, "we have much to do, and no time to sleep while there is daylight to work in these days! The fall will soon be upon us, and we must have our house ready before the rains come."

They saw that the plow that had been so long packed away in the bottom of the wagon had been taken out and Jim and Charley hitched to it.

"Now, Lige, I'll show you how to build a house out of dirt," he laughed, as, followed by the whole family, they set out toward the spot where the site for the house had been marked off on the grass.

"You don't do it with a *plow*, do you?" asked Lige, much puzzled.

"Yes,—partly," replied his father laughing. They all felt in high spirits this morning. The long, tedious, wearisome journey was over, the goal reached, and life lay before them like a clean new slate, upon which it was theirs to inscribe what they would.

Mrs. Peniman, much concerned about her new domicile, was carefully measuring off the ground and computing the space, while the children danced about as excitedly as if building a new home in the wilderness, miles upon miles from any other habitation, was the greatest joy imaginable.

When the plow was set upon the line and Jim and Charley started with a cheerful word of command it cut through the grass and turned over what was probably the first sod ever turned in that county.

The tough prairie sod was plowed about three inches thick in long furrows twelve to sixteen feet long. Joe, Lige, and Sam were then set to work with their sharp spades to cut it up into the required blocks.

"What are these for, Father?" asked Sam.

"These are the bricks of which we are going to build our house, my son," answered his father with a twinkle in his eye.

"But why don't we build our house of logs, Father?" asked Joe. "It seems to me it would be a lot nicer, and a lot less work. We have plenty of timber here. I think it would be much better."

"Which shows that you don't know anything about it, my boy. In the first place, we can't spare the timber. There is none too much of it at best, and what there is we want to save for fuel and shelter. In the second place, there is no house that is better for the hard weather of the prairies than a sod house. It is warm in winter, cool in summer, and about the only thing that will withstand the Nebraska blizzards and cyclones. Just wait until it is finished and you'll see. Don't you remember what a nice home the Wards had? Now take your spades and cut the sod as I am doing. Keep your squares even, and the edges of the sod straight and true. When we have the sod taken off this field it will be in fine condition to plow up, and perhaps we can get in a small crop of sod-corn yet this year."

The boys seized their spades and set to work manfully, and before noon had a good-sized pile of "Nebraska marble" piled up ready for use. After dinner, when they all felt somewhat refreshed, Mr. Peniman began laying the sods, which were about twelve inches square and three inches thick. They were piled one upon another, leaving open spaces for the places where the doors and windows were to go. When the walls were up to about the thickness of a couple of sods above the frames, lintels were laid across and the sod laid over them, continuing the walls right through. The vacant space above the frames was necessary to provide for the settling of the walls. When the walls were high enough, about seven feet, the gable ends were built up a few inches or a foot higher, for, to prevent the earth from washing off the sods by heavy rains, the roof was made almost flat. As the sods were laid Mr. Peniman trimmed down the walls with a sharp spade, to keep them square and trim. He shaved the top surface off each layer with a sharp hoe, and filled in the chinks between the sods with a kind of a cement made from the prairie clay and sand from the bed of the river.

All this, however, was not accomplished in one day. The work of cutting and laying the sods was hard and heavy labor, and before the day was over both the boys and their father were glad to quit for the night and go to their supper.

Here they found a glad and cheerful surprise awaiting them.

The open space between the semicircle of cottonwood trees had been cleared, and already was beginning to assume a homelike aspect. Mrs. Peniman and the girls, with Paul and little David to help them, had put in as busy a day at the camp as the boys and their father had on the sod house. When they arrived they found the table set, looking extremely neat and festive with its cloth of bright red, its dishes and silver, with a vase of wild-flowers in the centre of the table, and a great dish of fried prairie-chicken, mashed potatoes, gravy and hot biscuits steaming upon it, and Mrs. Peniman flying about in a big kitchen apron unpacking cooking utensils, getting out furniture, and making a cozy resting-place under the trees.

At their exclamations of delight she laughed happily.

"There's no use waiting until the house is finished before we begin to *live*," she greeted them cheerily; "we're all tired of hardships, and I, for one, want some kind of comforts around me again. Wait till you come home to-morrow night, you'll see what we have done then, won't they, girls?"

Ruth and Nina, busy as bees getting the supper on the table, answered with gleeful and mysterious nods. The place already seemed so pleasant and inviting that they were loath to go to bed when the time came, but pioneer boys and girls, as well as pioneer men and women, soon found out that it was not what they *wanted* to do, but what they *had* to do that was to be considered.

With grim determination Mr. Peniman and the boys returned to the building of the sod house the next morning. They all realized that while gypsying under the trees might be very delightful now, stormy weather would materially change its aspect, and that in the unprotected wilderness in which they were living the sooner they were sheltered behind thick walls and barred doors at night the greater would be their safety.

It was hard, slow work, and many days passed, while the piles of sod grew steadily and the walls went up higher and higher. The boys worked manfully, and Mr. Peniman, like the wise father he was, did not work them too hard or too long, but often sent them off for a walk or a swim, sometimes urging them to go and catch a mess of fish for dinner, sometimes pretending that he was hungry for meat and sending them off into the woods or out on the prairies to hunt for game. They found any number of wild turkeys about the place, some quail, and plenty of prairie-chickens, and once in a while a deer or an antelope was killed, although neither of the boys liked to shoot the pretty, graceful creatures, that seemed utterly without fear, and often came up quite close about their camp.

It took a month to build the sod house, during which time the family lived in the woods, sleeping in their beds in the wagons as they had done on their journey, and eating in the open under the spreading cottonwood trees.

The weather continued fine, and the family, in spite of their isolation, were very happy. They were busy all day long, and had always been one of those happy and united families who find their greatest happiness in one another.

Nina had come to be quite one of themselves now, and she and Ruth were seldom apart, while for Joe and Sam and Lige the girl showed a warm and grateful affection. She was devoted to Mrs. Peniman, and often sat at her feet or on the arm of the old rocking-chair with her arm about her neck, calling her "Mother Peniman," and showering upon her the love and tenderness she had always shown for her own unfortunate young mother.

When the walls of the sod house were completed the hardest part of the work was to come, and Joshua Peniman puzzled long as to how he was going to get the ridgepole in place without another man to help him. He felled a strong, straight young tree, about fifteen inches through, and carefully stripped the bark from it. To raise the pole the aid of the whole family was required. As there were no neighbors within many miles to call upon, the difficult and dangerous feat must be performed with what help was at hand. He first made skids and rolled the tree upon it. These skids he placed with one end resting on the wall, the other on the ground. Ropes were then fastened to it, and while Mrs. Peniman, Ruth, Nina, and Sam stood on the top of the wall and pulled the ropes, Joe, Lige, and their father, on the ground, lifted and pushed the pole from below.

Fortunately for the success of the operation life in the open air, constant exercise and hard work had hardened the muscles of all and made them equal to the exertion. It was a strenuous piece of work, but with much puffing and panting and laughter they kept doggedly at it, and before dusk had come they got the ridgepole in place, and the most difficult part of building the house was accomplished.

Next came the rafters, which were poles of young trees from four to six inches through, placed about fifteen inches apart. Over these were laid boughs, cut from the willow thicket, and these thickly overlaid with the dry prairie grass. When a thick, deep covering of this straw had been laid in place and carefully packed down, dirt to the depth of about a foot was piled upon it and beaten down hard with the spade.

Now they were ready for the doors and windows!

The proud architects of this mansion of "Nebraska marble"— consisting of every member of the family except little Mary and David— stood about and surveyed it with admiring eyes. Even Lige was converted and was now willing to admit that it was a great idea. The walls were even, straight, and true, its corners square, its whole appearance neat and workman-like.

Greatly to the boys' astonishment they found packed away on the very bottoms of the two wagons three sets of window-casings and two stout wooden doors.

"I never knew those were there!" cried Joe, as he saw his father haul them out. "How did you ever come to think of them?"

"It would be a poor sort of a pioneer that did not think about providing shelter for his family, my lad," he answered. "I knew, of course, that we should have to build a sod house, and knew also that though the house might grow out of the prairie itself that glass windows and wooden doors wouldn't, so I brought them along."

It was a sharp, snappy morning in September when the last window was in, the last door screwed to its hinges, and Joshua Peniman, with a great sigh of relief, laid down his hammer and turned over the new house to his wife.

"There!" he ejaculated, "there is thy house, now thee and the girls can do what thee please with it. The boys and I have done our part. We must get at the barn now, for if I don't miss my guess there is some stormy weather coming."

There was not much time for loafing in the little colony these days. The whole family felt the impending change in the weather, and while Mr. Peniman and the boys, profiting by their experience in building the house, started on the barn, Mrs. Peniman with Ruth, Nina, Sam and Paul, plastered the walls of the new "soddy" with a medium made of one-third clay and two-thirds sand, which, when dry, they covered with a neat coat of whitewash.

The "soddy" when completed was eighteen by twenty-two feet inside, and though it had no partitions, was divided into three rooms by means of curtains, which Mrs. Peniman had brought in her trunk.

The last coat of whitewash was applied late in the evening, and the next morning Mrs. Peniman could scarcely wait to get breakfast over before she began to move into her new house.

The boys and their father were off and away early, for they were straining every nerve to get in a crop of sod-corn before the coming of the fall rains. But with the help of the girls and little Paul, she went at it with a will, determined to make their home in the wilderness as pleasant and comfortable as it could be under the circumstances.

They had brought with them from Ohio a carpet, a cook-stove, two bedsteads and several cots, some chairs, among which were two comfortable old-fashioned rockers, a table, a great roll of matting, and books, pictures, and knickknacks, and when these were in place, with packing-cases converted into dressing-tables, cupboards made out of boxes, and a couple of roughly constructed benches placed against the walls covered with bright-colored chintz, the place assumed a cheery and homelike appearance that one would never have deemed possible from its exterior. The window ledges were wide and deep, and in the windows she hung pretty white curtains, covered the packing-cases and boxes with chintz, laid the matting over the dirt floors and covered it with the carpet, and when the pictures were hung on the walls, the books and knick-knacks on the table, with a vase of gorgeous goldenrod from the prairies, the little "soddy" looked like a real home.

The front part of the house, into which the door opened, was the living-room, with cot-beds covered in the daytime like couches furnished the sleeping accommodations for the girls. Curtained off from this the second part of the interior was divided in two, with the sleeping quarters of the boys on one side of the curtain and those of Mr. and Mrs. Peniman on the other. The back third, from which the back door opened out into the outdoor kitchen, contained the cook-stove, dishes and cooking utensils, provisions, and a table at which the family took their meals in stormy weather.

Profiting by his remembrance of the Wards' dugout, Mr. Peniman had decided to make a dugout for the shelter of his stock. He selected a spot where the steep incline of a ravine made a high embankment; he set to work digging back into it, and was gratified to find that the earth sloped downward under a wide ledge of rock, so that by extending the dugout for about twenty-five feet back under the ledge he could take advantage of it and convert it into an excellent natural roof. This plan lightened the labors of building the barn considerably. When a large square chamber had been dug they evened it up, built a strong sod wall in front and at the sides where they met the slope of the embankment, put in three stalls on each side, made of dead timber they found along the river bank, constructed feed-racks out of old boxes, and built in the back end a sort of attic or loft, for grain and hay.

As no door had been brought for the barn they were obliged to make one, using small saplings closely nailed together on a strong pine frame. This made a heavy and rather cumbersome door, but an exceedingly strong one.

"I guess no Indian will break through that to steal our horses," remarked Joe, regarding it proudly.

"No, I think not. We'll put a good strong lock on it, and then I think our horses will be safe. It behooves us to keep them so," went on Mr. Peniman, "for a settler's wealth is in his horses, and we are better off than most. Most of the movers we have met were driving oxen, while we have three good teams."

When the dugout was completed it was indeed a strong and safe shelter for the stock. Protected from above by the ledge of rock, and on both sides by the stout sod wall and the rocky sides of the embankment, with the sturdy log door across its entrance, it was a shelter that would have stood a long siege.

As the family stood about it viewing it with pride they did not dream how well it would serve them, or how glad they would be of its protection in the days to come.

CHAPTER XVI

IN THE HANDS OF THE ENEMY

The house and barn were completed none too soon. On the afternoon of the day on which the door of the barn was hung the clouds hung heavy and ominous in the northeast. About four o'clock it began to thunder.

"Just in time, my lads," cried Mr. Peniman with a glance at the angry blackness of the sky. "We're going to have a big storm. Thank heaven that both we and our cattle will have good shelter. Get up the horses, Joe. Lige, you fill up the racks with grain and hay. Sam, you'd better bring in the cow. If it should be, as I fear, a very bad storm we shall all feel happier to know that our faithful beasts are under shelter."

It was nearly five o'clock, and the cow and horses were comfortably settled in their new quarters, when the storm broke. It was the first experience of the pioneers in a severe electrical storm on the prairies, and glad indeed were they of the thick walls and substantial roof above their heads as the lightning flashed and forked over the prairies, the thunder crashed, and the wind howled and raged while the rain came down in torrents.

"Oo-ooh! if we were out in the wagons now!" cried Ruth, flattening her nose against the window pane and peering out at the driving storm.

"Yes, or even in a frame house," said Joe. "No frame house could last long in a wind like this. Whee-ee, isn't it a gale! I'm glad we're in a soddy."

"It *is* comfortable and cozy, isn't it?" sighed Mrs. Peniman, glancing about her with a little smile of content.

For three days the wind howled and the rain fell, while the gentle murmur of the river increased to a sullen roar and it rushed foaming and tumultuous over its rocky bed. On the night of the third day it overflowed its banks, and Mr. Peniman and the boys had to spend most of the night guarding their wagons, implements and other property that they might not be carried away by the flood. The rain had changed to hail on this night, and Joe and Lige wore inverted skillets on their heads to protect them from the pelting of the hailstones. On the fourth day the wind died down, the rain ceased, and the sun came out in an intensely blue sky, which looked as brilliantly clean and clear as if newly created.

With the first gleam of sunshine the pioneers left the shelter of the house and took up the work waiting them outside.

They found that the stock had weathered the storm in the greatest comfort. Dicky and Mother Feathertop, who had found shelter under the canvas covers of the prairie schooners, were sadly bedraggled, and Romeo and Juliet, though exceedingly muddy, and in a very wet pen, were squealingly protesting their desire for food.

"Their pen is all wet, Father," cried Ruth in a grieved tone; "they'll take their deaths of cold."

Lige and Sam burst into roars of laughter.

"*Pigs* don't take cold, you goosie!" chuckled Sam.

"They do, too, don't they, Mother?"

"I never heard of pigs taking cold," said Mrs. Peniman, "but they certainly do look most uncomfortably wet. Couldn't we take them out and put them in another pen until their house dries?'"

"I think we might. I believe the pen we made for them when we first came is around here somewhere."

"I know where it is," cried Joe, and ran to get it.

When the pen of saplings was placed in a comparatively dry place Joe, Lige and Sam, in high rubber boots, descended into the pit to capture the young porkers. The mud was deep and slippery, the pigs well coated with the clay, and the boys chased them round and round the pen, sometimes catching hold of one by the ear or tail, sometimes grabbing them about the body, sometimes managing to get hold of a leg, when with a flirt and a squeal they would wiggle away, too slippery to hold on to, while the would-be captor would sprawl face down in the mud.

"Talk about your greased-pig races," panted Sam, who had just lost his grip on Juliet for the fourth time, "I never saw one that was a patchin' to this!"

Joe caught Romeo by his tail, which was too short and curly to make a good handle, and after a violent struggle, during which Joe slipped and slid all over the pen, Romeo made his get-away with a shrill squeal of vengeance, while Joe sprawled on his stomach in the mud.

The girls, with Paul and their mother were watching the chase from above with shouts and shrieks of laughter. When Lige made a wild dive for Juliet, who slipped through his hands and dived between his legs, sending him head-over-heels, Ruth doubled herself up with shrieks of mirth, in which Nina joined. Nothing could have injured the feelings of handsome Lige more.

"Well, *stay* in your slimy old pen then," he growled, and began to climb out. Mr. Peniman, shaking with laughter, stopped him. He too had been watching the sport.

"Here's a rope," he called out; "you'll never get them that way, they're too slippery. Rope them and pass them up to me."

This was a new angle to the game, and one that suited the boys better. Sam grabbed the rope and made a lasso at one end. With a wild cowboy yell he made for the astonished young porkers. His first try failed, when Lige grabbed the rope, and after an unsuccessful cast or two succeeded in getting the festive Romeo firmly about his fat middle. Romeo protested with shrill squeals, but he was captured, and was soon hoisted up and dropped inside the other pen. Juliet, being a bit more spry, and perhaps, being a lady, a trifle more wary, was harder to catch. Each of the boys tried his hand, and it was Joe who at last made the lucky throw, and got her fast by the leg, after which it was an easy matter to get hold of her and hoist her up to their father.

By this time it would have been hard to say which were the muddier and dirtier, the boys or the pigs, but a swim in the river soon removed the mud, and the rubber boots and suits they had worn were washed at the same time, so that they were soon fresh and clean.

The next day was bright and clear, and soon after their early breakfast Mr. Peniman, Joe, Lige, and Sam set off for the far side of their claim to cut the prairie grass for hay.

Mr. Peniman had staked out his own claim of 160 acres, laying out at the same time a 160 acre tract for Joe on one side of it and Lige on the other, to be pre-empted as soon as the boys should be old enough.

They took all three teams, and while Mr. Peniman and Joe began cutting the long, rich prairie grass Lige and Sam guided the plows, turning over the sod for their fall planting.

As this side of the claim was quite a distance from the house they had taken their lunch with them, and had just finished eating, and Joe was tipping up the jug to take a swig of water, when he stopped short, the jug at his shoulder, staring with fixed gaze across the plains.

"Indians!" he shouted, "*Indians!*" and dashing down the jug leaped for the horses.

Joshua Peniman at the same moment had seen the horsemen dashing across the open plateau to the south of them.

With a leap he sprang to the other team and began loosing them from the plow.

Joe and Lige had by this time got Kit and Billy free and throwing themselves across their backs had started for home in a mad gallop.

In the minds of all was the same terrible thought. Mrs. Peniman and the children were there unprotected and alone.

Joshua Peniman, not so young or active as his sons, did not dare to ride bareback. With frantic haste he hitched his team to the wagon, and shouting to Sam to jump in, and lead the black team, leaped in and lashed the horses into a run.

None of them had any weapons. They had seen no Indians since coming to the Blue River country, and their fear of them had gradually subsided as their minds became filled with other things. Now as Joshua Peniman drove madly across the prairies he cursed his short-sightedness and stupidity.

Nearer and nearer the squat black house on the banks of the river came the naked, yelping savages.

"My God—will Hannah see them in time—will she get herself and the children into the house before they reach her!" The agonized thought hammered itself over and over in his brain.

As Joe and Lige dashed on, silent before the stark horror of the moment, they could see the children playing down by the river. It was evident that they knew nothing of their danger. Then as the boys dashed on, lashing their horses cruelly, they saw their mother come to the door.

For a moment she stood, and they could feel in their own hearts that terror that came over her. Then they saw her make a dash for the river. Even above the thudding of the horses' hoofs they could hear her wild, agonized calls. The Indians heard it, too, and answered with derisive whoops and yells.

With dry lips and a frantic unuttered prayer Joe ground his heels into Kit's sides.

Would they get there in time?

Joshua Peniman, standing up in the wagon and leaning far over the dashboard, lashed his horses and groaned aloud.

There seemed to be some forty or fifty of the savages, and as they wheeled and the sun shone full on their naked bodies Lige gave a loud cry.

"*Sioux!*" he shouted, in tones of horror, and lying forward over Billy's neck urged him forward with voice and whip. Joe had seen, and from his white lips came a hoarse cry.

Up to this moment he had hoped—even though faintly—that the band they saw might be a hunting party of Pawnees or Arapahoes, who seldom harmed white people unless first molested. But Sioux——!

He leaned forward over his panting horse and spoke in her ear.

"Oh, Kit," he half sobbed, "get me there—for God's sake get me there in time to save them!"

As if she understood the little mare laid back her ears and sprang forward like an arrow from a bow.

The Indians had reached the sod house by this time. Yelping and howling they were circling about and about it on their ponies.

As the eyes of the horror-stricken boys and man strained toward them a sharp "spat" spoke from one of the soddy windows, and a naked savage reeled and fell from his horse.

"Mother—brave, brave little Mother!" Joe sobbed in a choked, husky whisper. Then as he saw the band spring from their horses and make a dash for the soddy he leaped down from Kit's back, and followed by Lige dashed through the undergrowth along the bank of the river toward the house.

Before they could reach it they heard a wild shriek, and saw their mother dash from the house with David in her arms, dragging little Mary by the hand, and followed by Ruth, Sara, and Paul, and make for the dugout.

Joe's heart thrilled with pride as he saw tender Ruth, who loved all creatures, evidently covering her mother's retreat, backing toward the dugout, her face toward the Indians, a smoking revolver in her hand.

They heard its sharp angry bark, and saw another Indian fall. Then they saw that Mrs. Peniman had reached the dugout, and pushing the children in before her grabbed for the heavy door. As she did so an Indian in a war-dress of skin and feathers, with a great feathered war-bonnet on his head, made a grab for her, but Ruth was too quick for him. Quick as a flash she took deliberate aim and fired. Joe, who was almost behind her by this time, heard the grunt of the Indian as he fell face downward beside the door.

"*Inside—inside the dugout!*" he shouted, and grasping Ruth by the shoulders pushed her toward the door.

Ruth turned her white face and gave a quick, terrified look all about her.

"Nina," she shrieked, "where's Nina?"

With a stab like the thrust of a knife in his heart Joe heard the cry.

"*Nina?*" he shouted, "where is she?"

A wild, anguished cry was his answer, and whirling about he saw an Indian dashing past with Nina thrown across his pony in front of him.

Quick as thought he caught the revolver from Ruth's hand and fired. He had feared to aim at the Indian lest he should strike the child, but had taken aim at the horse, and saw it fall and roll over.

Joshua Peniman, with Sam, had now reached the scene, and brandishing a great club that he had caught up as he ran made for the Indians that were circling about the dugout, uttering their fiendish yelps and howls.

Mrs. Peniman and the children were inside now, the door firmly closed, and all the efforts of the savages seemed unavailing to move it.

As the horse fell the Indian at whom Joe had shot leaped with his burden in his arms, and fell free of the struggling animal. In an instant he was on his feet and started to run.

Joe was now past sixteen, tall, muscular, with every nerve and sinew in his body like thews of steel from his long life in the open and continual work and manual exercise, and he rushed after and sprang upon him like a young panther. The Indian staggered, and threw the girl he carried from his arms. Then with a snarl like a wild creature he turned and faced him. Joe had no time to train his revolver upon him. With a spring like a tiger the savage was upon him, but Joe, writhing himself free from the deadly clasp of his arms, grabbed his revolver by the barrel and with the butt dealt him a smashing blow on the head.

The Indian tottered, swayed and threw his hand to his head. As he did so Joe's horrified gaze saw under the edge of the war-bonnet a white neck and a *tuft of red hair.*

The boy leaped forward and tried to raise the screaming little girl from the grass. But as he stooped over her the other leaped upon him and dealt him a terrific blow on the temple. With a groan Joe fell forward and lay still.

As he collapsed upon the ground the Indian who had red hair caught up the girl, leaped upon the back of a riderless pony that was galloping by, and dashed away. As he rode he called out a sharp command in the Indian tongue. With a few wild whoops and yells the Indians who were scattered about the place whirled about and followed him.

As the Indians that had surrounded the dugout dashed away Joshua Peniman turned, and seeing Joe lie motionless upon the ground rushed to him.

"Joe, Joe," he cried in agony, lifting the boy's head.

Joe gasped and opened his eyes.

"Father," he panted, starting up wildly, "Princess—they got her—where is she——"

His father pushed him gently back upon the ground.

"Are you wounded, Joe?" he asked in anguish; "did they get you?"

"No, no," the boy sprang to a sitting position. "I'm not hurt—only stunned—but Princess—Nina—did they take her? Did they get away with her?"

Joshua Peniman averted his eyes and his voice was hoarse and shaken. "Yes," he answered reluctantly, "they got her. You did the best you could to save her, and I was just too late."

The boy staggered to his feet.

"I must go after her—I must find her," he cried, then reeled dizzily.

His father half led, half carried him into the house.

"You are hurt—you are not able to go," he said, pushing him into a chair. "And besides, you could never catch them now, Joe. They have half an hour the start of you, and they have swift ponies——"

Joe sprang to his feet. "I *must* go, Father—I must! I must find her—I must bring her back—Princess, Princess!" and collapsing into the chair he fell over insensible.

His father, who was a good deal of a doctor and nurse, bathed his wounded head and gave him a simple stimulant. Presently he opened his eyes. He sat up, gazed wildly about, then sprang up with a white, determined face.

"I'm going to find Princess, Father," he said in a tone that was not to be disputed. "I *must*—we can't leave her in the hands of that—that scoundrel. I'm all right now, I can ride Kit——"

"But Kit is not a riding-horse, Joe; you could never overtake them. By this time those Indians are miles away."

"Father"—Joe leaned forward and spoke low in his father's ear—"the man that carried Nina off *was not an Indian!* When I struck him I knocked his bonnet to one side, his neck was *white*—and *he had red hair!*"

Joshua Peniman started violently.

"*Red Snake!*" he muttered.

For a moment he stood lost in thought, then said rapidly: "This is worse than I feared. We must go after her. We must get her out of his hands. I don't see how I can go———"

"You *can't*, Father! You can't be spared. Mother and the children need you here. But I can go—I'm all right now—I *must* go—I *must* find her!"

Joshua Peniman had been thinking swiftly.

"The best thing we can do," he broke in, "is to get to the Missions and Agencies and get word to the Government about this degenerate white man who lives with the Indians and is inciting them to raids and assaults for his own ends. Of course it's a terrible risk, it is taking your life in your hands, but the only hope that I can see of rescuing her is for some one to go to Bellevue and get Government aid. If I dared to leave the family———"

"This has proved that you dare not, Father. You must stay here. It is my place to go."

"But, Joe boy, do you realize the danger? Do you remember how far it is—how desolate and barren—what a lone, wearisome, lonesome trail?"

The boy looked at him bravely. "I remember," he said. "But it can't be helped. It's *got* to be done—and I'm going to do it. I must take food and water. Get it for me, won't you, Father, while I go get Kit?"

He rushed from the house, and found both teams standing by the barn, the third tied, as Sam had left it, to the back of the wagon.

He rapped on the door of the dugout and called loudly, telling the quaking family inside that the Indians were gone and the danger over.

When the door was opened and his mother peeped out he hastened to reassure her.

"But they've carried Nina away and I am going after her," he cried, dashing into the barn, seizing a blanket, and throwing it over Kit's back.

"The Indians—they have carried off Princess?" shrieked Ruth.

He did not stop to answer them; throwing himself across Kit's back and snatching the revolver, the ammunition and the bag of food and water that his father handed up to him, he waved his hand to the family, and before they could utter a protest he was gone, riding at a mad gallop across the plains.

CHAPTER XVII

EAGLE EYE

When Joe had gone, riding madly away across the prairies, Joshua and Hannah Peniman stood looking after his receding figure until it faded into a mere speck and was swallowed up by the immeasurable distance of the plains.

The faces of both were grey and haggard, and in their eyes was mirrored the fear that they might never see their eldest son again.

"May the Almighty Father watch over and protect him," prayed the father.

"And bring him back to us alive and well," breathed the mother with quivering lips.

"I wish that I could have gone in his place!" were the words that forced themselves with a groan from the lips of Joshua Peniman. "But I dared not go—in justice to you and the children. I could not leave you here without my protection. But we could not abandon that poor child without making every effort to save her, so Joe had to go. But he is only a lad—it is a long, long trail—a wild and desperate mission———"

"But we, nor he, could not have done otherwise, dear." Hannah Peniman's eyes were dry, her tone steady. "It was a duty that was laid upon us. God will watch over him. He will permit no harm to come to our boy in the discharge of this sacred duty."

Her husband clasped her hand and looked tenderly into her eyes. "Thee is ever my inspiration and comfort, Hannah," he said with quivering voice. "Thy vision is ever more clear than mine, thy faith more fast and true."

She turned her face to him and began to speak, then stopped abruptly and stood listening.

"Hark!" she cried in a startled whisper, "what was that?"

Both stood motionless with heads raised, the fear of an unknown danger upon them.

Then there came to them again the sound that had arrested Hannah Peniman's attention. A low moan, scarcely more than a sigh, came from the tall grass near the side of the dugout.

Mr. Peniman caught up his musket and strode in the direction from which the sound preceded. His wife followed him.

"Be careful," she whispered cautiously, "it might be some trap!"

As they crept forward through the long, waving grass they came upon the body of a young Indian lying on his back, stark and dead. A little farther along both stopped abruptly as the moan they had heard before reached their ears. Joshua Peniman sprang forward. Suddenly he stopped, and with a motion to his wife to keep back, stooped in the grass.

Face downward in a tangle of weeds they saw an Indian lying, one arm extended, the other doubled under his head. As the white man stooped over him a shudder ran through his body and again the low, suppressed moan came from his lips.

Mr. Peniman lifted the body in his arms and turned it over. It was that of a young Indian, tall and powerful, in full war panoply, with a handsome copper-colored face. As the white man lifted him he groaned again and the blood rushed from a wound in his side. He was quite unconscious, the eyes half-closed, the lips blue and parted, the lean, keen-featured face ashen with the pallor of approaching death.

Mrs. Peniman, who had stolen up behind her husband, uttered a pitying cry, and quickly tearing off her apron tore it into strips and kneeling by the prostrate figure began binding up the gaping wound.

"Oh," she cried with a shudder, "oh, Joshua, perhaps it was I who did that! Oh, my God, to think of hurting a fellow-creature so desperately! But he was by the door—I was afraid he would get the children——"

"There were many shots fired, Hannah," her husband assured her, "it was probably not thee that hit him. But it is a terrible thing that we seem obliged to kill our fellow-men to protect ourselves. We who do not believe in slaughter——" He stopped, then went on quickly, "We must get him up to the house—he is badly wounded—he may die—and it is our duty to save his life if we can, even though we know that he is an enemy."

Between them they bore the unconscious form of the young Indian to their own home. Ruth met them at the door, and as her eyes fell upon the burden they carried she uttered a loud scream.

"It is the Indian I shot with Mother's revolver!" she cried, backing away in terror. Then seeing the gaping wound in the side she covered her face and began to cry.

"Oh, I did that, I did it," she moaned. "I thought he would kill Mother—I——"

"Hush, Ruth," her father commanded. "He is harmless now. He is badly wounded—perhaps dying. We must do all that we can to save him. You know we are told by the Master to help our enemies and do good to them who despitefully use us."

They laid the unconscious young brave on Joe's bed, and Hannah Peniman brought a pan of hot water and began to bathe and dress the wound in his side. Her husband bending down beside her examined the wound.

"I'm afraid it is fatal," he said sadly, "but we will do the best we can for him." From his earliest youth it had been the desire of his heart to be a physician. Circumstances had made him a farmer, but all through his life he had retained his love for the art of surgery and medicine, and by continually practising upon the stock on his place and on members of his family he had attained a degree of skill not possessed by many regularly licensed doctors. He probed and cleaned the wound, took the pulse and heart-beat and set about reducing the temperature.

For several days following the young Indian lay on Joe's bed burning with fever, delirious and muttering, sick unto death. Ruth, who seemed stricken with horror at the suffering her hand had visited upon a fellow-creature, devoted herself to his nursing, in which Mrs. Peniman and Sara shared, and Joshua Peniman waited upon and watched over him as if he were a friend or a relative instead of a deadly foe.

One morning as Mr. and Mrs. Peniman were bending over him irrigating his wound he suddenly opened his eyes.

For a moment he lay staring at them as if he believed that his mind was still wandering. Then he stirred, grunted, and tried to sit up.

Joshua Peniman pushed him gently back upon the pillows.

"Heap sick," he said, accompanying the words with gestures that left no doubt of his meaning.

The Indian stared at him, then turned his head and looked intently into Hannah Peniman's face. She bent over him with soothing words, took his hand, and stroked her cool, soft hand across his forehead.

"Heap sick," she said, smiling at him and speaking slowly, as one might to an ailing child. Then taking his hand she laid it over the wound, pointed to the bandages, then to her husband, then to herself.

At this moment Ruth came into the room carrying a glass of milk. Seeing the black eyes open and staring into her mother's face she started back, half-frightened. But she was too good and efficient a little nurse to let fear interfere with her duties, and going straight up to the bed put the glass to his lips.

He threw back his head, refusing it, then turned the glare of his fierce black eyes from her mother's face to hers. But Ruth was not to be daunted.

"You've got to drink your milk," she said firmly, "else you'll never get well. Take it now, this minute!" For a moment the young Indian continued to stare at her, then a grin came creeping over his brown face, and when she again put the milk to his lips he drank it obediently.

Mrs. Peniman smiled her approval. "Now go to sleep," she told him, and illustrated her meaning by placing her cheek on her hand and closing her eyes. The young Indian smiled again, and nodded. He was pitifully weak, and soon surrendered to the drowsiness that overcame him. When he woke again it was evening and the sunset was casting long wavering shadows into the windows.

All the next day he scarcely stirred in the bed, but the keen black eyes opened frequently and followed their movements. When Ruth came to his bed bringing a glass of milk and a plate of toast he looked up into her face and smiled. Later, as she was passing he put out a feeble hand and caught her dress. Drawing her nearer he took her hand and patted it gently.

He pointed to his own breast and in a feeble voice said: "Me Eagle Eye," then pointing his finger toward her he gazed at her inquiringly.

Ruth's brown eyes widened and smiled.

"*You* name Eagle Eye?" she asked, and when he nodded gravely she added delightedly, "My name *Ruth*."

"Woof!" he said, then smiled at her and closed his eyes.

Ruth ran to her mother in great delight.

"Our Indian isn't fierce or bad a bit, Mother," she cried, "he patted my hand and smiled at me. He likes me. His name is 'Eagle Eye,' and he wanted to know my name. I don't believe he's a bad Indian, I believe he was trying to tell me he was grateful to us for taking care of him."

For many days after that he appeared too weak and ill to pay much attention to them, but gradually the wound began to heal, and Joshua Peniman saw with much gratification that his patient was in a fair way to recover.

One day he indicated to Mrs. Peniman that he would like to get up. Pointing to the wound in his side he then pointed to the outdoors and the sun that was shining warmly, and by laying his head on his hand and pointing to the ground outside the window he made her understand that he wanted to go outside and lie in the sun.

"Why, to be sure," she cried, smiling at him, "you know what would be good for you, don't you? Wait, I'll call your doctor."

When Mr. Peniman came he repeated the pantomime. Joshua Peniman nodded.

"Yes, why not? Probably your instinct is a true one. I'll help you up."

While the Indian did not understand the words he understood the nod and smile that accompanied them, and with every sign of joy allowed himself to be helped out of bed and into the warm sun before the door, where he stretched himself at full length on the warm earth with a great sigh of contentment.

After that he spent most of every day lying in the sun, and his progress toward recovery was rapid. He could soon sit up, walk about, and at last wander from place to place by himself.

He had gradually been picking up a few English words, and during his convalescence Ruth and Sara became his teachers. It was no uncommon sight of an afternoon to see the tall young Indian stretched out on the grass in front of the sod house, with a little white girl on either side of him industriously teaching him English.

It was evident that he already understood much that was said to him, and remembered words and sentences that had been repeated in his presence while he was ill. One day he surprised them greatly by saying in fairly good English: "Heap good white folks."

Ruth laughed delightedly oven this, and Joshua Peniman found in the remark sober cause for congratulation. In the perilous position in which he and his family were placed he felt that every Indian who cherished a friendly feeling toward them was an immense protection.

No sign or word had come from Joe since they had seen him ride away over the plains, and his heart was sore and aching for the boy who had always been such a help and comfort to him. As the days went by and he did not return they almost despaired of ever seeing him again.

One day in the sorrow of his heart he spoke of him to Eagle Eye. He did not know how much of what he said was understood by the red man, but he looked at him intently while he spoke, and when Mr. Peniman finished the sad tale nodded gravely.

The next morning Eagle Eye came to them with his clothing and moccasins on and his bow and arrow in his hand. He solemnly held out his hand, and when Mr. Peniman accepted it shook it gravely. Then walking to Mrs. Peniman he shook her hand also, and without a word of farewell stalked away across the prairies.

"He's *gone!*" cried Ruth tragically, gazing after the receding figure with amazement.

"And without a word of thanks for all we have done for him!" cried Lige indignantly.

"You know he cannot express himself very well in our language," said Mrs. Peniman. "Perhaps he felt more deeply than he could tell."

"We'll never see him again!" cried Sara on the point of tears.

"Who can tell!" said Joshua Peniman, gazing after the tall blanketed figure with a strange light in his eyes, "who can tell!"

CHAPTER XVIII

A LIFE FOR A LIFE

Meanwhile Joe was having a thrilling experience.

While his father and mother stood gazing after him with prayers on their lips the boy was leaning forward over Kit's neck, urging her forward with voice and knees.

A great fear filled him. A terrible and undefined horror chilled his blood and knocked heavily at his heart.

"They've got Nina! *They've got Nina!*" he said over and over to himself until the words formed themselves into a kind of a chant that beat itself out in time to the thudding hoofs.

He had no consciousness of time or place or distance. His one frantic impulse was for speed, *speed!* It was not until he felt the mare heave and stumble under him that he came to himself and realized that she was nearly done.

"Poor Kit!" he murmured, checking her up and stroking the heaving sides and panting neck. "I mustn't kill you whatever happens."

He slipped down from her back, rubbed her down with grass, then cooled her mouth and sponged her nose with water from the precious flask he carried.

When she had ceased to heave and began to breathe more naturally he mounted again and tried to curb his urging spirit to her strength.

Kit had been born on the Ohio farm, and Joe had loved and tended and petted her from a colt. She knew every tone of his voice, and would come to him at his call. She was not, as his father had reminded him, a riding-horse. Her gait was not suited to the saddle, and as she had always been used for farm work, riding her was a painful and difficult matter. But Joe was not thinking of his own comfort now. He was thinking of Nina— Nina in the hands of the Indians! Nina in the clutches of the renegade with red hair!

As the sun began to droop low in the west he reined up and looked about him. Over the whole vast expanse of the prairies no living thing was in sight. Nowhere was there any sign of the Indians, and he recalled with a sore heart what his father had said, that with their swift ponies it would be impossible for him to catch up with them.

He felt weak and faint, and dismounting slipped the bridle over Kit's head and let her graze while he threw himself down on the grass and drank from the flask of water and ate some of the lunch that his father had put up for him.

Darkness fell swiftly these days. Before the son and purple in the western sky had faded the shadows of night were darkling over the plains. He urged Kit forward, determined that he would not sleep, that neither he nor she should know rest until he had reached Bellevue and set the Government agencies at work to rescue Nina.

Darkness was closing in about him when turning to scan the empty circle of the horizon he saw outlined against the fading sky a curl of smoke.

His heart gave a great leap.

Could it be the camp of the Indians?

His breath came quick and fast, and whirling Kit sharply about he dashed madly across the prairies toward it.

Boy-like, he did not stop to consider what he would do when he got there. Whether the encampment was that of friend or foe, or how, in case it should be the band who had abducted the little Princess, he should set about to rescue her.

All he thought about was to *get there*. The rest would come when he was on the ground.

Kit had got her second wind now, and traveled steadily, jolting and shaking the boy on her back cruelly, but covering the ground at a good gait.

He knew that he could not reach the point from whence he saw the smoke rising for nearly an hour, and realized that he must not approach it before darkness had completely enshrouded the plains and the camp had settled down for the night.

As he came nearer, his heart was gladdened, and at the same time shaken, by the sound of the tom-toms and the rhythmic chant of voices. Checking up his horse he rode more slowly, biding his time until the camp should be shrouded in darkness and sleep.

When darkness came he could make out the red glare of the camp-fire against the sky, and could see the silhouette of dusky figures dancing about it He got down, and muffling Kit's nose in his handkerchief, lest she should whinny, he walked beside her, ready at an instant's notice to check her slightest noise.

He could hear the singing plainly now, but did not know enough of Indian lore to realize that the song they were chanting was not a war-song, but the hymn of the buffalo hunt, appealing to the Great Spirit to bless the chase and give to them meat for their lodges and covers for their teepees before the coming of the big snows.

As the boy crept nearer his very heart was in his throat.

He saw presently that the camp was on a creek, that there were scrubby trees behind it, and a tangled thicket ahead.

Afraid to lead Kit any nearer he took her to the outmost fringe of the thicket and tied her securely, with the handkerchief still over her nose. Then he crept forward through the brush.

He could see the camp plainly now. The teepees were set up along the banks of the creek, the great fire in the centre of the half-circle, and on the ground was the newly removed hide of a buffalo, while the savory smell of its roasting flesh still hung in the air.

Creeping up as close to the teepees as he could and still remain in shelter he looked and listened intently.

Was Nina in one of those tents?

Which one?

Would she be alone? Would it be possible for him to reach her?

Doubts, questions, and anxieties struggled in his mind as he lay hidden in the thicket.

At last the feast was over, the music ceased, the fire died down, and squaws, bucks, and papooses slowly dispersed. The lean, cadaverous dogs, that are always a part of an Indian encampment, prowled about the fire eating the offal, but at last they too were surfeited and lay down to sleep.

Joe waited; his heart thumping so hard against his ribs that he feared the sleeping Indians must hear it.

It seemed to him that hours passed. Now and then a baby cried, a pony whinnied, a dog growled or barked. Gradually snores came to his ears. Long, sonorous snores, short, barking snores, but all of them snores that he was more than glad to hear.

After a time he moved his cramped limbs and slowly got to his knees, then to his feet. With cautious movements he parted the undergrowth about him and began to crawl through.

Whenever a bit of brush crackled he threw himself flat on the ground and tried to burrow himself out of sight. But at last, after much toilful and noiseless wriggling he got clear of the thicket and stood just within its shadow in the open.

Before him were the teepees.

He knew that if Nina were with this band she must be in one of them,—*but which?*

Cautiously, noiselessly, he worked his way around the edge of the thicket nearer to the teepees. Then on his hands and knees, crawling so close to the ground that he scarcely made a shadow, he wormed his way across the open space.

He knew that his life was not worth an instant's purchase if he was discovered. He felt positive that detection meant death. But Nina was there—in the hands of her enemies—he must get her!

At last he reached the teepees. Crawled nearer to their openings. Was listening before their doors.

From the nearest one came loud, deep snores. It was a man's snore—she could not be there. He crept on. From the next came the whimpering sound of a baby's cry. Something told him that she would not be there. With redoubled caution he wormed his way along to the next. Listening intently he thought he heard a stifled sob. His pulses leaped. Waiting and listening with bated breath he crept nearer. It came again. Some one inside the teepee was crying.

Some one was crying!

It was not a child—it could not be a squaw—squaws did not cry—*it must be Nina!*

How should he call her? How let her know that he was there?

Cautiously he raised himself, cautiously with slow, noiseless movement he raised the flap of hide that covered the opening of the teepee.

It was so dark inside that at first he could see nothing; then gradually as his eyes became accustomed to the blackness he made out a heap of leaves and branches at one side of the teepee, on which lay a grey-haired squaw, and his heart gave a great leap that almost made him cry aloud as he saw on the blanket beside her the white face and golden hair of the little Princess.

It was all he could do to stifle the cry that rose to his lips, but he knew that the least sound would be fatal now, so locking his teeth hard he slid forward like a great serpent and bent his face close to the sobbing little girl. Slipping his hand over her mouth he whispered rapidly, "Nina, it is I, Joe; be quiet, I've come to save you!"

Quietly as he had entered, soft, almost noiseless as was his whisper, it woke the squaw, who set up a great outcry and darted past him out of the tent. Before the boy could move or the startled girl rise from her couch of branches, a man in a long grey shirt rushed through the opening. As he came Joe thrust his foot between the long legs and tripped him, and as he fell headlong caught up the Princess in his arms and leaped over the prostrate body.

The teepees were placed on the bank above the creek, and back of them ran the line of scrubby timber and the tangle of thick undergrowth through which Joe had worked his way. The instant he found himself outside the teepee with Nina in his arms he darted back of it and into the brush.

Instantly the man in the long flapping grey shirt was on his feet and following them. Joe stopped long enough to catch his silhouette against the sky-line, and fire. He saw him fall, rise, press his hand to his knee with a groan of pain, then sink down into the brush.

Dragging Nina behind him he ducked between the legs of an Indian who was rushing toward him, bowled him over, and dodged behind a tree. He knew that he had not an instant to lose. Seizing Nina by the hand he dragged her behind the tree, then whispered rapidly:

"They're after us! They may get me, but Kit is just outside the edge of the thicket over that way," he pointed; "try to get to her and go on to Bellevue. It can't be very far now. We'll stick together if we can, but if you see me fall don't wait, make a dash for Kit——" a great whoop from the teepees above interrupted his broken whisper, and pushing Nina before him he rushed on through the thicket. "Through there—through there," he panted, "wiggle your way through the brush!" He leaned forward to push the undergrowth aside for her when a bullet whizzed through the air and his arm dropped to his side, while a stinging, burning pain shot through his chest.

"I'm hit!" he gasped. "Go on, *hurry*—whistle to Kit—you know my whistle—she'll hear and answer you!"

Nina cast a horrified look upon him, but he waved his arm impatiently, then staggered back and fell, slipping and sliding down the bank and into the water.

With a cry of horror she scrambled after him, but he was nowhere to be seen. The water at the foot of the embankment was ruffled, and she knew that he must have sunk to the bottom.

For a moment she stood with hands locked in agony gazing down into the muddy depths, then as a wild yelp sounded above her gave vent to a great sobbing cry and darted through the undergrowth, taking the direction Joe had pointed out to her.

Joe, badly wounded, probably owed his life to his plunge into the muddy waters of the creek. It brought him sharply back to his failing senses, and instinct made him crawl close to the bank, where, under a heavy growth of coarse reed-like grass and rushes he was entirely concealed from the bank above. He heard the rush of feet above him, the yelp and howl of voices, the loud, angry cursing of a man in the English tongue, then knew no more.

When he came to himself it was morning. There was no sound to be heard, and he was bitterly cold, shivering as if with an ague. He drew himself slowly and painfully out of the water and sat down on the bank. His left arm hung limp and useless at his side, and his shirt was stained and draggled with blood.

How long he sat there he could not tell. He was weak and dizzy, and his head was going around so fast that he could make no note of time. He stooped presently and drank a little from the stream, bathed his aching head, and shook the water from his clothes. Then he got to his feet, and weakly, warily, began making his way through the brush.

He wondered, with a sinking heart, what had become of Nina. Whether she had got away or whether she had been captured again by Red Snake. He could not go far at a time but, stopping every little way to rest and ease the agony in his chest, crept on. The sun was up and shining hot in the heavens when he reached the edge of the thicket. He called and whistled, but there was no answer. Kit was not there.

Suddenly he shrank back into the shelter of the undergrowth with a sickening heart. Across the flat surface of the plain he saw a troop of horsemen riding, and from the way they rode he knew they were Indians.

A groan burst from his lips. He supposed they were hunting him, and cowering back in the shelter of the scrubby undergrowth he gave himself up for lost. He thought that of course they had captured Nina, and the horror and agony of the thought, combined with the pain in his arm and chest, rendered him almost unconscious. Dropping down upon the ground he gradually drifted away into a blank, then into a wild, fevered dream, where all was confusion.

There was a great noise in the dream, a rushing and thundering of hoofs, a shaking of the ground, as if with an earthquake, whoops, yells, the crashing and smashing of timber, and a great crowd about him.

He cried out, and started up in terror. Outside on the plains a party of horsemen were thundering by, and not far away a great red animal lay struggling in its death-agonies, with a group of Indians about it.

Joe raised himself painfully, and creeping to an opening in the thicket looked out. Then suddenly he cried aloud.

These were not Sioux!

With all the blood in his body roaring in his ears he listened to the guttural tones of the Indians bent over the buffalo on the grass, quickly ending its struggles.

He had picked up a few words of the Indian language, and by the dress of these men, by the words that he could catch here and there he knew that they were Omahas and Pawnees.

With no further hesitation he crawled from his hiding-place and raising his hand above his head gave a weak call. The Indians whirled about swiftly and looked at him. One of them detached himself from the rest and came toward him.

He had but strength enough to point to his wound, to say "Heap sick," then stumbled forward and fell at the Indian's feet.

When he came to himself he was in an Indian wig-wam.

At first terror took possession of him, thinking that he had again fallen into the hands of the Sioux. But his first stir brought an Indian woman to his side, who, seeing his eyes open, uttered a guttural exclamation and ran from the wigwam. Immediately the opening was thrown back and a young buck entered.

Joe, half-expecting to see Red Snake, cowered down on the bed of boughs and skins. But the Indian who hurried to his side came with outstretched hand and a smile on his face. There was something strangely familiar about him, and as the boy gazed up at him he was struggling in his sick mind to place the face.

The Indian bent over him, smiled, then thrust his hand inside his shirt and brought out a bright red necktie. Joe's heart gave a great jump of joy.

"*Pashepaho!*" he cried, and grabbed the slim brown hand. Then gazing about him, "Where am I—how did I happen to get here?"

Pashepaho grinned at him and patted his hand.

"You with my people. Pawnee village on Platte River. Heap sick boy. Been here many sleeps."

"I *have*?" Joe rubbed his head confusedly. "How did I get here? I don't remember—oh!"—as memory began to come back to him—"oh, I was shot—and some Indian came——"

"My young men hunt buffalo. Fin' you heap sick. Bring you back Big Chief. Big Chief my favver."

"Oh, and I am in your wigwam? This is your camp?"

Pashepaho nodded.

"And you have been taking care of me, Pashepaho? I was hurt pretty bad, I guess. I believe I would have died there if your young men had not found me."

"Sure. Heap sick. Medicine man make you well."

Joe grinned weakly. He had not much faith in medicine men, but he cared little who saved him as long as he was getting well.

"I'm all right now, ain't I?" he asked anxiously, beginning to realize his great weakness and languor.

"Yep. Get li'l stronger. Eat heap meat."

Joe suddenly remembered his arm and lifted it gingerly.

Pashepaho saw the movement and grinned. "All ri' now." Then laying his hand on the boy's chest, "Here worse. Heap much hole. Bleed. Cough. Heap sick."

Joe put his hand to his chest. A rough poultice of leaves and herbs covered it. He could feel that it was still sore, but the burning, stabbing pain that he remembered the last thing before he became unconscious was gone.

He turned and grasped the hand of the young Indian tightly, and his gratitude shone in his sunken grey eyes.

"You're a true friend, Pashepaho, I guess you saved my life," he said fervently. Then, stopping now and then to rest when his breath gave out or a coughing spell came on, he told the story of the assault of the Sioux, Nina's capture, his own pursuit, his discovery of Nina in the teepee, and his shooting and escape.

"I don't know whether they got Nina again or not," he concluded sorrowfully. "I did the best I could, but when I got plugged in the chest I didn't know much afterward. I told her to get through the thicket if she could and find Kit, but I don't know whether she made it, and even if she did they might have got her afterward. To think of that poor little girl in the hands of that brute——"

His voice shook, and he stopped abruptly.

Pashepaho patted his shoulder. "No worry," he said. "She get home all ri'." Then, "Who get? Indian carry off girl?"

Joe's face flushed and his eyes blazed. "No, I don't believe there's any Indian mean enough. It was a white man. He lives with the Sioux——"

"Squaw-man?"

"I guess that's what they call him. He's got some kind of a grudge against Nina or her folks. This is the third time he has attacked her. He killed her father. Sometimes I have wondered if——"

"What kind man?"

"Oh, he's a *big* brute, tall and terribly strong, but thin, and he's got red hair and a"—then as a sudden flash of memory came over him—"why, say, you know him! That's the man that was trying to trade you out of that otter skin the first time I saw you!"

"Ai-ee, ai-ee! Big white man, red hair, live with Santee Sioux! Drink heap fire-water! Name Red Snake."

"Yes—yes—that's the man—Red Snake. Who is he, Pashepaho? What is he doing living with red men? What is his real name?"

Pashepaho shook his head. "*Red Snake* all name I know. Heap bad man. Make heap trouble."

Joe lay back on his blanket depressed and troubled. While he knew that he was now safe his heart was rent with anxiety for Nina and his parents. He had been gone "many sleeps"! He knew that by this time they must think him dead. And Nina—poor little Princess—what of her? Where was she, and what had she suffered while he lay unconscious in Pashepaho's wigwam!

He would have risen and tried to start forth at once, but Pashepaho and Petale-sharu, his father, the Great Chief, would not allow it.

"Me take you when you can ride," assured Pashepaho, and with that assurance Joe was forced to be content.

He found that he was in an Indian settlement on Buffalo Creek, where he was left alone day after day with the old men and squaws and papooses while the men of the tribe were away on the big fall hunt.

It was tedious business waiting for his wound to heal with so anxious a heart in his breast, and it took all the patience and fortitude he possessed. He played with the dogs and children, and talked with the squaws, whom he found to be kind and gentle, and who seemed glad to teach him their own language, learning, meanwhile, amid great laughter, a little of the English tongue. They had funny times making themselves understood by one another, and while his wound healed and his strength came back day by day Joe acquired a knowledge of the language and customs of the Pawnees which stood him in good stead at a later day.

The Pawnees lived in large circular houses called "earth lodges," with walls of dirt and a roof supported by trunks of trees set upright inside of the walls, the whole covered with poles, grass and sod. On the east side was a covered entrance, and on the west were the sacred bundle and buffalo skull. There was a hole in the centre of the roof to let the smoke out, and the people slept around the edge of the circle made by the walls, and gathered about the lodge-fire in the centre of the enclosure to eat and talk.

The women raised crops of corn, beans, pumpkins, squashes, and melons, and gathered the wild fruits and roots from the prairie and dried them for winter. As they were now busy with the drying process Joe often helped them, telling them in his boyish way how they could better their farming, and even taking a hand, when he grew strong enough, in showing them how to harvest their crops in an easier and more scientific manner.

He found them to be a very religious people, and as they came to know him better and to grow fond of him, he was sometimes allowed to attend their sacred rites. They believed in a Great Spirit, whom they called "Tirawa," the Father, who made the people, and who sent the corn, the rain, the buffalo, the sunshine, and all good things, and he was permitted to witness some of the dances and ceremonials held by the tribe for the purpose of gaining the favor of Tirawa.

In spite of his terrible anxiety about Nina and the burning desire he had to get back to his parents and relieve their worry about him the days went by not unhappily. He found the Pawnees to be a quiet, gentle people, friendly to the whites, and with high ideas of honor and honesty which surprised as well as delighted him. The women were very kind to him, gave him the best the lodges afforded to eat, and nursed and tended him until he was able to wait upon himself.

He had no means of knowing how time had gone by. To the best of his knowledge he must have been gone nearly a month, when Pashepaho, seeing his continual anxiety, told him one morning that they would set out upon his journey homeward the next day.

Joe could not sleep that night, and was awake and ready before even the first prowling dog of the encampment was astir.

After a good breakfast he bade them all good-bye, thanked the kind people over and over again for their care and hospitality, and mounting the shaggy Indian pony that Pashepaho had provided for him, and well equipped with food and water, they set forth toward home.

Joe could never have found his way alone. They wound along creek bottoms and by devious paths and trails which a white man would never have discovered, and as they rode they talked. Joe found that his friend Pashepaho was not only an exceedingly intelligent young Indian, but a man of courage and principle as well.

He told the boy that his people had lived in what was then called the Territory of Nebraska for more than two hundred years. That they had always been friendly to the white man, but that the white brothers who had come among them had robbed and deceived them and were taking from them all that they had possessed as their own for so many centuries. He talked sorrowfully of the condition of his people, and said in a tragic voice that he knew that their day was past. Standing upon a little rise and sweeping his arm in a slow circle all about him he said, "All once belong to my people. But white man come, and now my people are as the leaves on the trees in the winter, yours as the grass in the fields. If we rebel we get kill. If twenty your people fall, hundreds of mine must pay. No hope. The Indian must go. His day is ended."

The second day out they saw a great herd of buffalo feeding on the plains. Joe could see that it was hard for Pashepaho to pass them by unmolested.

"Can't we try to get a shot at them?" cried Joe, willing, boy-like, to risk anything for the sake of a stirring chase.

Pashepaho shook his head.

"No shoot," he grunted. "Bring trouble. We no want Sioux come now." Then glancing at the boy, who was still pale from his recent illness, "You no hunt now. Bime-by when you strong me take you big hunt some day."

"Oh, will you, Pashepaho?" cried Joe eagerly. "Hurray! And may Lige come, too? Jeminy, that'd be great. Don't forget, will you?"

"Me no forget," remarked Pashepaho, with a smile that showed how fond he had grown of his young white friend.

On the third day, or as Pashepaho expressed it, "three sleeps from the Pawnee settlement," Joe began to recognize the landscape.

"Oh, I know this road," he cried out excitedly, "we traveled over it when we were coming out! We made our noon camp right over there! Yes, sir, there's the signs of our fire yet! We go straight west from here, don't we?"

Pashepaho looked into the flushed, excited face of his young friend. "We no far from Blue Water now," he said with a smile.

Joe's heart beat hard and high as they came nearer and nearer to the homestead. What should he find when he got there? What might have happened while he had been away?

CHAPTER XIX

HOW JOE CAME HOME

When Nina saw Joe fall and heard him slide down the bank and into the water she thought he was dead.

When she could see nothing of him, and heard the Indians rushing through the trees and grass above her she fled like a startled rabbit through the undergrowth.

She saw an Indian dash down the bank and look up and down the creek, then she heard his footsteps recede and words called out in a language she did not understand. Twice while she hid and cowered in the undergrowth she saw Indians come down to the creek and look along its banks, then she heard them ride away.

Many times in her flight she stopped and listened. It was pitch-dark in the thicket, and the little girl, creeping forward through the underbrush, was half-crazed with fear. But she knew that her best protection from capture by the savages was in the tangled brush, and she fought her way gallantly through it, and just at dawn found herself at the edge of the thicket, with the broad, open prairies before her.

Remembering Joe's directions she gave the whistle he had always used in calling Kit, and to her unbounded joy heard a low, smothered whinny in answer.

In her terror and loneliness it sounded to the little Princess like the voice of an old friend. Guiding her direction by the sound she stole along in the shadow of the thicket and not long after came to where Kit, still tied as Joe had left her, turned her slender head and intelligent eyes toward her, pawing the ground with an impatient hoof.

Nina had never ridden horseback, but she was too terrified, too weary now to remember that. Clasping her arms about Kit's neck she managed to scramble on her back and started off, not knowing which way to go, but eager to put distance in any direction between herself and the horrors with which she had been surrounded.

She had to cling tight to Kit's mane to keep from falling off, and was afraid to let her go much faster than a walk, so that her progress was slow and difficult. Sunrise found her plodding on, a forlorn little figure on a big bay mare, tears running down her face, and muffled sobs shaking her.

SUNRISE FOUND HER PLODDING ON, A FORLORN LITTLE FIGURE ON A
BIG BAY MARE.— *Page 221.*

*SUNRISE FOUND HER PLODDING ON, A FORLORN LITTLE
FIGURE ON A BIG BAY MARE.*

Shortly after sunrise she was overtaken by a band of Winnebago
Indians laden with elk hides and buffalo skins, returning to their camp from
a week's hunt in the Blackbird Hills.

The surprise of the Indians may be imagined when seeing a solitary
rider ambling slowly and apparently aimlessly over the prairies, they
overtook it and saw that the rider was a beautiful little white girl, who cried
bitterly when they spoke to her and would not tell who she was, where she
had come from or where she was going.

None of the band could speak English, and as Nina knew no Indian
there was little chance of her being able to inform them. It was quite

evident, however, that the child was wild with terror when they approached her, and when they took her and her horse in tow she shrieked and fought, utterly unaware that they were doing their utmost to assure her that they were "good Indians," that they never hurt children and would take her back to her home and family if she could make them understand where she lived.

After much perplexed discussion among themselves the Winnebagoes decided to take her back with them to their encampment, where they would find some of their tribe who spoke English, and find out who the young stranger might be.

They tried to be kind and gentle to her, and the squaws did their best to comfort her, but the child was in a perfect panic of terror, and at the approach of every new person shrank and shuddered, looking with great agonized violet eyes into the faces of the Indians, and shaking and trembling with fear. To her all Indians were alike, and momentarily she expected the hated Red Snake to come and claim her.

As days passed, however, and Red Snake did not appear, when day followed day and no dreadful thing happened to her, and she saw the boys and men ride away leaving her behind with the squaws, old men and children, she began to be less afraid. Little by little the haunted look of terror left her eyes, and after a time she began to scrape acquaintance with the children that hung fascinated about her. The bright-eyed little papooses strapped to their rigid back-boards appealed to her wonderfully, and when she sat down before them and played with them, chucking them under their fat little chins and playing "peek-a-boo" with her apron, they squealed with laughter, and she too could begin to smile. After a while she began to play with the little Indian girls and boys, and little by little to learn their language and teach them hers.

Twice the camp was moved, and Nina was moved with it, helping the squaws with the babies, and feeling tremendous interest in the bustle of preparation, when the teepees were taken down, folded and tied with cords made of deer and buffalo hide, and fastened to the ponies, strong shaggy little beasts which dragged them after them in long traces, while the women carried the bundles, and the braves walked along smoking their pipes ahead of the procession, or nonchalantly rode their ponies, leaving the squaws and children to bear all the burdens and shoulder all the responsibilities of moving.

At first Nina could not understand these moves, but gradually came to know that the Indians were engaged in their fall hunt, and that while the men scoured the plains for the animals that provided them with food, clothing, and shelter for the winter, the women and children moved slowly along behind them with the equipment, so that the camp to which the hunters belonged was never far away.

The Indians were all kind to her, the women gentle and even motherly to the little paleface that had been thrust so unceremoniously among them, the men quiet and grave, but never cross nor severe.

Gradually as the days passed by she became fond of her little playfellows, and though she was desperately unhappy, and longed with a sick, yearning heartache for her adopted home, she did not suffer as she might have suffered if she had fallen among less quiet and gentle people.

One day when she had been romping over the prairie with the children and dogs they came back to find a great band of hunters just riding in, laden with the fruits of the chase. Some of them bore long poles on their shoulders from which were suspended the carcases of elk and deer, others carried great willow baskets, which the Indian women made, containing the meat of deer, antelope, and buffaloes which had been stripped from the bones to save carrying the huge bodies; others carried great baskets of grouse, prairie-chicken, and quail, and the whole camp was full of rejoicing.

Among the hunters was one tall, powerful Indian, who stopped short as the group of children came running toward them, and stared at Nina with an expression of utter astonishment on his face.

Pointing his finger at her he asked in the Winnebago dialect how she came to be there. A babel of tongues broke out among the children and squaws, each trying to tell her version of the story.

Nina, seeing him staring at her, was filled with fear. Her face paled, her great violet eyes widened with terror, and her bosom began to heave. But the red man walked straight up to her and put out a big brown hand.

"How, Nee-ah-nah," he said, and smiled down upon her.

Nina, with a trembling hand at her bosom, drew back.

The big Indian smiled, and putting his hand in his bosom, brought forth a little chain of blue beads which he held up before her.

The child looked, gasped, then looked again, then with a joyful cry ran to him.

"*Neowage, Neowage!*" she cried.

The big Indian grinned down at her and held her hand.

"How come here?" he asked gently.

Nina burst into tears. "I was captured by the Sioux," she cried. "They made an assault on the house—they got me—and Joe—Joe came after me to rescue me—and he was killed, Neowage, he was *killed!* Red Snake shot him."

Neowage threw up his hands. "Ai-ee, ai-ee! Keel? *Sho* keel? Ai-ee, that too bad. Tell."

Between her heartbroken sobs Nina told of the assault upon the sod house, of her capture, and of Joe's attempted rescue and what followed. When she had finished she clung to Neowage's hand sobbing bitterly.

"Take me home, Neowage," she begged, "oh, *take me home!* They've been good and kind to me here, but oh, I want to go back to Mother Peniman, and Ruth and Sara and Lige and Sam and little Da-da! I want to go back to them and try to comfort them, for if it were not for me dear Joe would not now be gone."

The big Indian stroked the golden hair with his great brown hands and patted and comforted her.

"Me take you home, Nee-ah-nah," he said, "me take you home."

The next morning Nina bade farewell to the squaws and papooses, the boys and girls that had been so kind to her, and mounted upon Kit's back, rode away by the side of Neowage in the direction of the homestead on the Blue River.

It was a soft golden day in early October, and the prairies were yellow with goldenrod and spangled gayly with sunflowers and St. Michaelmas daisies. As they rode the sun cast long shadows on the grass that looked like brown velvet in the distance, and the sky arched over them with a blue that is all Nebraska's own.

They talked little on the way. Neowage seemed to have fallen into a fit of deep musing, and Nina's heart was too sore with grief to feel like attempting conversation.

They rested that night at an Indian camp on the prairies, and started at daylight the next morning. It was almost evening when familiar landmarks began to come in sight, and quite dark when they rode up to the sod house.

The lamps were lighted inside, and creeping up to the windows Nina looked in, with a heart that was like to burst with mingled grief and joy.

The children had gone to bed, and on either side of the table sat Joshua and Hannah Peniman. The Bible was open on the table between them, and Joshua Peniman's head was bent forward on his hands while

Hannah sat with hands folded in her lap, her eyes on the fire, with an expression of heartbreak in their depths that made Nina sob aloud.

Somewhere in that land of broken dreams in which her thoughts were wandering Hannah Peniman heard the sound. She started, looked up, saw the face at the window, and with a sharp, gasping breath sprang to her feet, her hand pressed against her breast.

Nina dashed to the door, threw it open, and sprang into her arms.

"Mother Peniman, Mother Peniman!" she sobbed over and over, unable to speak any other word.

"*Nina*! Nina! My lamb! My child! Where did you come from?"

Joshua Peniman had sprung to his feet and stood staring like a man in a dream.

Before he could speak Mrs. Peniman had loosed Nina's arms from her neck and peered into her face.

"Nina"—she gasped, "Joe—*where is he?*"

Nina buried her head in Mrs. Peniman's bosom. "Oh, Mother Peniman, Mother Peniman," she wailed over and over as if she could not speak the words that must be spoken.

Joshua Peniman came to her, raised her head, and with his haggard eyes gazed into her face.

"What is it, Nina?" he said, with the gentle tone of authority she knew so well in his shaking voice. "Tell us. Anything is better than suspense."

It was some minutes before she could control herself enough to speak. Then, as gently as she could, she told her story. When it was finished there was no sound in the room. Joshua Peniman stood as if turned to stone, while Hannah Peniman's face turned from white to livid grey and looked as if stricken with death.

The sound of the talking had wakened the children, and they now came rushing out into the room; there was a wild shout of joy, which was changed to bitter tears as they heard the news she had brought them.

Suddenly Joshua Peniman raised his head.

"I have not thought to ask how you got here, Nina?" he said, in a voice she would scarcely have recognized. "Surely you did not come alone?"

"No, Neowage brought me."

"*Neowage?* Where is he?"

They found him squatted in the grass outside, with too much delicacy of feeling to obtrude himself upon the family in their grief.

Joshua Peniman grasped his hand in silence, unable to speak. In silence the Indian returned the pressure.

When he had greeted the family with his impassive "How," and had eaten the meal which the weeping Ruth provided for him, he lay down before the fire and gazed thoughtfully into its depths. Hannah Peniman had gone away into the night alone, Ruth had taken Nina away to bed, and Joshua Peniman sat with his arms on the table and his head bowed upon them, a prey to the agony and despair of losing an eldest and best-beloved son.

Suddenly Neowage looked up.

"Nee-ah-nah no *see* him die!"

Mr. Peniman raised his head, and his gentle face was seamed and seared as if a dozen years had gone over it.

"No, but I fear it is as she said. Joe would have been home before this if he was alive."

"Sho no dead!"

Again Neowage relapsed into silence, smoking his pipe and gazing steadily into the fire. Presently he rose, gathered his blanket about him, and shaking his host's hand solemnly strode forth into the night.

For three days the Peniman family mourned Joe as dead.

Mr. Peniman said little, but his hair turned white, almost in a night, and into Hannah Peniman's eyes had come a look of silent, patient suffering that none of the family could look upon without tears.

To Lige and Sam the blow had come with a shock that left them stunned for a while, then overcome with uncontrollable grief. Ruth and Nina clung to one another in a sorrow too sharp and keen for words, and the little ones wept without ceasing for the brother who did not come home.

On the morning of the fourth day the Chapter had been read, the silent prayer was over, and the family set mournfully about the work that had to be done, no matter how heavy the heart.

Going down to the spring for water Lige passed the dugout, and hearing the step outside Kit put her head out and whinnied.

The sound fairly unmanned him.

Kit had always known Joe's step, and had greeted him with that glad little whinny every morning.

"He can't come to you this morning, Kit," he whispered huskily, going to her and putting his arms about her neck, "he can't come to you—or to us—ever again." And leaning against the smooth brown neck he burst into a passion of tears.

To none of the family perhaps, except his mother, had Joe's absence brought more poignant grief. Always together, from their very babyhood, and dependent largely upon one another for companionship, there had grown up between the lads a comradeship so close, an affection so sweet and strong, that life seemed scarcely to be endured apart from one another.

Lige had striven nobly to fill Joe's place, hoping daily, almost hourly, to see him come riding home. But as the days and weeks passed that hope had grown gradually fainter and fainter, until the news that he had just heard was merely a confirmation of the fear that was in his heart.

So deeply was he plunged in grief that when he chanced to glance out and see two riders dashing across the prairies he took no interest in them. He glanced at them idly, then turned away as the blur of hot, bitter tears dimmed his eyes.

Brushing them hastily aside he took up his pail and went on to the spring.

Thus it was that Sam was the first to herald the approach of the strangers.

"Father," he said, in a sad, subdued voice, utterly unlike Sam's usual cheerful bellow, "here come two men on horseback. One of 'em looks like an Indian."

Mr. Peniman rose quickly and went to the door. He had no hope, yet something in the words of Neowage the night before had clung in his memory and said themselves over and over in his brain all night.

"Nee-ah-nah no *see* him die."

No one had seen him die! Perhaps—perhaps God in His infinite mercy—

———

As he stood in the doorway with his hand shading his eyes, his silvery hair glistening in the morning light, there was a strange tumult in his breast.

He shaded his eyes and gazed intently. Presently when the riders had come nearer he saw one of them lean forward and wave his hat about his head.

"*Hannah!*" he called in a queer, choked voice, "Hannah!"

Something in his tone brought her hurrying to the door.

The riders were now galloping madly. One of them, far in advance of the other, leaned forward on his horse's neck, and waved and waved, riding as if the horse could not carry him fast enough.

With a gasping breath Hannah Peniman clutched her husband's hand. Neither spoke. Both ashen pale, silent, tense, they strained forward, their eyes set on the riders galloping toward them.

Suddenly from Hannah Peniman's lips came a hoarse, "Merciful God!"

At the same moment Sam leaped through the door and began racing toward the riders with Paul at his heels, shouting frantically, "Joe, Joe, *Joe!*"

The riders were close now, and the foremost, with tears streaming down his pale cheeks, was lashing the little Indian pony with one hand, while with the other he waved and waved his hat about his head, shouting, "Home, home, home!"

None of them ever knew who reached him first, how or when or where he got off his horse, or how they all got back to the sod house, laughing and crying and clinging to one another, and saying over and over again as if they would never tire, "Joe's home, Joe's alive, *Joe's home again!*"

Down at the spring Lige had heard nothing of the excitement. He had splashed water over his face and eyes to remove the traces of tears, and close by the running water had sat down to get control of himself before he should go back to his mother and the house. As he came slowly up the incline carrying the pail he saw a crowd about the door. For an instant he stood motionless, then dropped his pail and ran swiftly toward the house.

Was it—-could it be—news of—of *Joe?*

When he was nearly to the house one of the children leaping and capering about stepped aside, and he saw a tall, slender boyish figure clasped in his mother's arms. Lige, tall young pioneer that he was, almost fainted. When the world righted itself he gave a hoarse, hysterical shout and dashing forward precipitated himself into Joe's arms.

Perhaps it was his shout of "*Joe*, Joe, Joe!" perhaps the general hubbub, that awoke Nina, who, exhausted by the trials through which she had passed, had been charged to remain in bed.

Startled by the noise she woke in a panic, leaped out of bed and ran to the window. What she saw outside held her there paralyzed, believing that she had lost her senses.

Joe glancing up saw here there, her eyes wide and fixed, her face white as a snowdrop, her head framed in a nimbus of golden hair.

Never while life lasted did he forget the picture.

"*Nina!*" he shouted, joy, amazement, incredulity in his voice.

The girl meanwhile was staring at him as if he were a ghost.

"J—J—*Jo-oe!*" her lips framed the word rather than spoke it. Then again, as if she could not believe the evidence of her senses—"*Joe!*"

Ruth ran to her and caught her in her arms. "Yes, Nina, yes, darling, don't look so scared. It isn't his ghost, it's just *himself*, our own darling, blessed, precious Joesy home again, alive and well, and not dead at all!"

Joe broke from his mother's arms.

"Nina, Nina," he cried stretching his arms toward the window, "oh, Nina, how did you get here? How did you escape? Oh, I've worried and worried and worried about you! Oh, thank God, you got home! I thought that the Sioux or Red Snake had got you again!"

Nina leaned from the window gasping and panting.

"But you, Joe—*you*—I thought you were dead! I saw you fall—I saw you slide into the water—and when I went to look for you you were gone. Oh, Joe, where did you go? I thought you were dead———"

She burst into a fit of hysterical weeping, and Ruth drew her back into the bedroom. A few minutes later, dressed, and a bit more calm, she burst from the door and ran into Joe's waiting arms.

It took a vast amount of talking, of telling and explaining and exclaiming, and tears and chills and thrills, before the whole story was complete, its two parts pieced together and all the events that had caused so much suffering and anxiety made plain.

It was a long time before Joe, with his hand clasped in his father's, his mother's arm about his neck, Ruth and Sara on either knee, Nina at his feet, and Lige and Sam and Paul and David crowded close up to him, had time to remember Pashepaho.

When he did remember him he ran to the door and called him. The handsome young chief was standing outside, his face wreathed in smiles.

Joe called to him joyously.

"Come on in here, Pashepaho," he shouted, "I want you to come in and join in the jamboree, and see all these blessed people I've been talking to you so much about." Then clasping Pashepaho's hand, "Listen, folks, I wouldn't be here now having you all make such a fuss over me if it wasn't for this fellow. If Pashepaho hadn't nursed me and tended me and doctored me like a brother I'd have been a dead one long ago."

You may be sure that Pashepaho received a warm and cordial welcome from the family. When Mr. and Mrs. Peniman shook his hand and thanked him with deep emotion for all he had done for their son tears sprang to his eyes. But when the children gathered about him and pulled the feathers on his dress and tugged at the beads and laid timid fingers upon his tomahawk he smiled, gave Sam his war-bonnet to look at, took little David upon his knee, and was soon happy and at home amongst them.

CHAPTER XX

EAGLE EYE REMEMBERS

When Eagle Eye left the Peniman family, striding away across the plains without a word of gratitude or farewell, Mrs. Peniman and the girls felt grieved and disappointed.

It would have comforted them perhaps if they could have seen his face; if they could have detected the surreptitious glances he threw backward, or if they could have beheld the moisture that blurred his eyes, which he hurriedly wiped away as if ashamed of his weakness.

He was not yet strong, and could not make rapid progress, and as he sat down in the grass now and then to rest his eyes turned ever backward to the homestead, while he turned over and over in his mind the story Joshua Peniman had told him.

Of that story he knew more than the white man suspected.

He was a Sioux, and had seen Red Snake among his people.

When, after many days' travel, he at last reached the Sioux village on the Missouri River, near the mouth of the Niobrara, he went at once to the head chief of the tribe.

"Where Red Snake?" he asked in his own language.

"I know not," answered the chief in the same language, "I have not seen him for many sleeps."

"Red Snake bad man," continued Eagle Eye, and proceeded to tell the chief the story that Joshua Peniman had told him, adding to it much that he had learned about the family while being nursed back to health among them.

When he had finished the tale the old chief looked thoughtful.

"Red Snake has a bad heart to the white brother," he said after a long pause. "He has done much harm to my people. He leads my young men into much trouble. He has brought fire-water among us, he has taught our young men to drink. And when my young men are drunk he takes them on raids on the white people. He make me much trouble with the white man's government. I wish he would come to my teepees no more."

Eagle Eye fervently echoed the wish.

"Where is the boy—the young maiden—he captured?" he continued.

Eagle Eye shook his head. "Gone!" he said laconically.

Both Indians puffed their pipes solemnly for a while. Then Eagle Eye asked the question he had been making ready to ask from the beginning.

"Does the Great Chief know what is Red Snake's name?"

The old chief shook his head slowly.

"I know nothing. One time when the big fire burn the grass of the prairies Black Bear brought a white man to our camps. He was drunk and had been caught in the great fire. He was heap sick, sleep two, three, many days. He gave Black Bear much presents, gun, knife, beads, many things. He gave other young men of my camp presents. At last he gave them firewater, and my young men were pleased. They gave the paleface a place in the lodge of my people. They called him 'Red Snake' because he moved so still and the Great Spirit had given him red hair. After a while he married Wahahnesha. He has been with my people ever since."

"And you never heard the true name of the white man?"

"No. He never told his name."

For some minutes they smoked in silence. Then rising slowly the old chief went to the back of the lodge and returned with a pouch made of deerskin in his hand. From it he drew a small red morocco-covered book, which he held out to Eagle Eye.

"He lose. Me find. Me keep."

Eagle Eye took the book and turned it over and over in his hands. As he turned its pages he could make out a lot of queer-looking marks and signs, which meant nothing to him. After scrutinizing it carefully but uselessly for a while he handed it back to the chief. The chief waved his hand.

"You keep," he said laconically, "give white man some day."

After another silence he burst forth: "He no red snake, he *black* snake. Heap bad man. Some day he make heap trouble for Sioux. Bring white soldier—shoot my young men. Wish he killed—wish he come back to my people no more."

Eagle Eye sat smoking silently for a time, then rose and left the lodge.

He heard the sound of voices, and following it came to a great campfire, about which a number of young men of the tribe were sitting cross-legged on the ground. He greeted, then joined them, listening idly to the talk that went on among them.

He learned after a time that they were talking about a great hunt that was to take place the next day, and that Red Snake, who had been suffering from a wound in the knee and had gone to Bellevue to see a white man's doctor, had returned the day before and was to accompany them. There was much joking about the presents he had brought them and the fire-water that was to be taken with them on the hunt, and which was to enliven their night camps.

"And where is the hunt to be?" asked Eagle Eye, a quick alarming thought running through his head.

"To the Minne-to-wauk-pala. He say heap much antelope, elk, buffalo out that way."

The eyes which had given the young Indian his name blazed hotly. In an instant he saw the plan. He knew as well as if he had heard the details that the drunken degenerate white man was planning to take these young men on a hunting expedition, and when they were crazed with fire-water lead them on a raid on the Peniman homestead, for which, if trouble arose, they would be blamed, and he would escape free, and yet would be enabled to work out his fiendish designs upon the family.

Without a moment's hesitation he resolved to join the hunt.

Long before the sun rose the next morning the young Indians were on their way. Red Snake, attired in his usual fashion, with his face stained red and great warlike emblems of red and blue and yellow painted on his face and breast, led the way.

He was not intoxicated this day, Eagle Eye observed with some interest, and the fire-water was kept carefully secreted until they made their night camp, when a demijohn was passed around and around among them until the Indians were all wild or stupid. He drank nothing. Eagle Eye, while making a great pretense of roisterous drinking, took little, but pretending to be stupefied lay down beside the fire with his blanket over his head and watched and listened until all was still.

The camp had sunk to silence, the whoops and yelps of the drunken Indians had gradually sunk to grunts and snores, when Eagle Eye saw Red Snake creep from his blanket and signal to Black Bear, a wild young buck who had already been in considerable trouble, and draw him away from the camp.

Eagle Eye lay still for a few moments, then rolling over and grunting, as if in a bad dream, edged himself away from the firelight until he reached the shadows beyond, then on hands and knees crept noiselessly through the grass until he was within earshot of Red Snake and Black Bear. They were talking in low, guttural tones, fortunately in the Sioux dialect.

After a jumble of talk, of which he could make nothing, he heard at last the thing for which he had been waiting; Red Snake and Black Bear were planning a raid upon the Peniman homestead, and to Black Bear was confided the details of leading the raid, while Red Snake himself would be free to carry out whatever nefarious designs on the persons or property of the settlers he might have in mind without danger of detection.

Eagle Eye's blood boiled hotly. Not only was his indignation aroused against the renegade by the feeling of gratitude for the white family who had nursed and tended him, but because of his loyalty and devotion to his own people.

He had been one of those who had been betrayed into making the assault upon the Peniman place before, and his life had nearly paid the penalty of his folly. Then, as now, the young Indians had known nothing of his plans, but maddened with fire-water, incited by wild tales of loot and treasure, they had followed him, ignorant of the fact that they were being made the cat's-paw to cover his crimes, and that should detection and punishment follow it was the Sioux who would be blamed and punished by the white man's law, while the white man who was responsible for it would escape, his villainy covered by the blanket and war-paint of an Indian.

All the next day the party hunted, bringing down many elk, deer, and antelope, cheered and enlivened by the prospect of the evening's carousal and the tales of the great herds of buffalo they would overtake the next day.

There was little sleep for any one in the camp that night. When darkness fell the camp-fire was lighted, and the supply of fire-water with which Red Snake had liberally provided himself while he was in Bellevue was sent around. No limit was put upon it, and after a time the prairies rung and the night was made hideous by the yelps and howls and wild orgies of the Indians, who, unaccustomed to the poisonous stuff, were made fairly mad and frantic by it.

When the start was made in the morning they were still drunk. Many of them were like mad men, while others were stupefied and logy, scarcely able to sit their ponies and utterly unfitted for the chase. Whether the tales of Red Snake in regard to the great herds of buffalo between them and the Minne-to-wauk-pala were intended as fiction or not they turned out to be true, and shortly after daylight they spied a vast herd feeding to the north of them, for which the Indians started with wild whoops of delight.

Red Snake followed, cursing. His plan was not working out exactly as he intended.

Riding like maniacs the crazed young warriors soon came close enough to the herd to fire, and a volley of arrows whizzed through the air, stinging and maddening the animals, and while not wounding severely making them ready to fight.

Instead of fleeing in terror, as they did from gunfire, they turned about and made a dash into the ranks of the drunken Indians, who, utterly unprepared for such action, became panic-stricken and many of those who sat their ponies unsteadily were thrown and trampled in the wild stampede that followed, while others fired wildly and recklessly, their arrows stinging and maddening the beasts, which gored and trampled the hunters that fell at their feet.

With wild shouts Eagle Eye urged his pony in among them, trying with all the might that was in him to rescue his friends, who, maddened and stupefied by the deadly effects of the liquor they had drunk the night before, were unable to help themselves.

As he stood with his bow curved, his arrow poised for flight, his eye chanced to fall upon Red Snake, the baleful and malign influence that had brought this and other troubles upon his people. Eagle Eye was a hereditary chief, and loved his people with the love of a father. Suddenly as he gazed upon the renegade white man a fierce anger burned in his breast. He saw red. His blood surged madly through his veins. And changing the aim of his arrow with the quickness of lightning he bent his bow strongly and let it fly, carrying his vengeance with it.

He saw Red Snake throw up his hands, heard above the uproar his yell of rage and pain, and saw him fall and the buffaloes charge on and over him, galloping away over the plains.

When they had gone the survivors of the disaster, sobered by their peril, drew close together and looked about them. On the ground were strewn the carcasses of a number of buffaloes, and among them, mangled and crushed out of all human semblance, were many of the young Indians who had set out that morning so recklessly.

Black Bear, who remained unhurt, went among them turning over those that lay face downward, lifting those that were alive, passing by those that were dead with a grunt. Suddenly he uttered an exclamation and stooped over a prostrate figure. Eagle Eye moved nearer. As Black Bear lifted the trampled and mangled form he saw that it was Red Snake.

"Is he dead?" he asked in his own language.

Black Bear put his ear to the chest of the wounded man.

"No, he is breathing," he answered in the same language.

"Then put him on your horse and take him home," thundered Eagle Eye. "He is your friend. You brought him among us to bring death and trouble and disgrace to your own people. Now look out for him. And you"—he pointed his finger in the face of Black Bear with a look that made him cringe, "go to the chief when you get there. I know what you were going to do. I heard your plan. The chief will settle with you for it."

Without a word the Indian stooped and picking up the body of Red Snake threw it across his horse, mounted behind it, and rode away. Eagle Eye stayed behind to bury the dead, look after the wounded, and see that the Indians who were too drunken to take care of themselves were mounted and started back toward their village.

When he arrived Black Bear was there.

"Does Red Snake still live?" he asked.

"He still lives," replied Black Bear.

"So much the worse for you," Eagle Eye told him, and driving Black Bear before him went straight to the lodge of the chief, where he told him the whole story.

When it was finished the old man turned to Black Bear.

"Have you no love for your people," he asked, "that you are willing to lead them to death and destruction? Well are you named 'Black Bear,' who sees not the danger when his nose is tickled by the honey-pots of strangers. You would have betrayed your people. You would have led your own kindred into the snare laid for you by the white man who has a bad heart toward Indians. You have caused the death of our young men. You are not worthy to live in the lodge of your people. Go; from this day forth you are no longer one of us. We cast you out. Now go!"

He slunk away, and at the same moment a young squaw entered the lodge of the chief in search of Eagle Eye.

"You speak the tongue of the white man," she said. "Come!"

Leading him to a teepee not far away she pushed aside the skin that hung over the door. He entered and saw Red Snake lying on a pile of skins and blankets in a corner, crushed and bleeding, the seal of approaching death upon his face.

As Eagle Eye approached him he opened his eyes.

"You die," said the Indian, looking down upon him sternly, his arms folded across his breast.

Red Snake looked up, the dew of death upon his forehead.

"Yes," he sneered. "It's all over. The game's up—and I'm glad of it."

"Who are you? What you name?" asked Eagle Eye.

"No matter who I am. I've sacrificed all claim to the name I was born with. I'll die as I have lived, as 'Red Snake,' a squaw-man, a renegade, a drunkard, an all-around bad egg."

As the words left his lips a shudder ran through his body, his eyes flew wide, and he clutched wildly at his breast; then with a gasping breath fell backward, the blood gushing from his lips.

Eagle Eye bent over him. The Indian head-dress had been lost or cast aside and his thick mane of red hair fell loose about his face. Beneath the buckskin shirt which he had thrust aside in his agony his skin was smooth and white, and, as if in immutable justice for the deed that he had done, a feathered arrow protruded from his breast.

The Indian stood looking down at the dead body for a moment, then spurned it with his foot.

He turned presently and cast his keen eyes about the wigwam. With a step as soft as that of a panther he skirted its walls, and from under a heap of hides, blankets and rubbish in a corner drew forth a battered tin box.

For a moment he stood holding it in his hands and gazing at it curiously. Then he tucked it under his arm under his blanket, and with a backward glance at the body and a muttered "Ugh!" lifted the flap and passed out into the night.

CHAPTER XXI

THE BLIZZARD

With the coming of November, bitter winds and cold rains began to beat across the prairies, and the thoughts of the pioneers were turned with deep concern toward providing for the winter.

On an expedition up the river one day Joe and Lige came upon a quantity of wild grapes and plums, and directly after the first frost the whole family made a day's excursion to the place and returned laden with bushels of fruit, a most precious commodity on the prairies, where other fruits were not to be had. Mrs. Peniman set to work the next day and made it up into jelly, jam, and preserves, which constituted a most welcome addition to their meals throughout the winter.

The pressing work at hand kept the whole family busy from daylight until dark, and December was upon them before they were aware.

Early in the month there came a break in the bad weather, followed by a series of mild, warm days.

Joshua Peniman, who had been carefully going through his stores and feeling some uneasiness in regard to the condition of their winter supplies, hailed this weather with joy, and determined to take advantage of it to make a trip to Omaha, then the nearest point at which they could obtain the needed commodities.

When Mrs. Peniman was told of the project she looked much troubled. "It has to be done, Hannah," he said, answering her look. "When the winter storms set in we are liable to be blockaded here for months, and we must be provided with sufficient supplies for our needs. Besides," he added with a smile, "you know Christmas is coming. Santa Claus must not fail to visit us this year—even if we are away out on the prairies."

"Dear man," she replied, patting his arm, "thee never fails to think of everything, does thee? Of course Santa Claus must come this year. But it chills my heart to think of thee crossing those dreadful prairies. Of course Joe must go with thee——"

"No, Joe and Lige must stay here to guard you and the little ones. But I will take Sam. He is a bright boy, and will be great help and company for me. Come now, let us make out our lists, for I would like to start this morning while the weather is bright and clear."

Before ten o'clock he was on his way, a long list of necessities in his pocket and Sam by his side, driving Jim and Charley, now sleek and fat and in fine condition from grazing on the rich grass of the prairies.

Joe and Lige were somewhat disappointed when they learned that they were to be left behind, but when their father told them that he was leaving them to take his place and act as the head of the house during his absence the pride they felt in the trust he reposed in them almost made up for the disappointment.

Sam, however, was jubilant. The prospect of the trip across the prairies with his father, of again seeing a town, thrilled him, and he chattered away gleefully as tucked cozily under the buffalo robes (made from the hides of the animals Joe and Lige had killed in a great buffalo hunt they had gone upon with Pashepaho), as they clattered away over the prairies.

The first night they put up at Lancaster, the little settlement on Salt Creek at which they had stopped on their way out, and the third day reached Omaha, after a rather wearisome and uneventful journey.

They put up at the American House, and his father gave him three dollars, and suggested that he might like to buy some things to bring to the folks at home, and also to purchase some Christmas presents for the family.

This was the first time that the thought of Christmas had come to him, and it brought with it something of a shock.

Christmas!

This would be a queer Christmas, away out there on the plains all by themselves!

He thought of the Christmases at home, of the comfortable old house wreathed with greens and holly, of the great Christmas tree in the parlor, the Christmas dinner, the stacks of presents, and the jolly crowd of aunts and uncles and grandmother and cousins and other relatives gathered about the board.

A wave of homesickness went over him, then the exciting thought of three whole dollars to spend took possession of him and he forgot his homesick feelings in planning what he should buy.

When his father set forth in the morning to make his purchases Sam, with his three dollars locked firmly in his hand, ran from store to store.

He bought candy and peanuts and apples and popcorn, a lace scarf for his mother, ties for Joe and Lige, ribbons for Nina, Ruth and Sara, a top for Paul, a doll for Mary, and a hobby-horse and a large candy cane for little David.

The candy cane took his last penny, and, in fact, he was obliged, greatly to his embarrassment, to change his order from a larger to a smaller candy cane, because the one he had selected cost three cents more than he possessed.

Well satisfied with his purchases he returned to the American House, where he found his father with the wagon loaded waiting for him, a fine new heating-stove for the living-room standing up grandly behind the seat.

"Jump in, son," he said quickly, "I have been waiting for thee. I want to get on the way. I'm afraid from the looks of the sky we are going to have a change in the weather."

They drove fast, and reached Lancaster by about six o'clock in the evening, by which time it had grown much colder. They awoke the next morning to find a grey sky and a high northwest wind blowing.

His father had bought an ear-cap and a pair of warm mittens for him in Omaha, and these he was glad to put on, and he noticed when he took his place in the wagon that hot bricks had been tucked away in the bottom under the buffalo robes.

As they drove he noticed that his father was unusually quiet and kept casting glances at the sky. He urged the team forward as fast as they could go, even using the whip, a thing he would never do except in extremities.

By ten o'clock the wind had risen and scattering snowflakes had begun to fall. By noon the sky had changed to a deeper grey and the wind had increased to a biting gale.

It was shortly after one o'clock, and they were clattering fast across the prairies, when a sudden blackness, almost as of night, seemed to fall upon them. For a moment the wind died down and a hush fell over all the earth that was like the hush of death. All about them over the vast, lonesome prairies came a tense, ominous silence, as if all nature were holding its breath. Then, with a whoop and a shriek that was like all the demons of the Inferno let loose, the blizzard was down upon them.

Its onslaught was so fierce and sudden that it staggered the horses and almost upset the wagon. The snow that came on the breath of the terrific gale did not fall in flakes, but in solid whirling *sheets*, which blinded, smothered, and utterly bewildered them. It stopped their breath, it stung their eyes, it slashed and beat in their faces like the beating of nettles.

All about them was a blackness almost like that of midnight, and the eddying wall of swirling, blinding snow, driven by a ninety-mile gale, caught them in its embrace, drove the breath from their lungs, froze on their mouths and nostrils, and buffeted them with a fury that almost left them senseless.

The horses, covered with snow almost as solidly as if it had been spread over them with a trowel, stood with drooped tails and heads, dazed and shivering, not knowing which way to go.

Through the demoniac shrieking of the wind Sam heard his father's voice.

"Get down in the bottom of the wagon under the robes," Joshua Peniman shouted, and tried to urge the terrified horses forward against the blast.

He knew that he dared not let them stop now. He knew that come what would he must keep them going as long as they could stand. He could not see a step before him. All about them was a maze, a stinging, dazzling, whirling wall of white, that blown on the breath of the fierce northwest wind pelted and buffeted the very breath from his body.

In a shorter time than would have been believed possible the prairies were covered with snow, all traces of the wagon-trail blotted out, and no indication anywhere which way to go.

The horses seemed utterly bewildered. Finding it impossible to keep them headed against the blast, and fearing that if they once swerved from the direction in which they had been traveling that he would lose his sense of direction and become lost on the prairies, he leaped out of the wagon, and grasping the terrified team by the bits led them forward, resolutely keeping his face toward the west. He knew that the wind was blowing from the northwest. If he kept it on his right cheek he knew that he was keeping in the right direction.

The breath of the horses froze on their mouths and noses, and walking beside them he had to continually wipe it away so that they could breathe. Stumbling along, now protecting his own face and ears, now the faces of the horses, he prayed continually for guidance and help.

Down in the bottom of the wagon against the hot bricks and under the buffalo robes Sam gradually recovered his breath and began getting warm. But fear and anxiety for his father made it impossible for him to keep still.

He wiggled out of the robes and suddenly appeared at his father's elbow.

"You get in and get warm now, Father," he shouted above the shrieking of the blizzard. "I'm warm now; let me walk by the team."

The temperature had fallen to thirty degrees below zero by this time, and warning prickings of his face, ears and feet told Joshua Peniman that he must take every precaution against freezing.

"Can you stand it for a few minutes?" he yelled, with his mouth close to Sam's ear. "I'm afraid my feet are freezing. I'll get on some more clothes and warm up a little, then I'll take them again. Keep the wind on your right cheek all the time. The horses don't seem to know which way to go."

Sam took the bits and his father climbed into the wagon. He rubbed his face and ears with snow, took off his boots and rubbed his feet, then warmed them against the hot bricks, put on his boots and wrapped his feet in pieces torn from the blanket. With another strip of the blanket he wrapped his head about, leaving only his eyes exposed. He knew that the one hope of their getting through this storm alive was for him to keep from freezing and able to direct their movements. When he had protected himself as well as he was able he again sprang to the heads of the floundering horses and sent Sam back into the wagon to rest and get warm.

In this way they kept their blood circulating, and relieved one another. He thanked his precaution of bringing the hot bricks many times. Under the buffalo robes in the straw in the bottom of the wagon they could escape the fury of the freezing gale, and by taking refuge there at short intervals they were able to keep from freezing.

Every moment the blizzard seemed to increase. They could scarcely see the struggling horses from the wagon now, and the snow, drifting on the biting wind, was growing deeper and deeper all about them.

Sam, protected like his father with strips of the blanket tied around his feet and wound about his head up to his eyes, was struggling at the horses' heads when suddenly the wagon gave a lurch, tilted perilously, then stopped.

The horses, up to their middles in snow, plunged and struggled, and Joshua Peniman leaped out, looked, and uttered a deep groan. One of the front wheels was broken at the hub.

For a single terrible moment the father and son stood gazing at the damage, and hope almost vanished from their breasts. Then Joshua Peniman set to work to liberate the plunging horses.

"We'll have to leave it," he shouted, struggling with his half-frozen fingers at the traces. "We'll have to trust to the horses."

"But our wagon—the supplies—our Christmas presents——" Sam shouted back, trying to raise his voice above the howling and shrieking of the storm.

"Can't think of them now," gasped Joshua Peniman; "we'll be lucky if we save ourselves!" And having got poor Charley loose from the disabled wagon he lifted Sam up on his back, and wrapped him about with blankets and one of the buffalo robes. Then taking the other robe from the wagon he mounted Jim, and wrapping himself up as best he could led the way straight into the teeth of the roaring, stinging vortex, that hissed and shrieked like ten thousand demons about their heads.

"Keep close!" he shouted to the boy, "keep Charley's head right up against Jim's tail! Don't lag, don't get out of my tracks or we're lost!"

The drifts were now up to the bellies of the horses, and growing deeper every moment. The wind had increased to a degree against which they could scarcely stand, and the snow came down in such solid sheets of blinding, dazzling white that they could not see a foot before them, could not keep their eyes open against its pelting fury, might almost as well have been stone blind, as they beat their way, struggling, stumbling, floundering, against the storm.

After a few moments of frantic struggling the horses stood still, shaking and trembling, instinct urging them to turn tail to the storm, yet kept facing its cruel onslaught by the firm hand upon the reins. Again and again one or the other of them stumbled and fell, and each time they got to their feet with greater difficulty.

Joshua Peniman had given up trying to ride, and was again walking at their heads, urging them on, patting, encouraging, helping them all he could. He knew that none of them could last long. He knew that the horses must soon fall and perish, and that no human creature could hold out long against the cold that seemed to grow more intense with every passing hour.

With all the strength, all the faith that was in him he prayed for help.

CHAPTER XXII

TO THE RESCUE

In the sod house on the prairies meanwhile there was fearful suspense and anxiety.

From the moment of the departure of her husband and son Hannah Peniman had watched the weather with an anxious eye. When the wind rose and the snow began to fall fear took hold upon her. With eyes scanning the horizon she went from door to window and window to door, hoping every moment to see the wagon approaching over the prairie.

But the hours passed on and they did not come. As the temperature fell and the wind rose her fears increased; and when the pall of darkness fell, and with a whoop and shriek and roar that she could never forget the blizzard swept down upon them, her heart almost died in her breast.

"A blizzard, a *blizzard!*" she moaned. "Oh, God, help them; God have mercy on them out there on those plains in this storm!"

The children, terrified at the blackness, almost like that of night, that had fallen over the prairies, and at the shrieking and howling of the wind, gathered close about her. She concealed her own fears to comfort them.

At the first approach of the storm the boys had put the cow and horses in the dugout and closed the doors. At five o'clock when they started out to feed them the door of the dugout was drifted half-way up to its top with snow, and the wind was so terrific and the whirl of the wall of snow so blinding and bewildering that they were unable to make their way from the house to the dugout.

Lige, who had started out ahead of Joe, became lost almost before he had left the shelter of the house, and were Joe not close behind him he might have wandered away and perished on the plains.

Battling their way back to the house, holding to one another, they sought the shelter of the kitchen, beaten, breathless, even in those few moments almost frozen. When they made another attempt to get to the dugout they were obliged to tie a rope to the handle of the door and clinging to it grope their way to the dugout, where they made the line fast, and when they had fed and attended to the stock were able to guide themselves by it back to the house.

As the hours passed on and the travelers did not return the anxiety of the family became almost unbearable. At last Joe drew his mother aside. "I can't stay still any longer, Mother," he said. "It is getting dark. Father and Sam ought to have been here long ago; they must have lost their way in this blizzard. Let Lige and me go out to meet them."

Hannah Peniman turned her white face upon him.

"What good would that do?" she asked. "You could not find them— perhaps you too would get lost—perhaps none of you would ever come home. Oh, God, have I not given enough, enough!"

Joe took her hands. "But, Mother," he said firmly, "we can't stay here and let Father and Sam perish in this storm without trying to save them! Lige and I are strong—we can take ropes—we'll tie ourselves to the house so we can always get back. We must go, Mother! They must have got nearly home before the blizzard struck them. They may be out there—not far away—lost and fighting their way through this storm——"

Hannah Peniman cried out and covered her face with her hands. A moment later she turned to the boy and said quickly, "Yes, you must go. It is thy duty—I would not keep thee from it. Go—go quickly! Thy father may be needing thee!"

It was bitterly hard for Hannah Peniman to send her two oldest boys—all that she and the little ones had to depend upon now—out into the howling blizzard. As she gazed out into the whirling, blinding, shrieking tempest it seemed to her almost like giving them up to inevitable destruction. But her husband, another child, were out there somewhere on those prairies in the blizzard. It was the duty of these boys to go to their rescue. All her life Duty had been her guide. So with prayers upon her lips and in her heart she wrapped them up and let them go, fighting their way into the storm inch by inch, unwinding as they went a great coil of rope that had been provided for a well-rope, but which, fortunately, had not been put in use.

As the two lads emerged from the shelter of the sod house the storm caught them in its icy embrace and almost drove the breath from their bodies. They had the wind to their backs, so fortunately were not obliged to head their way into it, but the cold was so intense that it froze the breath in their nostrils, the lashes of their eyes, and the wind so fierce that it fairly lifted them off their feet, causing them to stagger and stumble in the great drifts of snow.

They were warmly clad and well protected, but they had not gone many yards from the house when they began to realize how slight were the chances that their father and brother, caught out upon the prairies in this storm, could ever reach home. In twenty minutes their feet were like chunks of lead, their hands numb and aching, their faces, in the small space left exposed, tingling and freezing. Their breath was gone, their limbs numb and lifeless, and an exhaustion so great upon them that they were scarcely able to forge ahead and keep firm hold upon the rope.

As they stumbled and staggered forward, Joe, far in advance of his brother, stopped abruptly, while a muffled cry came from his numb lips. Spotty, whom they had taken with them, gave vent to a sharp, yelping bark and leaped forward in the snow. Under a drift, with something black protruding from its edges, lay a humped-up form.

Joe sprang to it with an agonized cry.

He bent and with his hands began to scrape away the snow, while Spotty, whimpering loudly, aided him by digging at the drift with his sharp claws. A body, lying face downward, was soon uncovered. Joe turned it over quickly, then gave a choked, quivering sob of relief. The body was that of an Indian.

Lige, fighting his way through the drifts with head bent almost to his knees, heard Spotty's whining bark and stopped.

"What's the matter?" he called out. Then seeing the body, "My Lord, *what is that?*"

"It's an Indian." Joe rose from his inspection shaking and trembling in every limb. "It scared me almost to death. I—I thought at first it might be—be—Father—or Sam."

"Who is it? Anybody we know?" Lige shouted above the howling of the blizzard.

"No, never saw him before. Poor fellow, I suppose he lost his way in the storm."

"I don't wonder," panted Lige; "I never saw such a storm. Lord, I wish we knew where Father and Sam were! They can't live long in a storm like this."

As they started forward there was a new fear, a new horror in their hearts. The sight of the Indian, young, strong, inured to the hardships of the plains, yet stark and dead in the drift, brought to them a hideous picture of what at that very moment might be happening to their father, older and not so agile and strong—and to Sam—their chum, playmate and brother—little more than a child!

Lige had not approached the Indian, but with a shuddering glance had pushed on. As Joe started forward his foot struck something imbedded in the snow. At another time he would have stopped to see what it was, but all his thoughts, all his fears were with his father out there in that whirling, blinding, shrieking blizzard, and his one thought to reach him if that was possible.

At the metallic click Lige turned and looked back.

"What was that?" he asked.

"I dunno, a tin can, I guess," answered Joe, and could not guess as he plunged forward through the blizzard that the solution of the mystery about which he had puzzled so much lay close at his feet.

When the two boys reached the utmost length of their rope they stood still, not knowing what to do next. They knew to abandon it and go forward would probably mean death, that they would soon become lost in the tempest, in which they could tell neither location nor direction, and probably perish in the storm.

They stood side by side, holding on to the rope and one another, their backs to the wind, gasping, panting, exhausted, half-frozen from the stinging blast that beat about them, half blinded by the snow that was almost waist-deep where they stood, and which covered them from head to foot while they stood still.

Spotty, crouched up close against them, whined and looked up in their faces as if trying to ask why they should be out in that storm.

"Do you suppose we'd have any chance of finding them out there, Joe?" Lige asked between chattering teeth.

"Not much," Joe answered huskily. "I don't believe anybody could live long in this."

"I wonder if we shouted——"

"They'd never hear us through this blizzard."

"Let's try it anyhow. The wind is blowing that way. They might hear—and if they were lost——"

Presently the two young voices were joined in a shout as loud as they could force from their aching chests. Spotty hearing it seemed to get some inkling that there was trouble and set up a loud barking. He ran round and round them in circles, nosing in the snow, and when Joe pointed off ahead into the reeling wall of the blizzard and cried "Go get Sam, Spotty, go get Father!" he looked up in his face, whined, barked, ran forward into the snow, then back to leap and bark about them.

Again and again they shouted, calling upon their father's name, upon Sam's, with all the strength that was in them.

After each shout they listened, straining their ears for a reply. But all that came to them was the wild roaring of the blizzard, the shrieking of the wind as it whipped up the snow and tossed it in blinding clouds over the plains.

For long they stood, the cold eating into their very vitals.

At last Lige spoke. "I can't stand it any longer, Joe, I'm freezing to death. Let's go on. They can't be very far——"

"If we ever get away from the rope we'll never get back home," answered Joe. "And you know we've got to think of Mother and the girls. If Father never comes back——"

His voice faltered and stopped.

"We'll have to go back then," gasped Lige; "we can't stand here any longer. We'll both freeze to death."

They stood, the two young, strained faces turned toward the cruel storm, their eyes trying to penetrate the reeling, swirling wall of white that eddied and whirled about them.

At this moment, when all hope was dead in their hearts, when they had both abandoned the last expectation of ever seeing their father and brother alive again, there came to their ears a far, faint cry.

They clutched each other.

"What was that?" whispered Lige, trembling like an aspen leaf.

Joe's only answer was to draw in his breath and send forth a shout so strong, so thrilling with the hope that awoke in his breast that even the tempest seemed to heed it. For a second the wind seemed to ease, and in that second they both called and shouted at the top of their lungs again and again.

Spotty too had heard the call. He seemed to know now what the trouble was, and what was expected of him. Barking loudly he plunged forward through the drifts, constantly looking back and stopping to bark and whine, as if begging the boys to follow him.

Only for a moment was he visible, then the storm closed about him and he passed out of their sight.

Presently the call came again.

"It's them—it's Father—it's Sam!" the boys shouted in chorus.

"It's them, it's them! They're alive! They're out there somewhere. Oh, Joe, let's go after them!" panted Lige.

For a moment Joe hesitated. All his heart was urging him to rush on into the blinding tempest toward the point from whence the faint calls came. But the judgment with which nature had gifted him, that judgment that was to mean so much to so many people in his after life, restrained him.

"No, we'd better stay here," he answered. "If we get away from the rope we might get lost ourselves, and make things worse. We'll do them more good by staying right here and shouting to them so we will guide them to us. I believe by the sound they're coming nearer. Listen!"

Again they sent forth a great shout.

For a moment there was no sound other than the roaring of the blizzard, then more distinctly than before came the answer.

"There!" shouted Joe, "it is nearer! They are coming this way. Listen! That's Spotty barking! I believe he sees them! All we've got to do now is to keep shouting."

With hope renewed they redoubled their shouts and yells. Nearer, and yet nearer came the answer, and at last, staggering out of the wall of white they could make out two huge shapeless bulks, which as they came nearer gradually developed into two floundering, staggering horses, with heads down and nostrils clogged and caked with ice and snow, and on their backs two shapeless creatures, which they at last saw, with a joy too great for expression, were their father and Sam, wrapped up in the buffalo robes and blankets.

Behind them, before them, around and about them leaped Spotty, barking and leaping upon them as if he could not express his joy. He it was who had reached them in their bewilderment and guided them back to the rope. They were hopelessly lost, had neither sense of location nor direction left, and had been wandering about for hours in circles when they heard, faint and far away, the sound of shouts. They answered, with all the strength that was left in them, but even then so paralyzed and bewildered had they become by cold and exhaustion that they should never have been able to follow it, but that Spotty came bursting through the storm like a guiding angel and barking and leaping about them had guided them on.

With the blizzard at its height the worn and weakened party would never have reached home but for the rope that anchored them to safety. Holding tight to it and leading the way Joe and Lige beat their way forward leading the almost dying horses, whose knees were fairly giving way beneath them from exhaustion, while the man and boy upon their backs were almost insensible from numbness and cold.

It seemed an endless fight against the tempest, but the rope held, and step by step they fought their way back by its aid, until suddenly out of the impalpable shroud that wrapped them in its icy embrace they fairly bunted into the walls of the dugout.

"*The dugout!*" gasped Joe, "thank God, oh, thank God! I began to fear we would none of us live to get home!"

Seizing Jim's bridle he led him up to the wall and lifted his father down in his strong young arms. Lige was already lifting Sam from Charley's back, so weak, so numb and exhausted that he could neither move nor speak.

As Joe was staggering toward the house with his father in his arms the door was burst open and Mrs. Peniman rushed out into the storm.

"Thank God, thank God!" she sobbed over and over, as together they lifted the wayfarers into the house, rubbed snow on their frozen faces and ears, got them into hot blankets, poured hot drinks and nourishment into them, and worked over them until life began to revive. Then they got them into bed with hot irons about them, and with a gratitude and thankfulness too great for words saw them gradually fall into a natural and healthy sleep.

Sam had a badly frozen ear, two frost-bitten toes, and a frosted finger, and Mr. Peniman's left foot was so badly frozen that it was many weeks before he could walk again. But these injuries were as nothing compared to the fact that they had come out of the most terrible blizzard ever known in the territory alive, and the thought that the lost was found, the dear ones given up as dead restored to life again, was joy enough to overbalance any amount of pain.

CHAPTER XXIII

CHRISTMAS ON THE PRAIRIES

The blizzard which so nearly cost Joshua Peniman and Sam their lives raged unabated for three days. When it was over the prairies lay a vast wilderness of unbroken white from horizon to horizon, the snow lying five feet deep on the level.

For several days Mr. Peniman was compelled to remain in bed, completely prostrated by the experience he had been through. But Sam, though somewhat frost-bitten in places, awoke the next morning as well as ever, and greatly exalted by the sense of being a hero.

The blizzard was followed by a spell of bitterly cold weather, the thermometer going down to thirty-six below. While the family all felt great anxiety about the abandoned wagon and its precious contents it was impossible to go after it until the weather moderated. In the meantime they employed the hours of the long cold days by making runners, one pair of which they affixed to Joe's wagon, carrying the other pair with them when a day at last came when the weather had so far moderated that they dared face it without danger of freezing.

They set out with all six horses, Jim and Charley drawing the wagon on runners, in which Mr. Peniman, Joe, Sam, and Lige rode, Joe leading his own team and Lige the Carroll horses, which had been rechristened Major and Nellie.

There was a hard, solid crust over the deep drifts, that carried them safely, and the sun sparkled like diamonds over the vast unbroken expanse of spotless white. On their way they saw three grey wolves and ten elk, which came within two hundred yards of them, driven to forget fear by hunger.

As the improvised sledge glided smoothly over the snow the thoughts of the whole party were busy with the dangers and terrors of the blizzard.

"It was just about here that we found that poor old Indian, Lige," said Joe, scanning the snow-covered prairies about them.

"Yes; I don't see any sign of him now though," replied Lige.

"What Indian?" asked Mr. Peniman.

"When we were coming out to meet you we came upon the body of an Indian, dead and half-covered by snow," answered Joe. "I thought after

- 165 -

we'd got you safe home we'd come back and bury him; but I guess the snow has done that better than we could, poor fellow!"

"Did you know him?"

"No, I never saw him before."

"Did you see any signs of any other Indians about?"

"No, he seemed to be all alone. And the funny thing to me was that we didn't see any signs of his pony. It seemed queer that an Indian should be way off here alone, on foot."

"If you'd looked far enough you would probably have found his pony in some draw or ravine. The poor fellow probably got lost in the blizzard, and feeling himself freezing to death deserted his horse in a drift somewhere, perhaps, and was making for some place of shelter when cold and exhaustion overcame him."

"Golly, it sure gave us a shock when we found him," broke in Lige; "I didn't see him, but Joe thought at first it was you or Sam."

"Thank God it was not," said Joshua Peniman fervently. "I know what the poor fellow must have suffered. I thought at one time his fate would surely be ours."

They found the wagon exactly where they had left it, completely covered over by a drift, its contents undisturbed, and practically uninjured by the storm.

When it was unloaded they removed the wheels and affixed to the bottom the extra pair of runners. They then replaced the contents, harnessed Kit, Billy, and black Major to it, while Jim, Charley, and Nellie were put to the other wagon. It was well for them that they had six powerful horses to pull the load, for weighted as the wagons now were they continually broke through the crust, and the journey back to the homestead required constant use of picks and shovels, and all the strength, initiative, and energy of both drivers and horses.

They reached home at last, and as soon as they had warmed, eaten, and rested a little immediately set to work to install the new heating-stove.

That night the family did not shiver about the stove in the kitchen, but clustered about in the warm glow of the new heater, cozy and comfortable, and thankful from the bottoms of their hearts, they enjoyed with the relish of appetites long denied the candy and popcorn and peanuts that Sam had brought to them.

That winter—the winter of 1856-7—will long be remembered on the prairies. From December until March storm followed storm, blizzard followed blizzard, the time between filled in with the coldest weather ever known in the west.

The young Penimans, who had run as free as wild antelopes over the plains ever since their arrival, were now compelled to stay in the house, which, small and circumscribed as it was, was sometimes almost too small to hold them.

One morning when the snow drove against the windows and a bitter wind howled across the prairies Mrs. Peniman looked across the breakfast table at her husband with a smile.

"Father," she said, "does thee not think that the time has come for us to begin our school?"

"I certainly do, my dear," replied Joshua Peniman. "I was thinking of suggesting it this morning. The children have been out of school too long now, but with all the work we had to do to make living conditions possible for the winter we have not had time to get our school started before. But now is the time to do it. They cannot be outdoors, there is little work about the place that can be done in this weather, and it will occupy their time and attention."

"But we haven't any school to go to, Father," cried Ruth, "nor any books or teachers!"

Mrs. Peniman laughed. "Just wait and see," she said. "Your school is going to be right here, and Father and I will be the teachers. Didn't you know that Father used to be a teacher in the Friends' School at home? And the books are right in the trunk over there."

"I don't want to go to school," grumbled Sam, "I want to play outdoors."

"I do," cried Joe. "I want to study. Can you teach us history and language and algebra, Father?"

Mr. Peniman smiled. "I have taught older and wiser boys than you, Joe, and I think I can teach you any branches that you will need to take up now."

"All right then, I'm all for it," declared Lige; "let's get our school started this morning."

It was quite a game after all, and they all entered gaily into the spirit of it, everybody helping to push the furniture about and arrange boxes and tables and chairs for the "school."

Mrs. Peniman took Sara, Paul, Mary, and David into the rear part of the sod house and drew the curtains between, and Mr. Peniman got out the school-books they had brought with them from Ohio and set Joe, Lige, Sam, Nina, and Ruth at work.

The program was so arranged that while some of the more advanced pupils, as Joe and Lige, were studying, the less advanced, as Sam and Ruth, were reciting. As Sam and Ruth had always kept pretty well together in their classes they were a great help to one another, but Nina was a problem. While far in advance of Sam and Ruth in English, geography, reading, and spelling, she was hopelessly behind them in grammar and mathematics. Indeed her whole curriculum of studies had been so superficially and sketchily acquired that Mr. Peniman scarcely knew what to do with her.

"I think I'll have to put you up a grade, Nina," he told her jokingly. "You are far and away beyond Ruth and Sam, yet I hardly think that on account of your arithmetic you could keep up with Lige and Joe."

"Oh, please do put me up with Lige and Joe, Father Peniman," begged Nina; "I have never really studied in my life, but I believe that I could keep up if I studied with Joe."

At first she made sad work of her lessons. Her work was brilliant but superficial, and Mr. Peniman, who insisted on thoroughness, was completely discouraged with her. On one occasion when she had signally failed in a recitation and had retired to her seat in tears Joe came to her side to comfort her.

"You don't know how to study, that's what's the matter with you, Princess," he told her. "Let me help you. We'll get our lessons together this evening."

Nina smiled up at him through her tears. "Oh, thank you, thank you, Joesy," she whispered. "I know I don't know how to study. I never really went to school, I always had governesses and tutors and never had to. But I can learn—I know I can—if you will teach me." And after that Joe and Nina always studied together, Joe's thorough, methodical mind acting as a balance as well as an incentive to the more brilliant but less logical mind of Nina.

Mrs. Peniman meanwhile with her little flock gathered about her knees had various and sundry milestones on the road of knowledge to start from. While Paul read and spelled well, wrote a fine large hand and had been initiated into the mysteries of addition, subtraction, multiplication, and division, Sara was only staggering through simple addition, stumbled sadly in reading, and was still scrawling huge hieroglyphics that only by the greatest courtesy could be called writing, Mary knew her letters and was in the c-a-t, cat, and r-a-t, rat, stage of development, and little David was still at sea in an ocean of letters, from which he could pick out a round O or a crooked S on occasion.

It was not easy teaching, but the parents had given up their home and friends and all the comforts of life to obtain for these young people greater and better opportunities, and were not to be balked by small difficulties. Day after day while the snow fell and the wind howled across the prairies the little school went on, and soon began to grow accustomed to the conditions, and the pupils to make rapid strides.

They rose early, and while Mr. Peniman and the older boys went outside to do the necessary work, Mrs. Peniman with Ruth, Nina, and Mary got the breakfast, washed up the dishes, made the beds, put the house in order, and arranged the two rooms for the "school" by nine o'clock, when the father and boys came in to begin the morning session.

At noon Mrs. Peniman dismissed her little pupils, with orders to play quietly and not disturb the students in the front part of the house, while she prepared dinner. At twelve-thirty Mr. Peniman closed the morning session, and they all ran out for a tussle with the wind or a frolic in the snow before dinner. When the meal had been eaten and cleared away the afternoon session was begun, and until four o'clock the little sod house was a very hive of activity, after which time they were all free, and while Mr. Peniman and the boys went out to do the evening chores and other outside work the younger children romped about until supper time, soon after which they all went to bed.

On the morning of December 24th Mr. Peniman announced at the breakfast table that they were to have a half holiday.

"As this is the day before Christmas," he continued, "I think we will have to go out and see if we can't find some mistletoe and greens of some kind, and a tree that might serve for a Christmas tree."

"*A Christmas tree?*" the children all shouted in a breath. "Are we going to have a *Christmas tree?*"

"Why, of course," smiled Mrs. Peniman. "Santa Claus has never failed to visit us yet, has he, Ruthie? And I don't believe he'll forget us this year, even if we are away off out here on the prairies."

Nina looked up with beaming eyes. "Oh, I'm so glad! I thought maybe we weren't going to have any Christmas. I've been thinking and thinking about it, but I didn't like to say anything, 'fraid it would make you feel badly."

"We'll have some kind of a Christmas, my dear," said Mr. Peniman. "It may not be the kind of a Christmas that you have always been accustomed to, but we will celebrate the dear day in some way."

Directly after dinner they all set off down the river bank, the boys in high boots, ear-caps, big coats, and mittens, the girls muffled to the eyes in coats, furs, scarfs, big Alaska overshoes, and leggings, and Mrs. Peniman looking very fat and pudgy in a pair of Mr. Peniman's trousers, over which she wore a huge woolly coat and hood, with scarf and mittens, and was bundled up so she looked like the Little Old Woman Who Lived in the Shoe.

They all set out in high spirits, and slid, slipped, coasted, snowballed and indulged in wild frolics over the snow, while Mr. and Mrs. Peniman took turns riding on the sled, which their wild young chargers took delight in upsetting as often as possible.

After long search they at last found a young pine tree which came to a fine apex at the height of about five feet, and in the woods they found bright red berries, mistletoe in the tops of some trees, which Lige and Sam were only too pleased to climb, and deep under the snow some kinnikinick, which with its dainty green leaves and red berries made wonderful decorations.

They returned home with the sled laden and in high glee.

The tree was set up in a corner of the soddy that evening after supper, and when pop-corn was strung from limb to limb, apples and oranges hung from the branches, small sacks of candy tied on, and the candles, which Mr. Peniman had thoughtfully provided on his almost fatal trip to Omaha, carefully disposed among the branches and lighted, it was a gorgeous sight. Beneath it on the floor were a great heap of queer-looking bumpy bundles, to which each one brought his or her contribution with great secrecy, and which were not one of them opened until the next morning.

It was scarcely light on Christmas morning when a great jingling outside (which *of course* no one recognized as the notes of the dinner-bell) announced the arrival of Santa Claus.

There was a great hemming and hawing, a great stamping of feet in the snow, and then the door opened, and Santa Claus, in a marvelous wig and whiskers (made out of the wool of a pair of old grey woolen stockings) and a wonderful costume (which of course no one recognized as a suit of red flannel underwear elegantly trimmed in strips of white cotton flannel), came prancing in with a sack on his back and began dispensing presents with a generous hand.

There were dolls for Mary and Sara, writing paper and ribbons and pretty handkerchiefs for Nina and Ruth, books and neckties for Joe, ties, handkerchiefs and a handsome muffler for Lige, balls and bats and tops and gloves for Sam and Paul, and a great lot of toys, including the remarkable hobby-horse that Sam had bought him, for little David.

But if the children had been remembered well neither Mr. nor Mrs. Peniman had been forgotten. Mrs. Peniman's heart was deeply touched by the gift of a beautiful white apron, made from one of her own pretty white dresses with infinite pains and secrecy by Nina, who gave Ruth a beautiful sash-ribbon with hair ribbons to match out of her own little store, Sara ribbons, a sash ribbon and a pretty white dress, and Lige and Sam her own gold pencil and a box of drawing crayons. But to Joe she gave her dearest treasure, a pretty red morocco book of verses, which her father had given to her on her last birthday, with an inscription written on the inside which deeply touched Joe's heart. For Mr. Peniman she had made a penwiper out of one of her own little felt shoes.

Joe and Lige had nothing to give their father and mother but their kisses and love, but for each of the children they had made or contrived in secret some little toy that added to the merriment of the day, and fully as welcome and as much appreciated as if they had come from a city store. Mrs. Peniman delighted her husband by bringing forth from one of the knobby bundles under the tree three fine new shirts, made at night and in secret with the labor of her own tired hands, and Mr. Peniman handed to her a bundle from beneath the tree, that had come all the way from Omaha the day of the blizzard, and had lain out in the wagon under the snow for more than a week. It contained a handsome new dress, which everybody praised and admired tremendously, and was as delighted over as if it had been given to themselves.

Altogether it was a most wonderful Christmas.

The dinner, at which a wild turkey took the place of the usual tame one, and at which the wild grape jelly and the plum preserves and a real plum pudding (made weeks before and hidden away for the occasion), was pronounced a grand success.

The afternoon was spent in games, winding up with a great snow-frolic, and snow-cream for supper. But when the evening came and the younger children had gone to bed the others gathered close about the fire and quiet gradually settled down upon them.

It had been a happy day, but now as the evening shadows gathered memories of other Christmases came out of the dusk and lingered about them.

To Mr. and Mrs. Peniman the memory of the little one they had lost, the tiny grave left behind there on the desolate loneliness of the prairies, was seldom out of their thoughts. And now as their thoughts traveled back over the past, bringing up to them the memories of Christmas at the old home, and the dear ones they were perhaps never to see again, there came a deep sadness that neither of them would permit themselves to express.

To Joe and Lige and Sam and Ruth this Christmas evening was also bringing memories. They could never forget the old home they had loved so well in the Muskingum Valley, nor the dear grandmother, the aunts and cousins and friends whom they had left behind.

But to Nina, sitting with her chin cupped in her hand and her lovely violet eyes gazing into the fire, came the saddest memories. She thought of her last Christmas, and of that dear father and mother whom she had so loved and who had always done so much to make her life a happy one, and the tears brimmed her eyes. She thought of her father's illness, the strange cloud that always seemed to be hanging over them, of their journey westward, and of the tragic death of both her parents on the plains. She remembered as if she had seen it yesterday the two long graves, side by side, with the wooden cross at the head and the morning sunlight shining down upon the fresh earth and newly-turned sod. Then her thoughts went forward over the months since, with all the mystery and terror that had surrounded her, and a great wonder and terror grew in her mind. Wonder of that mystery that hung about her; terror of that menace that seemed to so darkly pursue her; fear of what the years might have in store for her, who knew so little of who she was or where she belonged.

As the recollection of her lonely state came over her she heaved a deep, quivering sigh. The room was in darkness except for the firelight that threw its flickering light upon their faces, and as tears welled into her eyes she felt a hand slipped into her own and turned to see Joe sitting on a box at her feet and looking up at her with an expression of such deep tenderness and sympathy in his eyes that she knew he understood what was passing in her mind.

"It's all right, Joesy," she whispered, blinking the tear-drops from her lashes; "I was only thinking—and you know——"

"I know, Princess," he said, pressing her hand tenderly, "I know."

That was all. But it was enough for Nina. The pressure of that warm, strong young hand in hers, the sympathy in those honest grey eyes, banished the shadows that had been creeping round her as if by magic. Somehow the knowledge that Joe was near, that Joe understood, chased away the feeling of loneliness and mystery, and made her feel safe and happy again.

CHAPTER XXIV

RUTH MAKES A DISCOVERY

The winter passed swiftly. With the school to take up their time and attention in the daytime and games and talk and popping corn and telling stories in the evening the time crept by, and almost before they knew it it was spring.

March brought sunny days, thawing weather and big rains, with blue skies and balmy winds that soon melted the snow and sent it scurrying in foaming torrents down the beds of all the creeks and streams.

Very soon after the snows began to go a wonderful thing happened.

They woke one morning to see a train of emigrant wagons coming across the plains, and that day a new settler came to the Blue River, bringing with him a wife, two sons and a daughter.

They came directly to the Penimans' homestead for advice and directions, and the original settlers on the river were delighted beyond measure to find them refined and intelligent people, who, like themselves, had desired to better their condition and had dared the dangers of the frontier life to provide themselves with wider opportunities and a better home.

The name of the family was James, and they came from Iowa. The two sons, Herbert and Arthur, were seventeen and fifteen, while the daughter, Beatrice, was nearly the same age as Ruth, a pretty, fair-haired, slender girl, with soft brown eyes that looked like the heart of a pansy.

They remained with the Peniman family that day, and the two families fraternized immediately. It was a great joy to those who had been living in such lonely conditions to meet and talk with people from the outside world. Mrs. James and Mrs. Peniman exchanged confidences in regard to heating and housing and obtaining fuel and provisions, the men talked farm-land and crops and sod houses and dugouts, while the young people explored the river and became friends from the very beginning.

Few papers or news of any kind had reached the homestead during the winter, and Joshua Peniman heard with a sinking heart of the slavery agitation that seemed to be continually increasing and growing daily a greater menace to the security of the nation. Joe, too, was listening to the news from the outside world with great interest. Herbert James, a tall, fine-looking, manly young fellow of seventeen, who had been attending school in the East, was full of the threatening conditions of the country. He talked of the issue with keen, intelligent interest, and Joe listened with a strange thrill passing through his breast. The two boys soon became fast friends, while Lige and Arthur, who was past fifteen, also struck up a great friendship. Ruth, usually shy and quiet with strangers, expanded sunnily in the company of Beatrice, and she and Nina soon became fast friends with her, a friendship that endured to the very end of their lives.

Nothing else could have brought the satisfaction and joy to the Peniman family as did the coming of this pleasant, intelligent family. It brought to them companionship, added protection from the dangers that always surround the pioneer, and the added incentive of a new element in the making of their home on the prairies. The whole Peniman family went with them to select their location, which they had all decided should be very near, planned with them the site of their house, helped them in building it, assisted them in every way through those first hard months that are the lot of the pioneer in a new country, and gave them the benefit of their valuable experience. The James family settled on a tract of land about half a mile to the west of them, and it was a relief to each family to know that the other was within call.

The Jameses had brought with them a pony that Beatrice had always ridden and was exceedingly fond of, and one of the joys of the girls' early acquaintance was in taking turns riding on the back of gentle Flora.

Ruth took to riding as a duck to water. In a few days she could ride as well as her instructor, and was never so happy as when cantering over the prairies on Flora's back.

One day toward the first of April, when the sun was shining brightly and a pleasant breeze blowing, she asked her mother if she might not take a little ride.

Mrs. James remarked that it would be perfectly safe, as Flora was most gentle and reliable, and Mrs. Peniman gave her consent, cautioning her not to go too far away.

Ruth had always been a passionate lover of animals, and the feel of the horse under her, the curve of the soft neck under her hand, the swift, smooth pace, exhilarated her as nothing had ever done before.

The snow was going fast, only in places now were there remains of the great drifts that had covered the plains throughout the winter. As she cantered on she looked at them, wishing that they were all gone and that the beautiful wild-flowers which adorn the prairies in the spring would soon come to gladden their hearts and eyes.

Suddenly as she rode Flora started and swerved, and it was well for Ruth that she had a tight hold on the saddle or she would have gone off over her head.

"Why, Flora," she cried in surprise, "what's the matter?" then started violently herself, as she looked down and saw, partially concealed by the remains of a great drift, the legs and feet of a man.

She checked the pony abruptly and sat still, not knowing what to do. Then, being a brave girl and a true little pioneer, she scrambled down from the pony's back, slipped the bridle over her arm, and going to the body kneeled down and scraped away the snow that covered it.

It was still in good condition, the bitter cold of the winter and the snow packed about it having preserved it perfectly. As Ruth pushed aside the snow that concealed the face she screamed aloud.

"*Eagle Eye*! Oh, poor, poor Eagle Eye!" and being a real little woman she sat down beside the body and began to cry.

For a long time she kneeled beside the body of the young Indian whom she had so tenderly nursed back to health. The face looked just as she had seen it often, keen, thin, silent, the eyes closed, the grave lips motionless, the bronze-hued features set in the dignified mold of death.

"Eagle Eye, Eagle Eye," she called to him softly, placing her hands on his and bending nearer. "Oh, poor Eagle Eye, where have you been; how, *how*, did this terrible thing happen to you?"

The cold, immovable face remained impassive, the grave set lips made no reply.

She rose presently, and stood for a time looking down upon him. She knew that the body must not be left lying exposed on the prairie; that wolves, vultures, coyotes, the hideous carrion-crows would soon find it.

"I'll come back, Eagle Eye," she said as she left him, "even if you were not grateful to us for what we did for you, we will see that you have a proper burial." She mounted the pony and had started to ride away when a little distance farther on she saw a black object in the snow. Curious as to what it might be she rode to it. As she slipped from the pony's back and stooped over it she saw that it was a black tin box, which had once had a lock, which had been broken and torn away.

She examined it curiously, then tucking it under her arm rode home as fast as Flora could carry her.

"Mother, oh, Mother," she shouted as she burst into the house, "I found Eagle Eye—our Eagle Eye—lying out there on the prairie—*dead*—under a snowdrift!"

"*Eagle Eye?* You mean our Eagle Eye? The young Indian we took care of after he was shot?" cried Mrs. Peniman, running to her.

"Yes, yes," the tears were running down Ruth's cheeks now; "oh, yes, Mother, our own Eagle Eye; and oh, Mother, he was lying right under a drift, and I saw his feet, and when I uncovered his face I saw that it was Eagle Eye. He must have got lost in the blizzard——"

"What's this? Who was lost in the blizzard?" asked Mr. Peniman, who had entered the house in time to hear the last words.

Mrs. Peniman explained to him.

"*Eagle Eye?*" he ejaculated; "he must have been trying to come to us! He must have got lost in the storm! Perhaps he had some message to bring to us—perhaps he was not so ungrateful, so careless as he seemed——"

He stopped short, his eyes fixed with a strange stare upon the box that Ruth had entirely forgotten, and which she still clutched under her arm.

"*Ruth!*" he shouted, "*where did you get that box?* Where did it come from? How in the name of heaven——"

Ruth, startled half out of her wits at his face and voice, held out the box she had found on the prairies.

"I found it, Father—out there on the prairies—just a little way from where Eagle Eye was lying. Why, Father, what is the matter? What makes you look so—so——"

Her words died away as her father leaped forward and snatched the box from her hands. She saw him stoop and examine it, saw him stare into her mother's face, and saw her mother turn pale, as she murmured in a shaking voice, "The dispatch-box—the dispatch-box!"

Ruth had heard of the dispatch-box, although she had no remembrance of having ever seen it.

"*The dispatch-box?* Nina's dispatch-box—that we lost—that was stolen from us by the Indians?"

But neither Father nor Mother heard her. Tears had sprung to Mrs. Peniman's eyes and were rolling down her cheeks, as she murmured over and over, "Poor Eagle Eye, poor loyal, grateful friend, how unjust, how unjust we have been to you!"

Joshua Peniman was examining the box. The lock was gone, but the box had been roughly wrapped about and tied with a piece of deer-hide, and appeared to have remained undisturbed while it lay on the prairies.

"He was bringing it to us," he said in a low voice. "You remember, Hannah, that I told him the whole story. I did not know then how much he understood. But he must have understood it all. He went back to his own people and got the papers, and was bringing them to us when the blizzard overtook him. Poor Eagle Eye, poor loyal friend, he gave his life in our service." After a moment's thought he went on: "I wonder how he got it? I wonder what became of Red Snake? If he knows that this box has been taken from him he will never rest until he has his revenge and gets it back again."

"God protect us," whispered Mrs. Peniman, turning pale.

Joshua Peniman handed her the box quickly. "Put it away carefully," he said. "We will examine it more carefully when I come back. Just now our first duty is to Eagle Eye. Call the boys, Ruth. We must go after the body at once. I could not sleep this night knowing that the body of our faithful friend was lying uncovered on the plains."

When they reached the spot where the body was lying Joe uttered a surprised exclamation.

"Why, that's the Indian Lige and I found the night you were lost in the blizzard! I remember him perfectly. But I had never seen him before. You know I was away all the time Eagle Eye was at our house. Lige never looked at him at all, we were both so cold, and so scared and anxious about you. How do you suppose he came to be here?"

"He was coming to us, Joe," Mr. Peniman answered solemnly. "He was bringing to us a thing that we—all of us—would have been willing to pay any price to receive. And he gave his life in our service."

Joe stared. "What, Father? What was he bringing?"

"He was bringing Nina's dispatch-box. The box that was stolen from the wagon the night of the Indian raid."

Joe started, and a strange startled expression passed over his face.

"Where was it?" he asked.

"On the prairie, very near his body. Ruth found it there."

"Great heavens! I kicked it with my foot the night of the blizzard! I thought it was a tin can. *Nina's dispatch-box!* And it has lain all these months on the prairies!"

"God is good," murmured Mr. Peniman. But Joe answered nothing, but stared at his father with distended eyes.

CHAPTER XXV

THE DISPATCH-BOX

When they had brought Eagle Eye home and buried him under the willow trees on the river bank Joe went directly to his mother.

He was seventeen now, and the dangers and hardships he had been through and the responsibilities that had been thrust upon him made him appear much older than his years.

"Mother," he said in a low trembling voice, "have you told Nina—does she know?"

"Not yet, dear. There has not been time. It will of course be something of a shock to her, and I want to tell her when we are quiet and alone and I can prepare her for it."

For a moment the boy stood silent, his head bent forward on his breast. Then he burst out impetuously:

"Do you think we'd better tell her at all, Mother? She is contented and happy here, why should we tell her something that—that—might take her away from us forever? I have always known that she was—was—different, somehow, and this box probably contains the information about her own people and all that. If she gets it why—why she will probably go back to them—and—and——"

The troubled voice ceased, and his mother bent forward and putting her hand under his chin raised his face to hers.

"Why, Joe!" she exclaimed, "why, *Joe!* Is that my own boy speaking like this? You would keep the knowledge that must be of such inestimable value to Nina away from her because, perchance, we should lose her, lest she should leave us—to further her own happiness and prosperity in life?"

Joe bent his head and his face crimsoned.

"I know I'm selfish, Mother," he blurted out; "I know I shouldn't even allow myself to think of such a thing. But when I think of her leaving us—of—of going off to live with some one else—I—I just can't stand it." Then raising his head and fixing his deep grey eyes upon his mother's face, "I'd rather die than live without Nina."

When she had at last sent him away to bed Hannah Peniman sat for a long time before the dying fire.

Joe—her Joe—her son—her baby—was not a boy any more—he was a man!

The eyes that had looked into hers this night, the voice that had spoken out of a heart yet unknown to itself, were not the eyes, the voice of a child. And the knowledge left pain in her heart, and wonder.

She rose presently and going to the door called Nina.

As the girl came bounding into the room Hannah Peniman looked at her with new eyes. The little Princess was now a slender, graceful, beautiful girl of fourteen, with a head of rippling gold, eyes like wood-violets, and a face so entrancingly lovely that Mrs. Peniman's heart sank as she looked at it.

She drew the girl gently down on a chair beside her.

"Listen, dear," her voice was low, almost sad, as she spoke, "you never knew the Indian that Ruth found on the prairies to-day and that Father and the boys buried this evening, but he has done you a great, an inestimable service. You have heard us speak of him, and how we took care of Eagle Eye when he was wounded. That was at the time that both you and Joe were away, after you were kidnapped by the Indians. Father Peniman trusted Eagle Eye, and told him your story. He went away without a word, but in some way he got possession of the box containing your papers——"

Nina started up from her chair.

"The box—*the dispatch-box*—that Mother left me?"

"Yes, Nina. He got it, and he was bringing it back to us when he became lost in the blizzard. He gave his life in the effort to restore it."

"But the box—the box—Mother's box?" cried Nina, her hands clasped, her face white, her eyes wide and pleading.

"That was the box that Ruth found this afternoon lying on the prairie beside Eagle Eye's body."

"And you have it—you got it—it—it——" her agitation was too great for words.

Mrs. Peniman laid her hand over the little shaking hands that were clasped against Nina's breast.

"Yes, dear, we have it." She rose and going to her trunk brought forth the box and put it into Nina's hands.

The girl clasped it, bent over it, pressed it to her bosom, and burst into a flood of tears.

"It is all I have of them," she whispered, "all that I have to remember either of them. Oh, I hope there is a picture of Mother in the box, some letters, something to make me know more about my dear, dear father and mother!"

At this moment Mr. Peniman entered the room. He crossed silently to the table and stood beside it while Nina with shaking fingers unfastened the thongs that were wound about the box and raised the lid. On the top were two long folded papers. She opened these and glanced at them hastily, then threw them on the table. They were deeds, executed many years before, to Lee C. Carroll, by his father, Edgar M. Carroll, conveying to him and his heirs forever sole title to certain properties in St. Louis and New York.

There was a tray in the box, and with trembling hands Nina raised this eagerly, hoping to find the treasures she had coveted in the space below.

There was nothing in it but a heap of ashes.

The base, vindictive nature of the renegade, while leaving in the box the deeds to a property he dared not claim, incited him with devilish malice to destroy all the personal papers, all data, every scrap of information that could lead to the restoration of the child to her friends and relatives, or her place in society.

When the full realization of what had been done came upon her Nina uttered a heartbroken cry and cast herself into Mrs. Peniman's arms.

With eyes that could scarce credit the evidence of their senses the man and woman gazed into the box.

Nothing there but ashes.

Nothing to pay for the life that had been given. Nothing to bring to the helpless young girl the knowledge without which she was cut off from all family relation, or connection with the life from which she came. Nothing to help her to establish her identity, or enable her to claim the property, the deeds of which had been so sardonically left in the box.

The utter maliciousness of it, the cold, cruel, calculating vindictiveness of the deed left them stunned.

"Don't grieve so, darling," Hannah Peniman murmured, stroking the golden head and pressing it to her breast, "you have the deeds, and they mean a great deal. Property in those two big cities must be worth a great deal of money now."

"But I don't want money," sobbed Nina broken-heartedly. "I don't care anything about the deeds, he might as well have burned them, too. What do I want of property in New York or St. Louis? I'll probably never go there. I don't want to go there. I want to stay here with you. But what I wanted—what I hoped we would find in the box—were pictures of Papa and Mama, letters from them—things about them and me—so that I would know something about them—about myself, so that I wouldn't feel myself a poor forsaken, friendless waif, dependent upon your charity for all I have and am."

Joshua Peniman crossed the room and laid his hand upon her head.

"You are not a friendless waif, Princess," he said in his low, gentle voice, "you are our daughter, beloved, cherished, as much as Sara or Ruth." Then taking up the deeds from the table he examined them carefully.

"This is very strange," he mused; "I can't understand it. Why should he have left the deeds and destroyed everything else in the box? There is a considerable quantity of ashes here. The box must have been full of papers. Why should that villain have destroyed them all and left these deeds? I cannot understand it."

He puzzled over it long after Nina had sobbed herself to sleep in Ruth's loving arms.

Where was Red Snake?

Why had he burned the contents of this box?

How had the box come to be in the possession of Eagle Eye?

What had they to expect from this new complication in a mystery he was unable to unravel?

Little could he guess, as he went abstractedly about his work the next day, how those questions were to be answered, or how closely that mystery was to affect the lives of himself and those who were dear to him.

CHAPTER XXVI

TROUBLE BREWING

The spring of 1857 was a time of promise for the Nebraska settlers. Timely rains had fallen. The few little fields of wheat and corn promised good harvests. Elk, deer, antelope, grouse, and wild turkey were abundant. Buffaloes came close to their settlement and they were fortunate enough to get many hides and much meat. The Sioux had fought a great battle with the whites at Ash Hollow and been badly beaten and wanted nothing so much as peace. Fifty thousand dollars had been voted by Congress to build a capitol at Omaha, and fifty thousand more to build roads through the Territory.

With the advance of spring more settlers began to come in. There was now a little settlement at Beaver Creek, some five miles away, and during the summer several families located along the Blue, and a thriving settlement started up on the Little Blue, some three or four miles away, which was called "Milford."

Meanwhile the friendship of the Peniman family and their new neighbors, the Jameses, was growing apace.

To Mr. Peniman the presence of a neighbor, a man who was concerned with the same problems, the same dangers, and the same experiments as himself, was a great boon. He now had another man to talk to, to plan with, to rely upon in case the danger of which he was in continual fear should come upon them.

To Mrs. Peniman the companionship of another woman was a blessing almost beyond expression, and to the girls the presence of another young girl in the neighborhood brought a new interest in life.

But it was to Lige and Joe that the coming of the new homesteaders brought the greatest significance.

The James boys had always lived in towns and had a knowledge and sophistication of which the country-raised Peniman lads were entirely lacking. They had also had much better educational facilities, and there was much that Joe and Lige could learn from them. The four boys became staunch friends, and in talking with Herbert, Joe again felt his ambitions stimulated to study law.

When the snow had gone and the bright spring sunshine had dried up the prairies sufficiently to allow of travel Joshua Peniman proposed to Joe that he should go to Omaha in his place, have the wagon mended and bring back some spring supplies.

"There is so much work to be done this spring that I don't feel that I can go," he said. "I would not like to have you make the trip alone, but the Jameses are needing some things, too, and you and Herbert can make the trip together."

So it was arranged, and on a brilliant spring morning, when the sky arched like a bowl of sapphire above their heads, when the meadow-larks sang in the grass and the wind whispered softly over the prairies that here and there were already showing a touch of green, the two lads set off together.

It was a long drive, and on the way they talked of many things. Herbert, who was a fine, quiet, serious-minded boy, was thinking much of the political situation of the country, which this spring was showing signs of much bitterness and agitation.

"I tell you things are in a serious condition," he said. "We are going on indifferently living over a volcano. And it's going to burst out some day when people are least expecting it. Slavery is a curse that no civilized country can exist under. Are we going to keep quiet and let Kansas come into the Union as a slave State?"

Joe's eyes blazed. "Of course we're not. That would be a terrible thing," he cried.

"Then what are we going to do about it? Are men like Douglas going to blind the eyes and muffle the ears of the American people until we get all tied up in legislation that will give a preponderance of the Western States to slavery?"

When they reached Omaha they found the entire community asking the same question. On street corners, in stores, in halls, churches, meeting-places of all kinds the question of slavery was being discussed, not calmly and dispassionately, but with a bitterness that was disturbing business, separating families, setting father and sons, brother and brother apart.

Joe listened to it all with a growing feeling of anxiety. In spite of himself he found himself constantly being drawn into arguments, contending hotly on a question that he felt keenly that he knew too little about.

In a store where the two lads went to buy their provisions they ran into a group of a dozen men or more who were hotly debating the slavery question. They intended to do their trading and get out as soon as possible, but the proprietor of the store was one of the principal arguers, so leaning his back against the counter while he waited to have his order filled, Joe listened to the discussion.

Before he was aware of what he was doing he had answered a tall, gangling Missourian with a tuft of whiskers on his chin, who was arguing for State rights, and the first thing he knew he was in the midst of a fiery controversy, in which all the bystanders took violent sides.

Among them was a man whose appearance had drawn his attention from the first moment he entered the store. At his first glance it had startled him with a strange sense of familiarity. Then the argument had claimed all his attention and he noticed the man no more, until, having abruptly terminated his part in it he gathered up his provisions and was leaving the store when the gentleman stepped up to him.

"I congratulate you, young man," he said, holding out his hand. "You are a born orator. It does my heart good to hear the young fellows of our country take the stand that you just did. You are what I should call a real American. I'm afraid we have some tough times ahead of us before this thing is over, and it is to the young fellows like you that we may have to look for its settlement."

"Do you mean that you think it will come to war?"

"I begin to fear so. There is too much of a pull being made by the slave-owners and slave States,—and, I regret to say, by men in Congress, who ought to have a stronger sense of humanity and the country's danger."

"I agree with you," answered Joe eagerly, and before he knew it he was speaking out his thoughts to this stranger, the long, silent thoughts that had been forming themselves in his mind in the silence of the prairies, when he had brooded by himself about the subject of slavery and the danger of secession.

When they had remained talking for some time the gentleman laid his hand on Joe's arm.

"I like you, my young friend," he said; "you are a boy of much promise. Come up to my office with me. I am a lawyer. I'd like to talk with you further."

Joe hesitated. He had much to do, but something in the man's face and manner, some strange, haunting sense of familiarity, the fascination of his presence, his smooth and elegant manner of speech, made an appeal to him that he could not resist. They went together to the lawyer's office, and Joe saw for the first time a real law office and a law library.

When he saw the rows of shelves his eyes brightened.

"Oh," he cried, "what a library! How splendid! How I should like to read them all!"

The lawyer laughed. "I'm afraid you would find some of those books rather dry reading. They are all law books. A good many of them are reports."

"I know. That is what interests me so much. All my life my greatest ambition has been to be a lawyer."

"Is that possible!" cried the gentleman, evidently much pleased. "Well, well! So you would like to be a lawyer, would you? Why don't you, then? I am sure you would make a good one."

Joe's face flushed with pleasure.

"There is nothing in the world I want so much," he answered. "But we have a big family, my father is not a rich man, and we have recently homesteaded on the Blue. There is an awful lot of work to be done by pioneers, and I don't get much chance to read." Then, after a pause, "And besides I haven't any books."

"Would you read them if you had?"

"Yes, sir, I would, indeed," Joe answered so promptly that the gentleman smiled.

He rose presently and went to a case.

"Here," he said, taking down two volumes; "here's a copy of Blackstone, and one of Kent's Commentaries. I'll lend them to you. Take them home with you, and after you have read and digested them come back to me, and if I find that you have understood what you have read I'll lend you some more."

Joe's face crimsoned with joy. He stammered his thanks, and after shaking hands with his new acquaintance and promising to call upon him the next time he came to Omaha, he left the office and joined Herbert, who was waiting for him at the store.

When he told him of his experience and showed him the books Herbert whistled. "Looks to me as if that was a lucky strike," he said. "Do you know who that man is? I saw that he had taken a notion to you and asked about him. He is Judge North, one of the leading men of the Territory and the most prominent lawyer in the West."

Joe was not surprised to hear that the man at whose office he had called and whose books he carried under his arm was one of the leading men of the Territory. There was that in his manner and appearance that proclaimed him a leader of men. Absently he opened one of the books. On the fly-leaf was written in a bold flowing hand, "John M. North, Attorney at Law."

Joe pointed to the last words. "I hope to write that after my name some day," he said musingly.

"I'll be your first client," laughed Herbert.

"There's no telling but that you might," grinned Joe; "I might have to get you out of jail some day."

As they hurried back to the place where they had left the wagon Joe was overjoyed to find Pashepaho standing beside it.

He greeted them with a broad grin.

"Me wait," he said, "me know horses."

Joe grasped his hand and shook it with the cordiality of an old friend. Then he introduced Herbert, who looked with some astonishment upon this manner of greeting the red man of the plains.

"Pashepaho is one of my best friends," Joe assured him; "he saved my life once, and probably the lives of the family. What are you doing here, Pashepaho?"

"Come trade skin. What you do?"

"We came in to get some provisions and get the wagon mended. It broke down in a blizzard last winter."

"Heap cold."

"It was an awful winter. Father and Sam almost got lost in the big blizzard." Then suddenly remembering, "Did you know that Eagle Eye is dead? He was coming to us—-bringing Nina's dispatch-box—when the blizzard overtook him. We found him dead not far from our house this spring."

"Ai-ee! Eagle Eye dead?" The Indian's sharp face clouded. "Heap good man." Then suddenly, "You know 'bout Red Snake?"

"No," Joe turned on him sharply. "What about him? We have been awful uneasy ever since we knew that Eagle Eye got the box. We have been afraid he would come to take vengeance on us for it."

"He no come now," said Pashepaho gravely. Then with a tone of surprise, "You no hear?"

"No, we have heard nothing. We have been shut off there at the homestead with big snows all winter. What do you mean?"

"Red Snake dead."

Joe started, and leaned forward staring into his face.

"*Dead?* Red Snake dead? How? When? Where?"

"Eagle Eye keel heem."

"Eagle Eye killed him? When?"

"Many sleep ago. Shoot heem with arrow."

Joe stood as if transfixed, staring into his face.

"Eagle Eye heap white man friend," Pashepaho went on.

"I know he was, I know he was, he was our friend, our good, loyal friend; we felt awfully bad when we found him. But—how did it happen? How did he get the box, I wonder?"

In his halting, broken English Pashepaho told him the story as he had heard it from the men of his own tribe. Joe was deeply affected.

"Then he must have got the dispatch-box after Red Snake was dead, and was bringing it to us when the blizzard overtook him. Good, faithful Eagle Eye! We thought he was not grateful for all the folks had done in nursing him back to life, but look how mistaken we were! He was a faithful friend."

As Pashepaho shook his hand and rode away Joe stood still in a profound reverie. A relief so great that it was almost like the falling of a great load from his shoulders, came over him.

Red Snake was dead!

The danger that had hung so darkly and fearsomely over them was now removed, the menacing figure that had shadowed all their days and filled their nights with terror was gone forever!

He could scarcely wait to get back home and tell the glad news to the family. As he hurriedly began to load the provisions into the wagon two men in earnest conversation passed him.

"We shall have war," one of them was saying, "there is no escaping it. The South is bound to secede."

The South is bound to secede!

The two lads turned and looked at one another, and into the consciousness of both some strange prescience seemed to fall.

"War!" said Herbert in an awed tone.

"*War!*" repeated Joe; "I wonder what it would mean to me?"

CHAPTER XXVII

WAR

The news that Joe brought back from his trip to Omaha that Red Snake was dead and the dark menace so long hanging over them was removed forever, brought great relief to the whole Peniman family. To Nina especially did it seem to bring a sense of security she had never known since the day she had been kidnapped. She had recovered in a measure from the bitter disappointment of the violated dispatch-box, though many nights, and often when she was alone she felt deeply unhappy over her situation, and the unsolved mystery that seemed to cut her off from her own.

As the summer advanced the young people of the two families were much together, and Hannah Peniman noticed with a smile—and yet a sigh—that the boys no longer went off by themselves on hunting or fishing or exploring expeditions, but that wherever they went the girls were usually with them, and that as the party came home, strolling across the prairies or along the river bank in the moonlight, that Nina and Joe were always together, that Herbert walked with Ruth, and that Lige larked and sang and frolicked with pretty, gay little Beatrice.

Joe found little time for reading during the summer, but the law books which Judge North had lent him were his constant companions in the evening, and while he plowed and harrowed the fields in which their first crops were to be planted he propped the Blackstone up at one end of the furrow, and while he traveled its length he recited over and over again a paragraph he had read at the start. When he reached the end of the furrow that paragraph was usually committed to memory, and he took another, reciting it over and over all down the long black furrow and back. In this way he read Blackstone through, acquiring so perfect a knowledge of its contents that he knew it almost by heart, and could quote from it verbatim to the very end of his life.

His mind and thoughts were much occupied with the ominous news that continually reached them. Everywhere trouble seemed to be in the air. The violence and disorder in Kansas, where a state of civil war practically existed, as the result of the pro-slavery demonstration at Lawrence, communicated itself across the border to the sister territory of Nebraska, and bitter arguments and controversy were heard wherever two or three people were gathered together.

Such papers as they were able to obtain were full of menace. A seething current of excitement and unrest seemed permeating the whole nation. The North bitterly accusing the South of trying by trickery and treachery to force slavery upon the nation, the South maintaining that the North was fostering abolition, and that the real intent and purpose of the abolitionists was to arouse a slave insurrection and bring devastation to the whole South.

The decision in the Dred Scott case and the framing of the Lecompton Constitution in Kansas increased the agitation of the slavery question to a burning issue; and Joe and Herbert, sometimes accompanied by Arthur and Lige, fell into the habit of riding over to the little cross-road store at Milford evenings, to hear the latest news and listen to the discussion they always found going on there.

Joshua Peniman made few comments on the situation, but he seized upon the papers with an eagerness that showed his interest, and read them with set lips and frowning brow.

In October that year the little settlement of which the Peniman family had been the pioneers was increased by six families, who homesteaded upon the West Blue and Middle Creek.

A demand soon rose among them for a school which the children of the community could attend during the cold weather, and as there were no funds to provide such a school or pay a teacher the settlers all came together at the Peniman homestead to discuss the matter and see what could be done.

After much discussion it was agreed that they should build a little sod schoolhouse, large enough to accommodate the children of the neighborhood, and as Joshua Peniman was a natural leader among them and the best equipped for the purpose, that the men of the settlement should take upon themselves his work for certain hours of each day, while he in exchange should teach the school.

He was the more willing to accede to this proposal because he had never entirely recovered from the effects of the exposure he had suffered in the blizzard, and was subject to rheumatism and bronchitis, and was not sorry to have the heavy outdoor work done by some of the younger and stronger men during the severity of the winter.

A location was chosen on the prairies about midway between the different homesteads, and on a cold, bright morning in October the sod was broken for the schoolhouse.

There were men and teams enough to accomplish its construction quickly, and within a few days a solid little structure, about thirty feet square, was erected.

The question of heating and seating had arisen at the meeting, and it had been decided that each settler should furnish one desk or chair, and that each settler who had timber should cut a load of cord wood and those who had no timber should contribute their share by hauling it to the nearest market and selling it, buying a stove with the proceeds.

This program was carried out, two of the settlers who had no timber driving forty miles to Nebraska City, where they bought a good second-hand stove, which was set up in the schoolhouse.

The new schoolhouse was ready for occupation the first of November, and from that time on throughout the long, cold winter the little sod schoolhouse accommodated about twenty children, of all grades and sizes, of whom Joshua Peniman was the teacher.

Within a short time after the opening of the school a general feeling arose in the settlement that the Sabbath should be observed, and at the general request of the settlers Joshua Peniman consented to act as leader, holding services every Sunday in the sod schoolhouse. As the settlers were of all creeds and denominations the services were necessarily non-sectarian. The services were very simple, consisting of the reading of the Bible, prayers by members of the congregation, responsive reading from the Psalms, and hymns led by the clear, sweet voice of Hannah Peniman.

In the fall of that year another great boon came to the pioneers. A stage-coach line was established, the terminal of which was the Big Sandy station on the Little Blue. This line carried mail and passengers, thus doing away with the long, lonely, dangerous ride across the prairies to get mail, and bringing a postoffice, with mail and newspapers within about six miles of the Peniman homestead. After that it was possible to get papers not more than a day or two old, and to send and receive letters without the perilous journey hitherto necessary.

Joshua Peniman had proved up on his claim, and was holding fast to the claims he had staked out next his own for Joe and Lige, with two other 160-acre tracts which he hoped to hold for Ruth and Nina as soon as they should be old enough to take them. The harvest of that year was rich and plentiful, and the winter of 1858-9 saw the family comfortably established in a home that was beginning to have the appearance of a real farm, with hay, grain and corn stored in their granaries, a cow-house and chicken-house added to the buildings, and many substantial improvements added to their dwelling.

During the winter whenever Joe could snatch time from his other duties he and Herbert James trapped beaver, mink, and otter in the river. In Beaver Creek, where a beautiful little town was springing up, they got many fine beavers, the skins of which sold for from two to three dollars a pound, many of the beavers weighing from two to three pounds apiece. With the money he made by the sale of the skins he bought law books, adding one at a time to his precious collection, and studying them so industriously that when he went to Omaha to return the books he had borrowed from Judge North he rendered to the lawyer so good an account of his reading that the Judge called him a prodigy.

"You are the kind of a boy I like," he said genially, patting Joe on the shoulder. "I'd like to take you into my office to study law. You are highly gifted, and I believe will make a great success of the profession."

Joe glowed under his praise. Nothing would have given him greater happiness than to enter Judge North's fine offices as a student. It was a great temptation. But there was much work to be done at home, his father was no longer strong, and his work much interrupted by his teaching and ministerial duties, and much of the responsibility of the farm work had fallen upon him and Lige, who was now a tall, handsome, well-set-up lad of seventeen, while Joe had grown to the full stature of a man, and was approaching his nineteenth birthday.

"I can't come into your office now, Judge North," he answered regretfully, "but I would like to come and talk with you whenever I can, and have you advise and help me. I want to be a lawyer, and even though I cannot be spared from home now I can go on preparing myself until the younger boys get old enough to take my place on the farm."

"Good lad," said Judge North; "I like you none the less for your faithfulness to your duty."

As he smiled at him again that strange sense of familiarity came over the boy. Where had he seen that man before? Who was it of whom he so reminded him?

There was something about him that was not like a stranger, that carried a subtle sense of warmth, affection, to his heart. In the gleam of his deep blue eyes there came and went an expression that eluded him like an evanescent perfume. For some reason that he could not account for to himself the lad's heart warmed to him strangely. In the long, friendly talk that followed Joe told him of his ambitions, and of how that ambition had been roused in his breast by hearing a lawyer, a man by the name of Lincoln, make a Fourth of July speech in Illinois.

"Lincoln?" said Judge North, much interested. "Do you mean Abraham Lincoln? Well, well! So you heard one of those great speeches, did you? I wish it had been my privilege. Have you followed his debates with Douglas? He has a grip on this slavery question that no other man in the country can equal. Did you know that he is being talked of as a candidate of the new Republican party to succeed Buchanan as President?"

"No," cried Joe, much astonished. "*That* Mr. Lincoln? Why, he was only a country lawyer, a member of the legislature from Sangamon County, when I heard him!"

"He is the greatest man in this country to-day. A great lawyer. A great statesman. I hope that he may be elected."

Joe went home more eager and encouraged in his study of the law than ever before. He felt that if in so short a time a country lawyer like Mr. Lincoln should have become the nominee for President that there was hope for him in the years that lay before him.

A few evenings after his return there was a citizens' meeting at Milford, and he and Herbert rode over. His father, who had automatically become the leader of the settlement, had been asked to preside. Joe had had no intention of speaking, his purpose was to attend the meeting simply as a spectator. But before he was aware of it his blood was up and he was on his feet making a fiery anti-slavery speech.

He scarcely knew what he was saying. But with the first words he uttered all the long, deep thoughts that had been growing up within him while he worked in the fields in the vast silence of the prairies burst forth in a torrent, and he only came to himself when the little hall rocked with shouts and applause.

After that he was often asked to speak at meetings, and no one was more astonished than he when he was asked to accept the presidency of the Young Men's Republican Club, that was being organized in the county.

Feeling was running hot and high everywhere. And in the fall (1859) the torch was set to the smouldering powder of public opinion by John Brown's seizure of the national arsenal at Harper's Ferry.

Instantly the war-spirit of the country sprang to life.

Troops were hurried to the spot and the little band of hot-headed abolitionists seized. But though they paid the penalty of their well-meant but misdirected enthusiasm with their lives, the blaze was started. Nothing could stop it now.

War was inevitable.

The song,

"John Brown's body lies mouldering in the grave,

But his soul goes marching on,"

was born in a night and swept the country like wildfire, old men and young singing and cheering it.

The Republican party, born of the slavery agitation, grew apace, and "denied the authority of Congress, of a Territorial Legislature, or any individual to give existence to slavery in the Territories." It repudiated the doctrine of State sovereignty and the Dred Scott decision, and nominated Abraham Lincoln for President.

The nomination of the man whose anti-slavery speeches were read and quoted from ocean to ocean was a challenge thrown down to the slave-holding States, which responded to it with haughty defiance and the nomination of John C. Breckinridge, of Kentucky. The Northern Democrats, unable to endorse the attitude of their Southern brothers, split from their own party and nominated Stephen A. Douglas.

The nomination of Lincoln—his inspiration and guide—left no doubt in Joe's mind as to his course of action. He accepted the nomination of president of the Young Men's Republican Club, stripped off his coat and plunged into the campaign with the same energy, the same efficiency, the same unbounded enthusiasm that he had always brought to every task before him.

He spoke in sod houses, dugouts, schoolhouses, stores, churches, and halls, extolling the Republican candidate for President, and praising the man who seemed to him the very embodiment of the spirit of the freedom and democracy of America.

At many of these meetings Joshua Peniman presided. And as he heard the fiery utterances of his son his heart grew cold within his breast.

The campaign was a fierce and bitter one, but Lincoln was elected.

The South, angry, defiant, outraged by the election of a "nigger-lover," a plebeian, a country lawyer and rail-splitter, and the defeat of their own aristocratic candidate, Mr. Breckinridge, was incensed to fury. Many times they had threatened that the Southern States would no longer remain in the Union if the Republican party was successful, and on December 20, 1860, they made good their threat. A popular convention at Charleston passed an order of secession.

Throughout the intense excitement that followed Joe and his father had many discussions, in some of which Lige joined.

That war was inevitable they now knew. But how it was to be met by them—Quakers—was a thing upon which they could come to no agreement.

"We cannot take up arms," Joshua Peniman said firmly. "We are Quakers. Our religion, the Bible, the Word of God Himself forbids it."

"But it is our duty, Father," Joe urged passionately. "If we have to go to war with the South they will have all the advantage. They are ready for war. The Federal arsenals in the Southern States have fallen into their hands and furnished their soldiers with equipment. You know that we are not prepared. A great army will have to be raised and furnished with the munitions of war. Should we, whom you have always taught to love and honor the flag, sit still and see that flag torn down, our country divided, and left a prey to foreign nations?'"

Joshua Peniman blanched. "God forbid," he cried quickly. "But if it comes to that terrible pass there are others—not Quakers—who have not been reared in the faith that makes it impossible for them to fight. Let them go. Let them protect the country."

"It will take us all, Father," put in Lige. "This war is going to be no light matter. The South has the men, the money, the military training. It is going to take all the men the North can raise to hold the nation together if war comes."

And war did come.

Early in the spring Fort Sumter was fired upon.

This roused the North to the highest pitch of excitement. In April President Lincoln called for volunteers to suppress the rebellion.

The hour had come that Joshua Peniman and his sons had so long prayed might be spared them.

On the morning of June tenth Joe came and stood before him in the living-room of the little soddy.

Neither had slept. Joe's face was pale and his lips close set as he stood looking at his father.

"I enlisted last night, Father." He spoke in a hoarse, shaken voice, and his lips moved stiffly as if he could with difficulty frame the words.

Joshua Peniman started. He knew that it must come, yet the dart passed no less cruelly through his heart because it had been anticipated.

"Already?"

He looked grey and worn. Lines that had not been there a few months before had written themselves in his forehead and creased his cheeks. As the lad looked at him his heart rose up and choked him.

"Oh, Father," he cried, "I *had* to do it! It breaks my heart to go against your will. But I had no choice. I must go. Why, think what a skulker I would be if after all I have done and said I were to—to stay at home!"

"You were already under orders," Joshua Peniman said slowly. "You are a member of the Quaker Church. By your covenant with that body you have forsworn war. Your church and your God forbid you to fight. God Himself has commanded that 'Thou shalt not kill.'"

"Oh, but, Father, that means a different kind of killing. War is not *murder*!"

"War is always murder. The coldest, bloodiest, most terrible murder. Murder of the soul as well as the body."

"Oh no, Father, no, that isn't so!" cried out the boy. "Think of the men who have engaged in war! Think of Washington—his soul was not killed by war. This is a thing that must be done. It is a duty. We must fight for the Union—liberty—freedom—for our own homes and firesides."

"This issue need not have been met by war. It would not have been if war-crazy hot-heads had not forced it upon us. There is a better way for countries and nations to settle their difficulties than by war. Sometime men will come to realize its brutality and nations will combine to adjust their controversies by reason, not might."

"I don't believe that such a time will ever come. But if it does it is not here *now*. This issue is upon us. What are we going to do?—sit passive and let the South secede and break up the Union? Why, even Jesus did not suffer evil passively. He drove the money-changers from the Temple. And He Himself said 'Think not that I come to send peace on earth; I came not to send peace, but a sword.'"

"But the 'sword' that the Master speaks of in that passage of Scripture is not the literal sword, the sword used in war, but the sharp sword of conscience. Better that the Union be dissolved than that the hands of men should be stained with the blood of their brethren."

"Oh, Father," cried Joe, "how can you say so! Do you care nothing for the preservation of your country?"

Joshua Peniman flinched, and a hot flush passed over his face.

"God knows that I love my country as well as any man," he answered sadly. "But dearly as I love my country I love my God, my religion and the commands that He has given more."

"But remember what the Lord said to His disciples, in the twenty-second chapter of St. Luke: 'But now he that hath a purse, let him take it, and likewise his scrip: and he that hath no sword, let him sell his garment, and buy one.' The time has come, Father, when it is our duty to go to war, when the man who tries to escape that duty is dishonoring his God as well as his country. The time has come, when, as Jesus told His disciples, 'He that hath no sword should sell his very garment and buy one' and go forth to battle for the right."

Joshua Peniman gazed into the face of his son with sorrowful eyes. "Thee knows thy Scripture, Joe," he said in an unsteady voice. "I have striven mightily for thee. I thought I had brought thee up in the faith of our fathers——"

Hot tears sprang into Joe's eyes. "You have, you have, Father! As God hears me I would not take up arms against my fellow-man for anything less sacred than the preservation of our nation. I have studied deeply into this question. I have searched the Scriptures. And I feel that it is my sacred duty to go. Remember what the Lord said to Ezekiel, 'Son of man, speak to the children of thy people, and say unto them, When I bring the sword upon a land, if the people of that land take a man of their coasts, and set him for their watchman: If when he seeth the sword come upon the land, he blow the trumpet, and warn the people; Then whosoever heareth the trumpet and taketh not warning; if the sword come, and take him away, his blood shall be upon his own head. He heard the sound of the trumpet and took not warning; his blood shall be upon him. But he that taketh warning shall deliver his soul. But if the watchman see the sword come, and blow not the trumpet, and the people be not warned; if the sword come and take any person from among them, he is taken away in his iniquity; but his blood shall I require at the watchman's hand!'"

As the lad finished the long quotation from the book of Ezekiel, over which he had pored through many nights before, he fixed his gaze upon his father's face and said in a solemn voice:

"We are the watchmen, Father. If we rise not now, if we do not blow the trumpet, then should our nation perish, should the youth of our land be cut down, the Lord, according to His word will require their blood at the watchmen's hand."

Joshua Peniman gazed long and earnestly into his son's face. Then laid his hand on his shoulder.

"Thee has read thy Scripture carefully, son. I must confess that I have never read it in that light before. Perhaps thee is right. God knows. I am sure that it would grieve thee to go against the teachings of thy father, thy church and thy people. But I believe that thou art following what thou believest to be thy duty. It is breaking my heart, my son. But every man must settle an action of this kind for himself, according to his own conscience and his own God. If thou believest that the Lord sanctions thee, that it is thy duty to go, I will say no more; go, and may God go with thee."

The fire of youth and patriotism burned hotly in Joe's breast, but it was with bowed head and wet eyes that he left his father's presence.

All his life he had carried every pain, every grief and trouble to his mother, and he sought her now, kneeling beside her and burying his head in her lap.

She, too, had passed a sleepless night. Many hours of it she had spent upon her knees, praying for strength and wisdom in the trial that was to come upon her. She showed the strain of anxiety and labor of the past five years, and the suffering of the present had left her wan and pale, with heavy shadows in her eyes.

She clasped the boy to her and bowed her face upon his.

"Oh, Mother," he cried, "*you* don't blame me, do you? *You* don't think that I am doing wrong? I'm not deserting God, Mother, or the Friends' religion, or you! I love the old faith. I believe in it. I'll live and die in it. But oh, Mother, I *have* to go! No man who loves his country and is a man can hold back now!"

She held him close, tears streaming down her face.

Presently he raised his head. "I'll have to go, dear. They are waiting for me. I"—he hesitated, then said brokenly,—"I enlisted last night."

She gave a little gasping cry.

"You have enlisted—already? Oh, Joe, Joe!"

"Lige enlisted, too, Mother," he forced himself to tell her, "and Herbert. In the First Regiment of Nebraska Volunteers."

"Lige—Lige, too?"

Her cry stabbed him like a knife.

"Yes, Mother, he asked me to tell you. You know how soft he is. He said he—he couldn't."

"Lige—Lige, too!" she repeated in a stricken whisper. "Both my boys! My two eldest—my sons—my little boys! We came to this far country to save you this. We thought to keep you free from warfare and slaughter! And now it has come—even here! You—the descendants of old Quaker stock—you are going away to war!"

He caught her in his arms and held her close, whispering to her, consoling her, explaining over and over again the convictions and principles that actuated himself and his brother in this, the most difficult and momentous decision of their lives.

At length she was calmer, and withdrawing herself from his arms, said, "Send Lige to me."

As he was leaving the room she stopped him.

"Joe, dear," she said, "thee must not feel hardly toward thy father. He is not a fanatic. His belief in the wickedness and futility of war is as deep and strong as his belief in God. He could not change it now—even for thee."

When Joe left the room his heart felt ready to burst with pain. He knew that the call of his country was a sacred one. He felt in every fibre of his being that he was doing his plain duty as a man and an American. Yet the habit and training of years, the principles inculcated in him from babyhood, were not easily overcome. Even with a mind clear and positive upon his duty doubts and fears and questionings rose to torture him.

Blinded by the tears that would come in spite of all his efforts he walked toward the river.

So harassed and broken was he that he did not hear the murmur of voices in the little arbor they had built under the willow trees until he was very near it. Then he looked up suddenly, and stood still.

On the rough bench they had made on the river bank he saw Nina sitting, and Lige, with arms tightly clasped about her and his face close to hers, was gazing into her eyes.

He could not hear the words that were spoken, his heart was beating too loud and fast, but he saw that her arms were about his neck, that her face was wet with tears, and that her eyes gazed into his with a look of love and sorrow.

Up to this moment Joe had always thought of Nina as his sister. He knew that he had loved her devotedly from the first moment he had seen her; but it was only now, when the wild plunge of his heart, the wild fury in his breast, the hot, fierce current of blood that surged up to his brain brought the revelation to him, that he knew that the love he felt for her was not that of a brother.

For an instant a wild, mad rage against Lige filled him; made him want to strike him, to hurl him headlong from the arbor and down the bank of the river. Then the sense of fairness and justice that had always been a leading trait of his character asserted itself.

Why, he asked himself, should Lige not love her, as well as he? She was not their sister. He had the right. Handsome Lige. Merry, sparkling, generous Lige! No wonder she loved him!

He stole away unobserved. Then when he had reached the house he called out loudly, "Lige, oh, Lige, Mother wants you!"

When he saw Lige coming he turned away.

He hoped he was not selfish, but he could not speak to him then.

He made no effort to see Nina alone, but bade her good-bye the next day with the same grave, sad, brotherly kiss that he gave to Mary and Sara and Ruth.

CHAPTER XXVIII

IN FIELD AND CAMP

When the First Nebraska Volunteers embarked at Omaha under the command of Colonel John M. Thayer, on July twenty-first, Joe and Elijah Peniman and Herbert James went with it.

The troops were raw and undisciplined, the equipment poor, food scanty and hard to get.

The Peniman boys, neither of whom had ever been away from home before, were desperately homesick, and seeing the sordidness of war, its meanness, its dirtiness and its horrors at close range, and losing some of their high vision in the daily muck and grind, came gradually almost to believe that their father was right, and that they had gone against his will, violated the faith of their childhood, and broken their mother's heart to follow a chimera that could only end in utter defeat.

For weeks they got no nearer to war than a hot, dirty, disorderly, unsanitary camp, where they were drilled from morning till night with aching shoulders and blistered feet, marched and countermarched under a broiling sun, eating hard-tack and sow-belly, and drinking water from foul ponds and muddy streams, and sleeping in fever-ridden swamps under rain that poured down upon them continually.

For a long time Joe avoided his brother. The sight of Lige, so big and handsome in his uniform, with his bright brown eyes, his rich color, the dark curly hair that fell over his forehead under the vizor of his soldier-cap, roused in him a bitterness that he could not overcome.

The knowledge that had come upon him so suddenly was a well-established fact in his mind now. He knew that he loved Nina. Knew that he loved her with all the power and strength and passion of his young manhood. Not as a brother loves a sister, but as a man loves the one woman in all the world for him.

He could not banish her from his mind. In camp, in field, on march, standing guard in the rain at night, waiting for the signal to go into battle, her face was always before him.

It angered him to see that Lige was not suffering as he suffered. He did not appear to be eating out his heart for her. He larked and sang with the other boys (for they were boys—mere boys—these defenders of the nation's integrity), and before many weeks had passed had become one of the most popular men in the regiment.

Joe could not tell his trouble to Herbert—of whom he had grown very fond. That there had come an estrangement in his heart toward Lige, that brother who had always been almost like another self, was a thing of which he could not speak.

But Lige did not seem to notice. So far as Joe could see he treated him as he always had, with his jolly, careless affection. As soon as their drilling days were over and they were moved forward into action he seemed to become possessed with the spirit of war. The excitement, the danger, the fighting, the constant sense of adventure appealed to his spirited, adventuresome nature, and he threw himself into action with an ardor that raised him from a private to a corporal in a short time. Whatever his thoughts, whatever his emotions, Joe could see that he found no time to put them on paper or to dwell much upon them in his own mind.

Transportation was poor and the distance great, and they heard from home only at rare intervals. They had been gone two months when Joe received a small package one day, which, when he tore it open eagerly, he found to contain a daguerreotype of Nina.

Poor as was the early effort at photography, the face that smiled up at him from the shiny glass was so lovely that it caught his heart like a vise and left him gasping.

She was eighteen now—a woman! And in the proudly poised little head, the small oval face, the great violet eyes and the shining nimbus of golden hair there was that distinction that had always marked her as different from all others.

He was curious to know if she had sent a picture to Lige, but could not bring himself to ask. The letter, which reached him at the same time, was like all her letters, clever, witty, affectionate, sisterly letters, such as Ruth or Sara might have written, and did write on occasion.

The daguerreotype was in a little hinged case, which he carried in the pocket of his tunic over his heart for the remainder of the war.

Throughout the years of '61 and '62 the cause of the Union suffered many disasters. The defeat and rout of the battle of Bull Run had a most demoralizing effect on the Federal army. It demonstrated the fact that the soldiers needed more drilling and the army better organization before success on the field of battle was possible. General McClellan, in charge of the Grand Army of the Potomac, dallied and delayed, while the South pushed on winning victory after victory. In spite of the victories which the

Northern arms had gained in the West the winter was a gloomy one. But the campaign of 1863 brought new hope to the nation. The battle of Shiloh was fought and won, Lee was beaten back at Antietam, and the news of the proclamation of emancipation went flashing over the world.

At the beginning of 1863 the army in the West under General Rosecrans was near Chattanooga. Vicksburg and the whole Southwest was in danger, and the whole Union army was being pushed vigorously forward. The division of which Joe and Elijah Peniman and Herbert James were a part were rushed north to check Lee, who, after victories at Fredericksburg and Chancellorsville, was pushing north, even as far as southern Pennsylvania. The opposing forces met at Gettysburg, and the three boys were hurled into one of the most stubborn and bloody battles of the war. The battalion with which they were connected had to cross a valley several hundred yards in width. On the left rose a hill which was being riddled with shot and shell. Joe, who was now a sergeant, was on the extreme left of the advance, his platoon being the supporting platoon of the left assault company. Along the steep slope of the hill facing them not thirty yards away was a cannon. They swung their guns around and opened a fusillade on the attackers. Joe, who was commanding the platoon, was ordered to advance with his men and cover the left flank. Suddenly as they pushed forward the valley became a shrieking Bedlam. A company of Confederates on a hill far to the rear of the Union men sensed a new menace in the advance and opened up wildly against their position. The air was filled with howling bullets and shrieking shells. Some of the men dropped flat on their stomachs, many of them were killed. It was a clear day. There had been mists in the valley in the morning which shrouded the hills, but as the sun rose they lifted so that the movements of the Union men were perfectly visible to the enemy along the ridges. They went stumbling upward through the leafy jungle, bullets whipping and snipping off the leaves and branches about them.

Finally they debouched upon a path veering to the left in order to get behind the enemy. Joe's detachment made preparations to charge. But before they could move it seemed to them that all hell broke loose. Joe caught a glimpse of Lige, who was now a corporal, leading his men, his cap gone, his hair blown back from his forehead, his eyes filled with the lust of battle. The next moment he saw him fall.

In that one second all the love that he had ever had for his brother came sweeping back in a great overwhelming flood. He rushed toward him, but the demands upon him were too great, his responsibility too terrible for him to stop even for his brother. Officer after officer was falling around him. Colonel Baker went down with a shot through the lungs, Captain Young was shot in the stomach, Sergeant Ellton had three bullets through his left arm, Private James, who fought beside him, had a wound in his shoulder. He caught a wild glimpse of him, fighting with his left arm, while a huge Confederate with clubbed musket rushed at him. Then Joe was swept on and saw him no more.

They fought madly, blindly, desperately. At last but seven of his platoon were left; yet he must cover his position. The little band drew grimly together, and the strain was so great, the excitement so terrible, that Joe had no time to feel even a thrill of surprise or joy when he found Lige fighting beside him. As in a dream he saw him crouch in the grass. Then he became aware that his rifle was cracking as regularly as the crack of a whip. For a brief instant he turned and looked down. Crouched low in the tall grass, with his rifle at his shoulder, Lige sighting as carefully as he was wont to do at home when he shot the heads off wild turkeys, he was potting the Confederates who manned the gun, dropping them one by one with the regularity and precision of clockwork.

Suddenly an officer rose up near one of the guns, and with perhaps a dozen men behind him came charging down the hill. The young sergeant had no time to count his men, to see how many were left of that platoon that started out so gayly. Fixing his bayonet, he dashed at them. When the skirmish that ensued was over and he had time to look about him he and Lige stood alone on the hill. The lieutenant with all his men lay scattered about them.

It was not until the mad hell that raged about them was over and the battle won that the two boys realized that they had done anything out of the ordinary. Then they learned that they had cleaned out a position, routed the enemy, and left open the channel through which the Union troops rushed in and saved the day.

It was a desperate battle, desperately fought and gallantly won. The Confederate army was defeated and beaten back, and Lee never tried the invasion of the Northern States again. That battle, bloody and terrific as it was, was really the turning-point of the war. From that time the Confederate army began to languish. The end of slavery was at hand.

Then came victories, victories, and more victories for the North. Grant was made Lieutenant-General and entered upon his "hammering campaign" at Vicksburg. Sheridan was in the Shenandoah Valley; Sherman was marching through Georgia. His telegram, "Atlanta is ours and fairly won," gave a new courage to the whole country. Lincoln was reëlected by a large majority.

Through it all Joe fought his battle with himself as silently and bravely as he fought the battle with his country's foes.

When a moment of leisure came and the two brothers could be together for a few uninterrupted moments he sought Lige's society, talked with him of home and parents and brothers and sisters, spoke lovingly and tenderly of Nina, and gave him every opportunity and encouragement to tell his secret. But Lige did not speak. After many trials Joe, hurt to the quick, gave up the attempt and kept his own counsel.

Sharper and fiercer grew the fighting. Lige was captured, made a brilliant and spectacular escape, was wounded once in the leg and twice in the shoulder, and came out a Colonel, the most adored man in the regiment.

At last it was over. The long, bitter, bloody struggle was ended. The South, impoverished, exhausted, beaten, was obliged to surrender, and Lee handed his sword to Grant at Appomattox, on a day which the United States will never forget.

When the troops were mustered out the Peniman boys, men now, with the stain and smirch of battle upon them, laid down their arms and returned to the homestead on the prairies, where anxious hearts, loving and weary hearts, were waiting to welcome them home.

CHAPTER XXIX

HOME AGAIN

Those terrible four years of war had been an anxious, sorrowful time for the pioneers on the Nebraska prairies.

Rumors reached even to the homestead of the unsanitary condition of the camps, of the thousands of deaths from fever, and the hearts of the parents were rent with anxiety for their two brave lads, lest even should they escape shot and shell they might fall a victim to disease.

With the two older boys, upon whom he had depended so much, away at war, Joshua Peniman found the labor thrown upon him almost more than he could bear. Sam, who was now a fine, well-grown lad of seventeen, full of fun and energy, had done his best to take Joe's place, and Paul, whom the family had previously looked upon as "one of the little ones" was now a big boy of fourteen, strong and agile, intelligent beyond his years, and able to do a large part of the work that Lige had always attended to.

As the years of the struggle went on Hannah Peniman's shining brown hair turned grey, and the deep blue eyes that gazed out over the lonely prairies came to have in them the look of those who wait and fear.

Nina and Ruth clung together as if some deep, unspoken bond of sympathy lay between them, and day after day pored over the newspapers, read the few letters that came together, and lingered over them with clasped hands and tearful eyes.

Mrs. Peniman noticed that many of these letters that Ruth watched and waited for so eagerly were addressed in a different hand from those of her brothers. Seeing that the postmark on them was the same as those on the letters of Lige and Joe she asked who they were from. Ruth blushed deeply and said they were from Herbert.

She was seventeen now, dark and slender, graceful as a young fawn, with soft, tender brown eyes and a color like a prairie rose. Between her and Nina there seemed to be an affection that was deeper and closer than that of sisters. Nina had not seemed cheerful or well of late. The horrors of war seemed to weigh upon her with crushing sorrow. She grew thin and pale, read the news of every battle with feverish intensity, and often went away alone, wandering by herself for hours over the loneliness of the prairies.

Mr. Peniman had long since set inquiries on foot both in New York and St. Louis in regard to the property the deeds to which had been found in the violated dispatch-box. But as yet nothing had come of them, and the girl was as much in the dark as ever in regard to her past and future.

Beatrice James came to the homestead often, and the three girls seemed to have much to talk about together, frequently banishing Sara and Mary, whom they considered too young to share their confidences.

"All they talk about is the soldiers, Mother," indignantly protested Sara, who was now thirteen and resented the indignity of being shut out; "and they cry and snivel and get as sentimental as mush."

Mrs. Peniman smiled. "Don't mind, Sara, they're at the sentimental age," she comforted. "You and Mary and I have more sense, haven't we?"

Mary, who was now ten, glanced up from her task of dressing Spotty in a gingham apron.

"They all want to be *nurses*," she commented scornfully. "Huh! I'd like to see Beatrice—or Nina either—put on a bandage! They'd faint away, both of 'em. Ruth is the only one who would make a good nurse. I guess"—with a wise little nod of her curly head—"I guess they'd only want to take care of *certain* patients, don't you think so, Mother?"

Mrs. Peniman laughed, though a bit sadly, her heart quailing at the mention of wounds. "You're a wise little owl, Mary," she said, thinking to herself that Mary was probably right.

There were periods of fearful anxiety, bitter disappointment and deep depression as the first year of the war went by, and times when the issue looked doubtful and the hearts of loyal Unionists grew sick with fear.

In the early spring of 1864: a terrible day dawned upon them. The Sioux, Cheyennes and other hostile Indian tribes united to exterminate the white settlers, and a great Indian outbreak ensued, during which the entire frontier was paralyzed with terror.

With the aid of Mr. James and Arthur a stockade about twelve feet high was erected about the house and dugout, made from the young timbers along the creek, which were driven into the ground so close together that no living creature could pass through them.

For days and many weary nights they feared to sleep, but with the whole James family as well as their own crowded into the house, watched and waited, fearing momentarily to hear the war-whoops that would mean their destruction. Dozens of settlers in the western part of the Territory were murdered, their homes laid waste and their women carried away by the savages, and the settlers from the Blue Valley, the Platte Valley, and Salt Creek left their homes and fled to more protected counties.

Many of their neighbors abandoned their newly located homesteads and fled for protection to the agencies or towns, but this Joshua Peniman refused to do.

"We have worked too hard and sacrificed too much to get what we have here, to abandon it," he said. "If thee and the little ones think best to go into the town with the others, thee must do so, Hannah, but the boys and I, with Mr. James and Arthur, will stay here and protect our homes and property."

"Then I will stay with thee, Joshua," answered his wife. "I have never yet deserted thee in danger or trouble, and I will not do so now. The stockade is high and strong and will act as some protection, and we will trust in the One who never forsakes us to keep us safe from harm."

For many days they lived in terror, with weapons ready to give battle at a moment's notice from inside the stockade.

The Governor of the Territory had called out troops, and the First Nebraska Volunteer Cavalry company was assigned duty in that locality.

The Indians were no match for the United States troops, and after burning, destroying and massacring the homes and families of many settlers were finally overcome, and sent flying across the border, while peace settled down over the distracted frontier.

With April of the next spring came the glad news of Lee's surrender, and then the letters which told them that the boys were coming home.

The boys were coming home!

The lads whom they had prayed for, wept for, feared for, agonized over all these weary four years, were safe—well—*coming home!*

The news ran like wildfire over the prairies. Every soddy, every dugout, every town and village and crossroads store was vibrant with it. In the Peniman household the joy was too great, too deep for words.

It was decided that the whole family should go to Omaha to meet the returning soldiers. And on a glad morning, when all Nature seemed to laugh with joy, when the very earth seemed to be rejoicing that the cruel war was over, they set out, Sam driving Kit and Billy, no longer young and skittish, but sobered by years and the exigencies of pioneer life on the plains.

The former trading-post had now developed into quite a city. Brick buildings were going up here and there, streets were laid out, and the "squatties" and shanties that had done service in the days of the trading-station for Indians and trappers were giving place to good shops and stores.

As the family passed through the little settlement on Salt Creek, at which Mr. Peniman and Sam had spent the night before the great blizzard, they were astonished to see its growth. It had developed from a straggling settlement into a town, was now called Lancaster, and not many years afterward was rechristened *Lincoln*, and made the capital of the State.

The troops were ferried across the Missouri, and as the Peniman family, with hundreds of others, stood watching the transports laden with the cheering, yelling, waving boys in blue, their emotions grew too strong to be controlled. The girls wept, the boys yelled, but Hannah Peniman could only gaze and gaze, her whole soul concentrated in her eyes.

They saw them at last. Lige, mounted on the railing of the ferry-boat, was waving his forage cap around his head and shouting himself red in the face, and Joe stood beside him. He was very thin, very white, and had a great scar across his cheek. Leaning against the railing his eyes were fixed intently on the shore.

When the eyes of the long-parted ones met there was a great shout, a tremulous, half-sobbing cheer, and discipline was utterly forgotten as mothers and sons, sisters and brothers, sweethearts and lovers rushed into each other's arms.

Lige reached them first, in a rush that bore every one in the way before him, and caught his mother in his arms and held her to his breast. Joe was directly behind him, and grasped his father's hand. There was no need for words between them now. Both knew that the war and its issues had answered all arguments, and as they held each other's hands, gazed into each other's eyes, both knew that the past was passed and over, and that there existed no differences of opinion between them now.

Lige rushed from one to another, kissing and hugging them all, laughing, sobbing, half beside himself with joy. But Joe was more quiet in his demonstrations. After he had held his mother in a long, close embrace, shaken hands with Sam and Paul, kissed and hugged little David, and kissed and embraced Sara and Mary and Ruth, he turned to Nina, and shook her hand.

It was not until long afterward, when the first excitement was over, that he asked himself impatiently why he could not greet her as he had greeted his other sisters.

Every one was too excited to notice her pallor, or to see that Ruth's great brown eyes were wide and terror-filled, and her face white and drawn. She waited her opportunity, then clasping Joe's arm, said tremulously: "Herbert, Joe—where is Herbert?"

Joe started and looked down into her face. For the first time he realized that Ruth was no longer a little girl. For the first time he realized the thing that had been in Herbert's heart, that had drawn them so close together through the war.

With a quick, indrawn breath he bent and clasped his arm about her. "Oh, Ruth," he said in a low voice, "oh, little Ruth!"

Every vestige of color faded from her face.

"Was he killed?" she whispered huskily. "We have not heard anything from him in so long——"

"No, no," he hastened to assure her. "He was not killed. He was captured at Gettysburg, but I heard that he had escaped. I haven't seen or heard from him since, but I think he's all right. He will probably turn up soon. Perhaps he may come home as a casual. He never got back to our regiment."

The boys had been granted a furlough of a week, and the journey back over the prairies was a happy one, every one talking at once, so much to see, so much to hear, so much to tell, so glad and thankful to be together once more that words would not begin to express it.

In the general hubbub of voices no one noticed that Nina was very silent, that the color had faded from her cheeks, and the light that had shone so transcendantly in her eyes since the news of the home-coming of the boys had faded, leaving them dark and still.

Joe, stealing a glance at her, thought that she had never been so beautiful; and when he turned to talk to her her laugh was so gay, her chatter so light and merry that he thought he had fancied the shadow in her eyes.

When they reached the homestead Joe leaped down and patted Spotty, who came leaping and barking about the wagon, as if he too knew that the boys had come home and was wild with joy. Then he went to the team and put his arms about Kit's neck, laying his face against her smooth neck. Dear old Kit! Memories of all they had been through flooded over him and almost unmanned him.

Both the returned soldiers were amazed and delighted to see the changes about the place. It was a wilderness no longer. Vines grew up over the little sod house, shading its windows and throwing their green tendrils and shining new leaves over the door. Trees had been planted about the place, walks made, and the fertile fields were already green with winter-wheat.

Romeo and Juliet had departed for that bourn from which no piggy returns, but were succeeded by a large and thriving progeny, that were rapidly increasing in weight and value.

Cherry was the mother of a fine two-year-old calf, and Mother Feathertop and Dicky, the progenitors of the poultry yard, were no longer there to greet them, but had been succeeded by many fine broods of chickens, which had multiplied and accumulated wonderfully under Ruth's tender care.

It was almost evening before the transports of rapture subsided and the boys went to their old place in the sod house to wash up and get ready for supper.

When Joe entered he found Lige making a careful and fastidious toilet.

"I suppose you are looking forward to a happy evening with Nina," he said, trying manfully to keep the pain that was wringing his heart from sounding in his voice.

Lige was shining his shoes. He turned his head and looked up at his brother.

"Nina?" he said interrogatively, then going on with his shining with bent head. "Why—a—no, I—I thought I would go over to the Jameses—that is if I won't be in the way. I—a—I thought I'd like to ask if they had heard anything about Herb."

Joe stared at him.

"Go over to the Jameses? Your first evening at home! Why, Lige!"

Lige looked up with rather a red face.

"Well, why not? We've been with the family all day, and I haven't seen Beatrice, and——"

"But Nina—what will she think—how will she feel——"

"*Nina?* What the deuce——" Lige suddenly suspended operations on his boots and straightened up, holding the brush extended and staring at his brother.

"Good Lord!" he ejaculated suddenly.

For a moment he continued to stare, then dropped the shoe-brush and caught Joe's arm.

"What d'you mean—you don't mean—you don't think—that I—that Nina—that there is anything between *us*, do you?" he demanded.

Joe turned white to the lips.

"Why I—I——" he managed to stammer.

"*Great Jehoshaphat!*" ejaculated Lige. "That—*that's* what's been eatin' you! I couldn't understand it. I thought it was Beatrice——"

"*Beatrice?* What the dickens do I care about Beatrice!" panted Joe. "I thought you loved Nina—and that she loved you. I saw you kiss her——"

"Well, Lord A'mighty, why shouldn't I kiss her? She's my sister, isn't she? I kiss Ruth and Mary and Sara; why shouldn't I kiss her?"

Joe's heart was pounding so he could hardly speak.

"Yes, but that's different. She *isn't* our sister, you know. I saw you together the night before we went away, and her arms were around your neck and she was——"

"And she was talking about *you* every minute of the time, you big booby, begging me to take care of you and bring you home safe and all that! Oh, gosh, this does beat all! Why here was me trying to do the noble brother act and forget all about little Beatrice because I thought you cared for her, while all the time you were hating me like the old Harry because you thought I'd cut you out with Princess! Why, Lord love you, boy, what's the matter with you? Are you blind as a bat? Can't you *see* how she feels toward you? Why, there never was any one else in the whole world for Nina but just you, ever since that first day when she refused to ride anywhere else in the wagons but beside you!"

Joe's face was as white as chalk, his eyes fastened on his brother's face, and his breath coming quick and short.

"Is it—is it true, Lige?" he asked after a little interval, in a strained whisper.

"*True?* Well, you are a duffer if you haven't seen it yourself. Didn't you see her face when you gave her that cold little hand-shake to-day? She could hardly keep from crying all the way home. I thought you didn't care about her at all. I thought all the time you cared for Beatrice——"

"Beatrice! As if I could ever think of Beatrice when Nina was around! Do you really think she cares, Lige? That she doesn't care for me just as a brother——"

"Go along and ask her, you old gosling," cried Lige, busily adjusting a new tie. "As for me, I'm going over to the Jameses so fast you can't see me for the dust. I've been afraid to even write to little Bee for fear I'd be making trouble for you, but now that I know what a goose you are——" He clapped on his soldier-cap and shot through the door, leaving Joe standing motionless beside the window with wildly beating heart.

Twilight was coming before he found courage to wander down to the river. He found Nina sitting in the little arbor alone. She had been with Ruth for the past hour, trying to comfort her, and her eyes were red and her heart cold as she sat gazing down at the water.

Joe came so quietly that she did not hear him. For a long moment he stood gazing at her, his very heart in his eyes. She was more beautiful than ever, startlingly, exquisitely lovely, as she sat with bent head, the sunlight flickering through the golden waves of her hair, the pure oval of her cheek and chin a little sharpened in the years he had been away.

He entered the arbor noiselessly and sat down by her side.

"Joe!" she cried, and started violently.

Very tenderly he took the little hand that lay trembling in her lap.

"Nina," he said, bending his head close to hers, "are you really glad I have come home?"

"*Glad!*" The tears she had been trying to conceal rushed into her eyes. "Glad, Joe? There are no words that can tell how glad! Oh, we have all missed you so! Sometimes I have thought that Mother would die of grief and longing. And Father—oh, Joe, his patience, his gentleness, his suffering, his noble and generous admission of his mistake——"

"But you, Nina, you——"

She lowered her lashes and gently drew her hand away.

"I, Joe? Why, of course I am glad! Why shouldn't I be glad? Both my dear brothers back from war——"

"But I am not your brother, Princess. I don't want to be your brother." Then suddenly the denial that he had so long set on his heart burst its bonds and cried to her, "Oh, Nina, Nina, dearest, sweetest, loveliest girl in all the world, I don't want you for my sister. I love you, I love you! I want you for my love, my sweetheart, something nearer, dearer, sweeter than a sister—I want you for my wife!"

From Nina's parted lips came a little smothered cry, and she covered her face with her hands.

Joe drew them down gently.

"I have always loved you, Princess. Ever since the day that I first saw you out there on the desolate prairies, lying on the graves of your father and mother. I have always loved you——"

Nina looked up at him, tears flooding the purple splendor of her eyes.

"Oh, Joe, Joe, why didn't you tell me so before!" she cried. "You went away to the war—and I might never have known. I thought you cared for me only as a sister, and I have suffered—my God, how I have suffered—thinking that you did not care for me, while I—while I——"

He caught her in his arms and pressed her to his heart.

"While you—say it, darling, say it; my heart has been breaking for those words! I thought I should never hear them from your lips. I thought you loved Lige. I could not speak because I thought he loved you and you cared for him. The night before we went away I saw you in his arms, and I thought—I thought——"

She drew herself from his clasp and gazed into his eyes.

"You thought I cared for *Lige*?"

"Yes, dearest, yes, I truly, truly, did."

"And you went away without a word! You gave up your own chance of happiness because you thought you were adding to mine—and his! But what about me, Joe? I almost broke my heart trying to make myself love you like a sister. Oh, Joe, Joe, how like you! And you never suspected about Beatrice? Oh, Joe, you dear, darling old simpleton, how *could* you think such a thing? Didn't you know that there never was—never could be—any one else in all the world but *you*?"

Darkness had quite come when they went back to the house together. As they entered the kitchen hand in hand Hannah Peniman looked up, and a little cry escaped her lips.

Nina ran to her and hid her head on her breast. Joe took her hand and slipped his arm about her.

"I've been a great fool, Mother," he said tenderly, "but I've come out of it better than I deserved. I thought that Lige cared for Nina, and I was going to just step aside and never let any one know how I felt. But I find I was mistaken, and that Princess cares for me. Are you glad, Mother? Tell us that you are glad she is really and truly going to be your daughter."

"She could never be more truly my daughter than she is now," said Mrs. Peniman, kissing the white brow that nestled against her shoulder.

"But I am glad that she and you have found each other, for true love is the greatest thing in the world."

It was long after midnight when Lige came home, bursting into the room where Joe lay in the darkness with a tumult in his heart too great for sleep.

Lige rushed up to the bed and grasped his hand.

"Congratulate me, old boy," he cried; "by golly, I'm the happiest chap in all Christendom to-night. She loves me, Joe, she really loves me. I can hardly believe it even yet. And she's loved me all the time I've been away. I'm so happy——"

"I'll bet you're not any happier than I am," cried Joe, returning the grip of his hand.

"You are? Bully! Then you and Nina have fixed it up all right? Good! I'm mighty glad. Lord, Joe, I wish I'd suspected it sooner; it would have saved us both a lot of heartaches. But no matter, they're all over now, and perhaps we fought all the better for feeling that we hadn't so much to live for at home."

And while the boys lay in their old bed exchanging confidences and talking in whispers of the happiness that was to be theirs, and Nina, glowing with a happiness she had thought to never know, kept watch and ward through the silent night, little Ruth lay at the other side of the curtain and wept for the boy who did not come home.

CHAPTER XXX

RUTH RECEIVES A SURPRISE

With the return of the young men of the West from the war the settlement and development of the new country made rapid strides.

The Free Homestead Law, which had been signed by President Lincoln, took effect in 1863 and provided that any man or woman twenty-one years old or the head of a family could have 160 acres of land by living on it for five years and paying about eighteen dollars in fees.

Joe and Lige, who were now of age, immediately filed claims on the tracts of land that their father had staked out for them near his own eight years before, and proceeded joyfully to build upon them the houses necessary to hold the claims, which each fondly hoped would shelter a bride before another year had rolled away.

Ruth was not yet old enough to file a claim, but Nina, who had passed her twenty-first birthday, filed a claim on a beautiful tract of land next to Joe's, near the river. Sam, who was only twenty, had already taken out a timber-claim, and was planting trees upon it in his spare time, and both he and Paul had pieces of land located upon which they meant to preëmpt as soon as they were old enough.

In spite of the thankfulness she felt for the return of her brothers Ruth could not be happy. She tried to enter into all the joy of the household, but the sight of Joe and Nina walking hand-in-hand in the moonlight, of Lige and Beatrice scampering across the prairies on their ponies, caused an ache in her heart that kept her sleepless many nights and wet her pillow with tears.

She had kept her secret while Herbert was away, feeling that they were both too young to become formally engaged, but she knew that she loved him as she could never love any other man, and that if he never returned there would be a grave in her heart for all eternity.

Joe and Lige did their utmost to comfort her, but felt as the days crept by that there was little chance of Herbert's return.

Joe's ambition to become a lawyer had never faltered, and as soon as he had received his discharge from the army he immediately set to work to prepare himself for his examination for admission to the bar.

He studied hard, and the reading he had done during the long days while he plowed in the fields now stood him in good stead. A month after his return he went to Nebraska City and took his examination, which he passed with high honors and was admitted to practise law in the State.

He left the building with his certificate in his pocket and pride and exultation in his heart. He was a lawyer! The ambition of his boyhood was fulfilled. It now remained with him to make the rest of his dreams come true.

As he walked along jubilantly he saw a group of men coming toward him wearing the familiar blue uniform. He had returned to citizen's clothes, but the sight of the old uniform still thrilled him, and with the feeling of comradeship that it always inspired in him he stopped and waited for them to come up.

They walked very slowly, and as they came nearer he saw that they supported between them one of their comrades, who tottered like an old man.

"That fellow ought to be in an ambulance instead of on foot," he thought, and walked toward the group. As he reached them the man who was being supported raised his head.

"*Herbert*—my God, Herbert!" he cried, and clutched the yellow, skeleton-like hands.

The gaunt figure raised a haggard, ashen face, with hollow eyes and unshaven cheeks.

"*Joe!*" he whispered in a weak voice; "thank God!"

Joe had his arm about him by this time supporting him. Casting a swift glance up and down the street he saw a man coming toward them in a wagon.

"Here," he shouted, "take this soldier to a hotel, won't you? He's sick—wounded—he is not able to walk."

The war was too fresh in the minds of the people for any one to hesitate. Willing hands lifted the emaciated frame of the young soldier into the wagon, Joe sprang in beside him, and a few moments later Herbert James was in a hot bath, laid in a clean bed, with a doctor and nurse beside him.

When he could speak he told Joe that he had been captured and held in a Southern prison, where the conditions were so terrible that it was a miracle a single man came out of it alive. He had just been exchanged, he said, and he and the companions whom Joe had seen with him were on their way home when Joe met him.

Joe saw that there was something on his mind of which he hesitated to speak, and after a little time he asked for Ruth, so bashfully, and with an expression of such wistfulness in his hollow eyes that Joe's heart rejoiced. He told him that Ruth was well, but very unhappy at his failure to return, at which a faint color stained the boy's thin cheeks, and he turned his face to the wall and lay silent for many moments.

When he had fallen asleep Joe asked the doctor how soon he could be taken home, and was told that the sooner he reached home the better. "All he needs now is food and rest and care," he continued, "and it will take a lot of that, and considerable time before he is much better."

When the young soldier awakened it was to find a new suit of citizen's clothes laid out upon a chair, his filthy, tattered old uniform destroyed, and a barber waiting to shave him.

When he had eaten, was bathed and shaved and dressed he looked better.

"Now we're going home, old chap," Joe told him, whereat the poor broken youth began to cry.

Joe now had a side-bar buggy, to which he drove Kit, and with Herbert beside him made as comfortable as possible with rugs and pillows, they started for the Blue.

When they came in sight of the homestead Herbert gave a glad cry. "I never thought to see it again," he cried.

Joe lifted him out of the buggy and supported him into the house. Fortunately Ruth had gone for a walk with Nina. Mrs. Peniman received him almost as joyfully as if he had been one of her own sons. He seemed too exhausted to go farther, and a message was sent to his parents by David, who almost caused the death of Mrs. James by bursting into the house and yelling at the top of his voice that Herbert had come home.

The James family arrived at the homestead a few minutes later, and Mrs. Peniman went out and closed the door, leaving the young soldier to meet and greet his mother.

Half an hour later Ruth and Nina came home. It was evident that Ruth had been crying, and they walked slowly, with Nina's arm clasped about her waist.

Mrs. Peniman sent the children away and stood in the door awaiting them. As they came up to her she put her arms about Ruth and drew her to her side.

"Ruth," she said gently, "I have news for thee. A message has come——"

Ruth started forward, the color ebbing out of her face.

"From Herbert?" she whispered.

"Yes, there is a message from Herbert. Is thee strong enough to bear a shock——"

"A *shock*? Then he is dead?"

"No, no, I did not mean that. But we have news—some one has come——"

"Some one has come—*Herbert*?" and without waiting for the preparation that her mother had intended, she rushed into the house. For an instant she stood inside the door with white face and distended eyes. Then, hearing the low murmur of voices, she dashed aside the curtains, and saw Herbert lying on the bed.

The two young people uttered a simultaneous cry, and a moment later were locked in each other's arms. It was not for many minutes that Ruth could look at him, that she saw the wreck that war had made of the handsome boy she had loved. But when she did see it made no difference in her love. With the wealth of mother-love that had always overflowed her gentle heart she soothed and comforted him, told him that he would soon be well, and promised that she would nurse him back to life and health.

The next day she went quietly to her father and told him that she wanted him to marry them.

"It will take months to nurse him back to himself, Father," she told him, "and I am the one who can do it best. I can give him better care as his wife than I could as his sweetheart, and I want to marry him right now."

The family protested, but Ruth was never known to abandon an idea once she had set her mind upon it, and after some argument on the subject her family at last gave in.

"She might as well be nursing Herbert as a chicken with a broken wing or a dog with a sore foot," smiled her father, "for you know Ruthie will always be taking care of something. We all know and like Herbert, and have no objection to her marrying him sometime, and I know no reason why, if they both desire it, Ruth should not be given the privilege of nursing her husband back to health."

Mrs. Peniman finally agreed to this, and that evening as the sunset glow shone into the little soddy Herbert was propped up in his bed, and

Ruth, in a simple little white dress, with the flush and glow of radiant happiness upon her face, stood with her hand in his while her father spoke the solemn words that made them man and wife.

CHAPTER XXXI

JOE HEARS A STRANGE STORY

Civilization was now moving westward with rapid strides.

The part of the Territory in which the Peniman family had cast their lot had been organized into a county, and a thriving little town had sprung up about five miles from their homestead which had been made the county seat.

It was here that Joe decided to open his law office and begin the serious business of his life.

Sam and Paul were now old enough to take his place at home, and he saw no reason why he should not begin his life-work, continuing to live at home, and doing what work he could mornings and evenings.

He had managed to save up a little money, and with it he rented a small one-story frame building containing two rooms, and after building his book-shelves with his own hands he disposed upon them his precious library, bought a table and two chairs, and hung out his shingle, "Joseph Peniman, Attorney at Law."

One of his first cases was that of an Indian, brought to him by Pashepaho, for whom he obtained justice against a white man for fraud. This case received wide notice in the Territory, and before long the young attorney had a large Indian clientage, whom he served with fairness and honesty, demanding for the red men the same justice that the law provided for white settlers.

By this time Joshua Peniman was considered one of the leading men of the county, and the family were all well and favorably known. Joe's anti-slavery speeches had made him many friends, and it was not long after his admission to the bar before he had a good practice.

In the fall of '65 the first election was held, and he was nominated for floating delegate to the legislature.

He had been too busy since his return from war to go to Omaha to call on his friend Judge North, but shortly after his nomination, while he was sitting in his office one day busily preparing a brief, the door opened and Judge North walked in.

Joe sprang up to meet him joyously.

"I heard that you had returned safely," said the Judge, warmly shaking his hand, "and I've been expecting that you would drop in to see me. But as you didn't, and as I had business here in the county, I thought I'd come to see you."

Joe expressed his pleasure in seeing him.

"Thought you were coming up to study law in my office?" smiled the Judge, casting a glance about the modestly furnished little office.

Joe colored, then smiled. "I took my examination a few weeks ago," he answered, "and as I got my certificate and felt that I couldn't lose time I thought I'd better not study any longer, but begin work on my own hook."

"You're right, my boy," and as he spoke the same strange, illusive resemblance that always tormented him when in the Judge's presence again flashed through Joe's mind.

They talked for a long time, Joe telling of the war and his experiences, Judge North informing him of many things that had taken place during his absence, and were soon to take place in the State.

As the sun declined Joe looked at his watch.

"Come home to dinner with me, Judge, and meet my family," he said. "I have often talked to Father and Mother about you and I would like you to meet them. It's only a short ride, and I have my buggy here."

The Judge, who had contemplated spending the night at the little cross-roads hotel, gladly accepted the invitation.

It was twilight as they drove across the prairies and approached the little soddy. The warm rosy afterglow was lingering in the sky, and silhouetted against it a figure moved toward them across the prairie, a light, graceful figure, the after-glow touching its crown of golden hair into gleaming splendor.

As they drew nearer Judge North fastened his eyes upon the girl who was coming to meet them, with a strange, intent expression.

When she raised her hand and waved to them he turned to Joe swiftly. "Who is that girl?" he asked.

"It is my—my—a—foster—sister," Joe answered, his face flushing a little.

"I asked"—explained Judge North,—"because as she came toward us in this light she bore such a strange, such a remarkable resemblance to some one I—some one I loved very dearly."

The girl had drawn nearer now, and seeing that there was a stranger in the buggy was about to turn back when Judge North leaned forward and stared at her, then leaped out and ran to her.

"*Marion!*" he cried, "*Marion!*"

The girl stopped, then turned to him inquiringly.

The lawyer was breathing quickly, and his face was pale, his eyes intent as he leaned forward staring at her.

"My God!" he breathed. "Her face—her voice—her hair! It must be—I can't be dreaming—Marion, Marion!"

Nina came toward him. For some reason she too appeared greatly moved.

"My name is not Marion," she said; "my name is Nina, but Marion was my mother's name."

"*Your—mother's name?* Then you are her daughter—you must be the child of Marion—Marion North!"

"No, of Marion Carroll."

"*Marion Carroll!* Oh, thank God, at last, at last!"

He sprang forward and clasped Nina's hand.

"Your mother was Marion Carroll—Marion North—my sister—my precious little sister—who was lost, and whom I have been searching for all these years! Where is she? Where is she? You are her living image. I thought when I first saw you that it was she. I had forgotten the lapse of years. I should have known you were her daughter anywhere!"

Nina had turned white, and Joe, who had thrown the lines to Paul, now came up to them.

"Come into the house," he said quickly, slipping his arm about her. "This is very strange. There must be much to tell and much to hear. Come, Nina, you are shaking so you can hardly stand."

He led the way swiftly to the house. Inside the door Mr. and Mrs. Peniman were waiting to receive them. After a hasty introduction Joe explained to them what had just taken place.

"I know now," he cried; "I have always seen a resemblance in Judge North to some one I had seen. Now I know that it was to Nina—to Mrs. Carroll—whom I have never forgotten. Don't you see it, Father? Isn't it so?"

Joshua Peniman had been gazing at the stranger with keen scrutiny.

"Yes," he said, "I see the resemblance to the unfortunate young mother very plainly. I also see a certain look that is like Nina, which is only natural, as Nina is the image of her mother." Then, turning to the stranger, "I was with Mr. and Mrs. Carroll in the last hour of their lives. I buried them on the prairies, and took their child with us in our wagons. Sit down, friend, this is a strange dispensation of Providence. Tell us what you know of this strange tale."

Judge North seemed unwilling to let go of Nina's hand. Drawing her close to his side he sat down at the table. Joshua Peniman in his clear, calm fashion told the story of the arrival of the Carrolls in their wagon at their camp on the prairies, of Lee Carroll's tragic death, of the subsequent death of Mrs. Carroll, and their taking charge of the child. Of the raid upon the wagons by the Indians, the taking of the dispatch-box, and the kidnapping of Nina by Red Snake.

The lawyer listened with intense interest.

"And this white man—this 'Red Snake'—what of him? Did you ever see him?" he asked eagerly.

"I saw him several times," said Joe.

"What was he like?"

"He was tall, powerfully but slenderly built, with red hair, a long, red, dissipated face, and a short, sandy mustache."

Judge North brought his hand down upon his knee with a sounding blow.

"A *red Carroll!*" he ejaculated. Then turning to Nina, who stood with blanched face and parted lips beside him, he led her with gentle, old-fashioned courtesy to a chair.

"Sit down, child," he said, "I have a strange story to tell, that touches you nearly."

The family had all gathered about him now, anxious to hear the solution of the mystery that had baffled them so long.

"I know who 'Red Snake' was," he began; "his name was Bernard Carroll. He was a brother of the Lee Carroll whom you buried on the prairies."

"A *brother?*" cried out Joe; "why, it was he that killed him!"

"I don't doubt it at all. He was a bad man; a degenerate, a scoundrel, from his very boyhood. The two brothers were descendants of a splendid old family, the Carrolls, of Virginia. But every few generations there appears in that family a *red Carroll*. The family are all of dark complexion, and whenever a red-haired Carroll appears among them there is sure to follow trouble and disaster. Before he was twenty years old Bernard Carroll had broken his mother's heart and caused her death. When he was twenty-three he fell wildly, madly, passionately in love with my sister Marion."

"Marion—*my mother*! That was why he stared at me so! That was why he called me 'Marion'!" panted Nina.

The Judge turned his eyes upon her. "Yes, no doubt it was. You are marvelously like her. Startlingly like what she was at your age. He wooed her with the same fiery zeal, with the same ardor and passion that he carried into every act of his life. For a time his good looks, his native charm, his passionate wooing attracted her. Then as she came to know him better she turned from him with loathing. It was just at this time that Lee came home from college. He too fell in love with Marion, and she returned his love. In a short time they became engaged."

He paused, as a short, broken sob escaped from Nina's lips. He laid his hand over hers affectionately, then resumed:

"Bernard never forgave either of them. For Lee he developed a hatred that was shown in every act of his life. He was drinking heavily at the time, and as his extravagance threatened to ruin the family his father put him on an allowance, which no amount of whining or bullying would induce him to increase. He laid all his father's sternness at Lee's door, and set deliberately to work to ruin him in his father's affections. With the cunning of the snake, for which he was so well named, he crawled and wormed himself into his father's confidence, and then with devilish malice began to poison his mind against his younger son. Lee and Marion had married by this time, and were starting out in life together. Bernard forged his brother's name to a check, and made his father believe him a criminal. The father denounced him and turned him out of the house. Lee, indignant, hurt, grieved to the heart that his father should doubt him, high-spirited and stubborn, as all of the Carrolls are, left home with his young wife and went to New York to earn his living. A short time afterward a child was born to them, and they went abroad. It was while Lee was abroad, and all communication between himself and his family had been cut off, that Bernard again began to go the pace. He forged another check, which was traced to him, he was arrested, and fled the country. His father was relentless. Bernard had prejudiced him against and separated him from his younger and dearer son, had caused the death of his mother, and the old man was determined to punish him to the full extent of the law. But Bernard was never found. Once he was heard from in Iowa; some one who knew him saw him on a wagon-train headed for the gold-fields of California. Then all trace of him was lost. I presume that growing more and more degenerate he took to using drugs as well as liquor, became a squaw-man and settled among the Indians."

When his voice ceased there was deep silence in the room. Nina, with her violet eyes fixed intently on the face of her uncle, had scarcely stirred during the narrative. The keen mind of Joshua Peniman was busy putting two and two together.

Suddenly he rose from his chair and going to a chest in a corner of the soddy brought out the two deeds that had been found in the dispatch-box.

"This would indicate that the father forgave Lee, and deeded this property to him," he said, handing the deeds to Judge North.

The lawyer examined them critically. Then he looked up with an eager light in his eyes.

"Have you ever done anything about these?" he asked.

"Yes," answered Mr. Peniman; "I have done all that I could with the limited knowledge and means I possessed. I have tried to set inquiries on foot regarding them, but as yet have had no results."

Judge North put the deeds in his pocket. "I will take this matter up at once," he said. "This should be valuable property. Bernard would never have allowed it to fall into the hands of Lee's child if he could have used it himself, but he knew that he dared not claim it."

Turning to Nina he laid his hand on her head.

"And so, after all the search of years I have found my niece at last! I had almost believed I never should do so. And then," breaking into a genial smile, "I accept an invitation to dinner with my young friend here, and find my beautiful young niece—the very image of the little sister I lost and for whom I had so grieved—awaiting me!——"

He put out his arms, and Nina, with a glad little cry, ran into them.

"Of course you must come and live with me now——" he began, but got no farther, for from the whole Peniman family there rose a cry of simultaneous protest.

Nina, blushing rosy red, turned a shy glance on Joe.

He at once came to the rescue. Crossing the room he laid his hand upon the Judge's shoulder.

"I—a—I hope you won't mind, judge," he said awkwardly, "but—but the truth is that Nina has just promised to—to live the rest of her life with me."

The Judge turned and looked at him, then burst into a roar of laughter.

"Well, well, well!" he cried, "to think that the young man I have liked so much would steal such a march as that on me! So you have promised to live the rest of your life with this young chap, have you, niece? And I suppose you'd much rather do that than come live with a lonely old man like me?"

Nina could not truthfully deny the statement, but softened the blow by putting her arms about his neck and kissing him softly on the forehead.

It was Judge North's wish to give the young couple a fine wedding in Omaha, but this they firmly declined.

Lige and Beatrice had decided to be married soon, and the two young couples had planned a double wedding, at which the gentle Quaker father, minister, justice, should officiate.

It was while the preparations for the double wedding were going briskly forward that Joe received a letter from Judge North one day, asking him to come to Omaha at once, and bring Nina with him.

When they arrived the Judge met them at the door and led them into his private office. They saw that he looked very grave, and they were no sooner seated than he turned to Nina and took her hand.

"My child," he said, in a tone that sent premonitory chills of trouble into the hearts of the two young people, "you must prepare yourself for a great blow."

"A blow?" Nina turned pale. "What kind of a blow?"

Joe too had whitened. "What is it, Judge?" he asked, wondering if some insurmountable barrier to his marriage with Nina had been discovered.

"I have been very busy tracing back these deeds and looking up the estate that I hoped your grandfather Carroll had left his son," the Judge went on, "and which you, as his only heir, should inherit. But to my deep regret and sorrow I found that the property, the deeds of which were found in the dispatch-box, had long ago passed into the hands of some distant cousins, and that the fortune which we supposed Colonel Carroll to possess was so wasted by his spendthrift son, and so dissipated by his long search for Lee and his own long illness, that there was nothing of it left when the will was probated."

"Is *that* all?" Nina drew a deep breath and loosed the grip of her hands in her lap. "Great heavens, Uncle, you nearly frightened me out of my wits. I thought—I thought something terrible had happened."

"But—but it *is* terrible, my dear," said her puzzled uncle. "You don't seem to understand. There is no money for you to inherit. I thought you would be a great heiress. I hoped you would get a large sum of money from that property——"

Nina burst into a ringing laugh.

"Nonsense, Uncle! Who cares! What would I want with a great lot of money? I don't care a button about the fortune. I've found you—and know all about my dear father and mother now—and I've got Joe, so what more could I ask?"

"But, my dear——" cried her distressed uncle, gazing at the shining eyes and smiling face with amazement.

Nina sprang across the room and threw her arms around his neck with another burst of laughter.

"Don't bother any more about it, dear," she cried. "Just let's forget all about the money part of it, and be happy. I'm sure it will never give me another thought—if Joe doesn't mind taking a penniless bride."

Joe's expression as he gazed at her would indicate that he did not mind in the least.

"As a matter of fact," he admitted, "I feel rather relieved. I don't know whether I should feel equal to living up to a rich wife or not." Then more seriously, "No, Judge, don't let's lose any sleep about that. Nina and I have grown up poor, and I guess we shall never be any happier than we were in the little soddy back home. I have my profession, the State is growing, new business is coming in, I have my homestead and the little house on it where we can begin, and I guess we'll manage to get along and be pretty happy with that."

Judge North, who had been exceedingly worried and unhappy since he had received the news in regard to the property, looked at the young couple with surprise, and his face cleared.

"Well," he ejaculated, "I think you're a great pair of young simpletons, but I'm glad you take it that way. I don't think, however, that you need feel much uneasiness about your future. The new West is opening up, there are going to be great adventures and opportunities for young men, and Joe has a good start and the prospect of a brilliant future."

"Of course he has," cried Nina; "why should we worry about a little old money! Joe is going to be one of the biggest men in the new State."

The Judge patted her head and sighed while he smiled. "He ought to be, with a love and belief like that behind him," he said, a little wistfully.

It was now fall, and Herbert was once more almost himself again, thanks to Ruth's good nursing. She entered into the preparations for the double wedding with all the interest and enthusiasm she had had no opportunity to expend on her own wedding.

It was a glorious autumn morning when the little party left the sod house and walked quietly across the fields that were just beginning to put on their robes of brown and russet and gold, splashed here and there with brilliant dashes of color made by the goldenrod and sumac, and starred with St. Michaelmas daisies, while the great yellow sunflowers lifted their proud heads to the kiss of the morning and the meadow-larks poured forth their thrilling melody through the golden, sunlit air.

Joe walked with his mother, his arm about her waist, his tall form bent to hers, as he talked in low and tender tones of all that he meant to do for her and his father and the children in the days that were to come.

Nina, radiant and lovely as the morning, dressed in the soft creamy white she loved, was with her uncle, leaning lightly on his arm, while she chatted with Ruth and Herbert, who walked beside them, and Sara and Mary, who as bridesmaids to the party were charming in their garlands of wild-flowers and their simple little dresses of virgin white.

Lige walked with Mrs. James, his handsome head thrown back, his face shining with happiness and his eyes turned continually upon Beatrice, who skipped gayly along by the side of her father, lovely as a picture in her bridal white.

Sam and Paul, who were to act as best men to the wedding party, felt just a bit out of it as they trudged along behind, and David, now a sturdy little chap of ten years, skipped in and out, now with one group, now with another, the pet of the family, welcomed and admired by all.

At the door of the little church on the prairie Joshua Peniman awaited them. His hair was grey, his face lined and pale, and in his eyes was the expression of one who had been communing with another world.

As the friends and relatives crowded into the pews and the two young couples approached the altar there was a little bustle and stir at the back of the church, and Joe looked back to see a sight that touched him deeply. About the door was crowded a large party of Indians, the friends whom he and Nina had made in their captivity among them, and those he had made in later days.

They were all there, squaws, bucks, papooses, grinning at him from the door, and among them was the tall form of Pashepaho and the stately Neowage, who had come many, many miles to witness the wedding of their friend.

Joe rushed to the back of the church to meet them, insisted that they must all come inside, and ushered them down the aisle to the front pews, as proudly as if they had been the mayor of the city and governor of the State and their staffs.

They wore no hats, their hair was braided with beads and feathers in honor of the occasion, and Pashepaho bore on his arm a magnificent otter skin as a wedding present, while Neowage carried a wonderful pair of elk-horns that adorned Joe's home for many years.

Slowly the gentle patriarch mounted the pulpit, quietly the two young couples took their places before him, and with solemn voice he read the ceremony that united their lives.

When the wedding was over they all returned to the homestead, where a wedding feast had been prepared, and the Indians were among the most honored guests. They refused to sit on chairs, never having become accustomed to that luxury, but squatted on the grass they enjoyed the feast as well as any of the guests.

When it was over Joe and Nina left for Omaha, where his legislative duties were soon to begin. Lige and Beatrice drove over to the county-seat, where Lige, now a cashier in the bank, had built a modest home for his gay little singing-bird. Ruth and Herbert left for the home that had been built on their homestead, and as the shadows of night came down Joshua and Hannah Peniman with their shrunken household were left alone.

"We have given much to the New West, Joshua," she said, gazing with moist eyes about the little soddy that looked so lonely and empty in the waning light.

"It was that for which we became pioneers," answered Joshua Peniman, laying his hand over hers.

THE END

- 232 -

Milton Keynes UK
Ingram Content Group UK Ltd.
UKHW050035220624
444555UK00004B/401